Dedalus European Antholoɠ
General Editor: Mike Mitchell

The Dedalus Book
of
Lithuanian Literature

The Dedalus Book
of
Lithuanian Literature

Edited by

Almantas Samalavičius

Dedalus

Published in co-operation with The International Cultural Programme Centre programme: "Books from Lithuania" and Arts Council England, London.

Published in the UK by Dedalus Limited,
24-26, St Judith's Lane, Sawtry, Cambs, PE28 5XE
email: info@dedalusbooks.com
www.dedalusbooks.com

ISBN printed book 978 1 909232 42 6
ISBN ebook 978 1 909232 90 7

Dedalus is distributed in the USA & Canada by SCB Distributors,
15608 South New Century Drive, Gardena, CA 90248
email: info@scbdistributors.com   web: www.scbdistributors.com

Dedalus is distributed in Australia by Peribo Pty Ltd.
58, Beaumont Road, Mount Kuring-gai, N.S.W. 2080
email: info@peribo.com.au

Publishing History
First published by Dedalus in 2013
First ebook edition in 2013

Printed in Finland by Bookwell
Typeset by Marie Lane

The Editor

Born in 1963, Almantas Samalavičius is a cultural historian, critic and essayist. The author of eleven books and seven collections of essays he is a professor at Vilnius University. He has served as president of PEN Lithuania and is currently its vice president.

His books, articles and essays have been widely translated. His most recent book to appear in English is *Ideas and Structures: Essays in Architectural History* (2011).

The Translators

Jūra Avižienis has a Master's degree in Lithuanian literature from the University of Illinois. Jura is a Fulbright Scholar (Lithuania, 2000), and has been teaching at Boston University since 2008. Her translations of contemporary Lithuanian literature appear regularly in *The Vilnius Review.*

Aušrinė Byla is the granddaughter of Balys Sruoga. She has a Master's degree in English from Arizona State University and is currently living in Vilnius, Lithuania, where she is working as a translator and language instructor.

Violeta Kelertas received her PhD in Comparative Literature from the University of Wisconsin Madison. She was Endowed Chair of Lithuanian Studies at the University of Illinois at Chicago 1984–2008. She has translated and edited widely, mostly Soviet era Lithuanian prose fiction, focusing on Aesopian language, used to evade Soviet censorship. Currently under the auspices of the University of Washington Baltic program she is engaged in preparing a translation of the 19th C. feminist Lithuanian writer Žemaitė.

Elizabeth Novickas has a Master's degree in Lithuanian Language and Literature from the University of Illinois. She has worked as a bookbinder and fine printer in Urbana, Illinois; as a newspaper designer and cartographer in Springfield, Illinois; and as editorial system administrator at the Chicago Sun-Times. Besides translating Lithuanian into English, she is the editor of the journal Lituanus. In 2011 she won the St. Jerome Prize from the Association of Lithuanian Literary Translators.

Medeinė Tribinevičius holds a MA in creative writing and an MA from the Centre for European, Russian and Eurasian Studies at the University of Toronto. She is a writer, editor and curator, as well as a translator of Lithuanian literature and poetry.

Ada Mykote Valaitis is a writer, editor, and translator with a Masters degree in Literature from George Mason University. In 2007, Ada was awarded a Fulbright Fellowship to study and translate Lithuanian literature. She currently works as a Writer-Editor in the Office of the Secretary of the U.S. Department of Transportation and lives in Alexandria, Virginia.

Jayde Will has a master's degree in Fenno-Ugric languages from the University of Tartu, and is currently an assistant at the Department of Translation and Interpretation Studies at Vilnius University. His poetry and prose translations of Lithuanian, Estonian and Russian authors have appeared in a number of anthologies, including the most recent *Best European Fiction 2012 Anthology*. He is currently working on a collection of selected poems by Estonian poet and prose writer Eeva Park. He resides in Vilnius.

Contents

Introduction: Time Lost and Found

Almantas Samalavičius

The great social changes that occurred in Lithuania in the 1990s were triggered by the collapse of the Soviet empire, which had colonised the Baltic nations and ideologically controlled the whole of central and eastern Europe for half a century. This, along with the onset of Gorbachev's *perestroika*, hastened the events that led to the start of a second hard-won independence for Lithuania. For the first time my generation – born and raised in the Soviet era – had the opportunity to breathe in the life-giving and heady air of freedom. The current crop of twenty-year-olds, born in an already independent country, accept what for us was an intoxicating independence as something natural and ordinary. Though many Lithuanians had long dreamed of life in a free country, for my generation and our elders, it was most likely something that would occur and be experienced only once in a lifetime, and only under favourable historical circumstances.

Similarly, for most writers of the 20th century, freedom and independence were not self-evident truths, and nor was independence seen as guaranteed to last; it was only in the second decade of the 20th century that Lithuanians succeeded in shaking off the yoke of the tsarist Russian empire. This ancient and at times vast country, which at one point stretched from the Baltic to the Black Sea, bore this subjugation from the very end of the 18th century, when the Polish-Lithuanian Commonwealth – a union which was constantly undermined by external forces and internal disagreements – was weakened and collapsed. In the end, having lost its sovereignty, it was an easy prey for an expanding Russia. For nearly 150 years

Lithuania was ruled by a foreign colonial regime that consciously and maliciously ravaged and ruined the country's cultural and religious institutions, crippled collective historical memory and fiercely suppressed (but fortunately did not extinguish) even the merest manifestations of a desire for freedom.

As the storms of the First World War raged, all of the regional representatives in Lithuania gathered in Vilnius for a conference. It was there that the Lithuanian people announced their decision to reclaim their independence. On 16 February 1918, the Council of Lithuania proclaimed the historic Act of Independence of Lithuania and quickly took action to consolidate independence. This event was a natural outcome of the formation of a national consciousness that started at the beginning of the 19th century – a process later described by Czesław Miłosz, the Polish poet of Lithuanian origin and Nobel Prize laureate, as bordering on the miraculous.

The same could also be said about the incredible, phoenix-like reconstruction of the Lithuanian language, which formed the basis of the intellectual programme of the 19th century national liberation movement. It had been pushed out of public life and into the cultural fringes by the Russian colonial regime and its use had been entirely forbidden in public, in print and in schools after the second of two uprisings in the 19th century. But through great and often brave efforts spanning just a few decades, the Lithuanian language had been reborn.

Throughout the decades that the ban was in effect, the life of the Lithuanian language was maintained by way of books, mostly of religious content, which had been smuggled in from Prussia. However, even this could not effectively stop the degradation of the language. Many of the works published in Lithuanian in the 19th century clearly reflected that foreign vernacularisms and words had been imported into, and were undermining, the Lithuanian language. Elements of the Russian and Polish languages relentlessly penetrated into the structure and vocabulary of written Lithuanian, turning an archaic language into a combination of native and foreign tongues that quickly lost its characteristic identity and life. After the colonial regime brought into effect the ban on the Lithuanian language in 1864 that would last another forty years, the written word continued to grow sickly and wither, becoming a caricature of its former self. Fortunately, the national newspaper *Aušra* (*Dawn*), which was established in the 1890s, and later *Varpas* (*The Bell*) took up the mission to revive the Lithuanian language, strengthen national consciousness and rebuild historical memory in order to strengthen the foundations of Lithuanian identity. In a relatively short period of time, both periodicals played extremely meaningful and unexpectedly successful roles in the achievement of these goals. Even after the newspapers ceased publication, the work towards establishing an independent state and a shared sense of nationhood did not stop. It was taken up by other periodicals which continued to foster the seedlings of modern Lithuanian consciousness and identity. It would later become clear that this work was indispensable to the restoration of the lost institutional foundations of Lithuanian statehood.

It is therefore unsurprising that the themes of history and national identity have often been reflected by Lithuanian prose and poetry. It is probably also not difficult to understand why, for a nation deprived of its independence on several occasions, untangling these problems is so important. After nearly two centuries of Russian subjugation that witnessed the erosion of national traditions and identity, the inter-war period of independence only lasted a little over two decades. It was marked by a rapid, even feverish, period of creation of culture and cultural institutions but was followed by the occupation by the Soviet Union in 1940, which resulted in a new fifty-year period of colonisation. All of this left significant marks on the collective memory of Lithuanian society, culture and the body politic. The lasting mentality and institutional legacy, though sometimes bemoaned, are still felt in Lithuanian culture today.

In the 1940s the hopes held by some of the country's leftist intellectuals – that the composite nature of the Soviet Union would protect the most essential elements of Lithuanian society and provide an element of cultural autonomy – were dashed. The onset of the first Soviet occupation brought with it mass deportations of citizens to

Siberian gulags. Although the deportations targeted representatives of the intellectual class, the ensuing suffering was not inflicted solely on adults but also on children, even infants – a fact which graphically demonstrated the true face of the communist regime and the real aspirations of the occupiers. This experience also encouraged a second significant loss of Lithuanian intellectuals when a large number of writers and other artists moved to the West at the end of the Second World War. Following the movement of the front lines, they understood that if they remained in their homeland, they would be condemned – if not to death, then to prison, exile and other forms of repression. Their suspicions were soon confirmed. The post-war communist regime proved to be particularly brutal and the returning Soviet government initiated a fresh wave of deportations. Writers whose pasts, works or views raised even the slightest suspicion or doubt were questioned, tried, deported to *gulags* and condemned to a long exile. Those who had managed to avoid repression – typically as a result of their social origins, the expression of an outlook more acceptable to the Soviet state or a chameleon-like ability to adapt – were left with two options: either sing the praises of Stalinism or remain silent for decades on end. However, just keeping quiet was a dangerous option. A silent (non-writing) writer could be accused of harbouring a conscious desire *not* to glorify Joseph Stalin, *not* to support the ideology of the Communist Party and *not* to enact its requests. That mindset was a prelude to new types of persecution. As a result, the first decade after the end of the Second World War was the most difficult for the survival of Lithuanian literature. Some writers retreated underground or joined anti-Soviet fighters in the forests and lived in bunkers where they wrote poems in their notebooks that rarely reached the wider masses. For most of these writers, their fates ended tragically. In 1953, when the armed anti-Soviet resistance was finally quelled, the occupying regime made short work of free speech.

Soviet censors used every means at their disposal to control literary content and form. Any deviation from socialist realist norms was severely punished. Many of the works written in the post-war period were in reality the fruit of forced 'collaboration' between authors and censors. In certain cases writers were forced to re-write their novels or short stories several times in accordance with suggestions made by censors, especially in those instances when the writer's family or loved ones were imprisoned in Siberian *gulags*. In exchange for this literary collaboration, the writers were offered the promise that the suffering of their incarcerated loved ones would be lessened or shortened. It was in this way that the work of the inter-war writer Antanas Vienuolis was compromised: his son was serving time in a Soviet *gulag*. He wrote a second version of his socialist-realist novel *Puodžiūnkiemis* under the strict supervision of a Communist Party 'co-author', paying careful attention to the 'editing' provided.

Some writers became victims of both physical and intellectual oppression. The talented writer Kazys Boruta, whose excellent novel *Baltaragis' Windmill* (*Baltaragio malūnas*) was widely acclaimed and has been translated into English, was imprisoned in independent Lithuania for his membership of the outlawed socialist-revolutionary party; in the post-war period he was incarcerated by the Soviet regime for defending his position on national independence. Poet, dramatist, critic and professor at Vilnius University, Balys Sruoga was incarcerated along with other Lithuanian intellectuals at the Stutthof concentration camp by the Nazis. He died before the publication of *Forest of the Gods* (*Dievų miškas*), a memoir of his time in the Nazi camps. A book which critics later hailed as staggering and ironic, it was banned by the censors and languished for decades in a publishing-house drawer.

Censorship greatly affected the literary climate, spreading mediocrity and opportunism whilst studiously assisting in con-solidating the socialist-realist literary canon. Conditions changed somewhat after Nikita Khrushchev's famous speech at the 20th Soviet Party Congress in 1956. Encouraged by the new, apparently more moderate tone emanating from Moscow, Lithuanian writers became bolder in liberating themselves from the clutches of the compulsory canon and searched for new literary forms as well as more diverse creative motifs. An interest in literary techniques such as impressionism, interior monologue and increasingly individualised styles of expression began to appear in Lithuanian prose. At the same time growing attention was being paid to themes that had earlier been forbidden such as forced collectivisation as well as sudden and massive urbanisation, while there was also rising interest in drama depicting post-war existence. Lithuanian filmmakers also attempted to crack open this latter genre and a fine example of this trend came in the form of art film *No One Wanted to Die* (*Niekas nenorėjo mirti*), by the renowned director Vytautas Žalakevičius. Unfortunately, the 'thaw' in the Soviet regime's stance towards any kind of independent thought was short-lived, shattering the naïve illusions held by writers and other intellectuals that it was going to be possible to create 'socialism with a human face' in the Soviet bloc.

One might expect that there might be a search within literary forms for ways to express one's true feelings and ideas in a society where free speech is restricted and repressed. However, unlike in other central and eastern European countries where fierce censorship created stronger preconditions for the blossoming of self-publishing (*samizdat*), nothing of the sort occurred in Lithuania. Although banned periodicals and regularly issued self-published editions did appear in the country such as the multi-volume *Chronicle of the Catholic Church* (*Katalikų Bažnyčios kronika*), most publications of this type reached only a very small circle of readers.

Furthermore, the heavy repressions enacted in the first post-war decade and the suppression of the anti-Soviet armed resistance had considerable long-term effects on the collective memory. Many writers, creators and intellectuals imagined their role in the legal public sphere as one of being devoted to fostering and protecting Lithuanian culture, particularly language, while at the same time safeguarding its continuation. However, this type of thinking had controversial consequences on the development of Lithuanian culture and literature. A communist nomenclature rapidly formed in all spheres of cultural production. The Communist Party elite began to wield significant influence on creative development, retaining an iron grip on these institutions and blocking the way into the public world for braver, more original thinking authors and non-conformist literature. Even after more than two decades have passed since the end of the Soviet period, the question of collaboration and conformism still remains relevant because post-war habits of thinking and behaviour rooted in official culture continue to be felt today. They are also evident in the evaluation of literary development of the past few decades and in the bestowal of the most prestigious prizes for cultural creators based on criteria that developed in the late Soviet era and remain alive today.

The only writers to be unaffected by the array of controls over literary forms were those who chose exodus at the end of the Second World War. After spending some time in German displaced persons camps, they eventually travelled west, often ending up in the US. For quite some time, these prose writers and poets living in emigration, a few of whom had managed to become well known in independent Lithuania and were even regarded as having written classics, rallied together in a strong group. They established Lithuanian literary presses, literary journal editorial boards and other institutions of literary life. Some of these writers, having seen with their own eyes the process of Sovietisation in 1940 in Lithuania and upon finding themselves on the other side of the Atlantic, conveyed their experiences in literary form, with Vincas Ramonas telling his story in the 1947 novel *Crosses* (*Kryžiai*). Writers Algirdas Landsbergis and Marius Katiliškis used other aesthetic means to describe the themes of exodus, and the existential dimensions of exile were strongly and dramatically revealed in one of the most famous novels by a Lithuanian émigré: *The White Shroud* (*Balta drobulė*, 1958) by Antanas Škema. In this novel the narrator seeks to speak with an eternally silent God "whose presence reveals itself only in the suffering and total destruction of man", as the well-known critic of émigré literature, Rimvydas Šilbajoris, observed when commenting on this work.

For most of the works created by emigré writers, the path back to Lithuania was difficult. A large part of their readership was in

Lithuania and these works could only find domestic readers through illegal means. As a consequence, their impact on the literary consciousness forming in Soviet Lithuania was unavoidably limited. Works by emigré authors, for example, were not included in the literary programme at secondary schools or universities, and so an entire generation of readers only became acquainted with this part of Lithuanian literature after 1990. Eventually the production of émigré literature slowed, although the last few decades have witnessed the emergence of several prominent English-speaking Lithuanian writers in the United States and Canada.

The Soviet period in Lithuania nurtured its own literary leaders who, regardless of certain controversies, played a meaningful role in the formation of Lithuanian historical consciousness and national identity. When discussing Lithuanian literature of the Soviet period, it is impossible to ignore the poet and dramatist Justinas Marcinkevičius and his historical trilogy *Mindaugas* (1968), *Mažvydas* (1977), and *Cathedral* (*Katedra*, 1971). These plays strengthened the foundations of national identity and pride despite the hostile environment created by Soviet ideology and cultural colonisation. As a writer recognised by the regime and awarded the most important literary prizes, he had a huge impact on several generations of readers and became an object of adoration for a large part of the public. Many Lithuanian authors explored the processes of destruction affecting traditional village structures and communities, describing the incremental loss of the traditional ways of life and examining the consequences of collectivisation. In the 1990s these literary themes were woven into Romualdas Granauskas' literary opus. Granauskas presents an epitaph for the village epoch in Lithuanian culture, his realism tinged with more than a hint of sadness. His short story *Life under the Maples* (*Gyvenimas po klevu*), which was later made into a popular television film, showed the ideologies and political processes of the Soviet period irrevocably damaging the Lithuanian village. Characters in the village who are repositories of traditional wisdom end up disappearing, while the newly developing *homo sovieticus* is shown losing his cultural memory.

Introduction

As a result of rubbing up against the ideology and censorship of the Soviet regime, authors in the Soviet period perfected the Aesopian manner of speaking. This was the case not only for poets, who were used to juggling complex metaphors, but also for prose writers of that era who found individualistic ways of expressing encoded meanings in their texts. Some wrote about madness, split consciousness, and the development of dualism, while others skilfully wove ambiguous post-war episodes or historical dates important to Lithuanians into their stories. For example, in one of his stories Romualdas Lankauskas describes the dealings his character has with Satan: he is being pressured to accept huge material gains in exchange for altering the ending of the book he is writing. The reader, knowing how to read between the lines, no doubt understood that to use such a metaphor was to speak about the relationship between the writer and the KGB. Censorship stifled freedom of speech, but it also played a role in stimulating writers to perfect their artistic voice, to arm themselves with inventive modes of expression that would not be noticed by censors, and to create multiple meanings, the nuances of which were only revealed in the process of encoding and decoding.

An important characteristic of late Soviet-era literature was the marked increase of women writers in a literary domain traditionally belonging to men, and along with them new themes pushed their way into the literary sphere. Women writers paid more attention to relationships, revealed the dominance of male philosophies and stereotypes, and wrote about the fate of women and other Soviet-era realities with a more subtle hand that sparkled with new colour. It is reflected in this anthology by the work of contemporary women writers such as Birutė Jonuškaitė and Giedra Radvilavičiūtė.

In 1989, as the national reform movement, known as *Sąjūdis* in the West, was actively expressing its opinions – though no one had yet publicly dared to declare independence and most of the participants were still talking about supporting Gorbachev's 'reforms' – Ričardas Gavelis' novel *Vilnius Poker* (*Vilniaus pokeris*) appeared. It was destined to become the most significant late Soviet-era work of Lithuanian literature, crossing aesthetic and psychological thresholds as well as becoming a paradigm for post-modern discussion. The novel, which was written over nearly a decade and sections of which were hidden in the homes of the author's most trusted friends, examines the nature and mechanisms of power and coercion. Gavelis writes about what he called eternal conspirators against humanity, who are found in various forms throughout all periods of history from the time of Plato onwards. The novel, which sought to solve the mysteries of power and mind control, also revealed a new type of human – *homo lithuanicus* – who, in his wretchedness, cowardice and duplicity, surpasses his older spiritual brother, *homo sovieticus*. In this gloomy, post-modern text, full of sexual coercion, moral perversions and images of violence, the author attempted to answer the question: what happened to this nation which had lost its dignity, and spiritual orientation, one which safeguarded only empty symbols of past greatness that had lost their essence? Gavelis was also the first Lithuanian novelist who, quite early on, openly discussed the experiences of Lithuanians in the Siberian *gulags*, specifically in his story *Handless* (*Berankis*). *Vilnius Poker* broke all the literary sales records set in the previous decade; when the novel was released, nearly 100,000 copies were printed at lightning speed. A comparable print-run has only been seen since with the publication of a poetry collection by the well-known, previously banned émigré poet, Bernardas Brazdžionis, and was released to mark his triumphant return to Lithuania on the eve of independence.

The final years of the Soviet Union are often referred to as a period of 'stagnation'. It was during this time that I, having become a literary critic, encountered a strange and especially paradoxical situation: though the intellectual atmosphere of the time was gloomy and grim, with no prospect of changes to freedom of expression in sight, the regime's facade was manifesting signs of weakness. At that time I had published several critical reviews of the literary press and the literary situation in Lithuania, and I was scolded and accused of 'slandering Soviet Lithuanian literature' at the official annual meetings of the Writers' Union (ironically, an organization I was invited to join just a few years later). However, unlike the bravest critics of previous generations who in earlier decades, after similar public condemnations, had lost their right to publish for a few years or sometimes more, no one even tried to block my career. An obvious lack of vigilance in censorship was also apparent in the fact that in 1988, the popular weekly *Literature and Art* (*Literatūra ir menas*) quoted insights from *Encounter* magazine, which was widely known to be a Western, anti-Soviet magazine. The regime had wasted away from the inside and, as demonstrated by the bloody events of January 1991 in Vilnius, was desperately relying on its military strength. Its days were numbered.

This anthology attempts, admittedly fragmentally and without laying claim to any panoramic vision, to convey the more essential developments in Lithuanian literature over the last few centuries, a period that was closely connected to the evolution of statehood – its creation and loss – and the quest for freedom and independence. In the last century Lithuanian prose was dominated by themes related to agrarian life, bearing witness to the social and cultural developments taking place on the colonised edges of Europe. Many prominent writers of the past century observed, reflected on and wrote about the fate of traditional village culture in a modernising society (this view is exceptionally rendered in the work of one of the most prominent modern Lithuanian writers, Vincas Krėvė). They responded sensitively to the historical calamities that tormented the country – both of the world wars, the Holocaust, the Soviet occupation, the *gulags* and exile as well as the Sovietisation of the nation's identity and the controversies created in a late-forming urban culture. Under these circumstances, many writers, even into the present day, have used their work to examine both the distant and the not-so-distant past because it is connected not only with individual existential experience but also with questions about the future of society. Clearly, literature has many different objectives; it should not and cannot be reduced merely to elementary social commentary. However, keeping in mind the copious complicated historical changes that are a part of Lithuania's cultural development, one can see that it is entirely natural that writers often seek answers to the questions that eternally plague literary creators: Who are we? Where did we come from? And where are we going? It is my hope that the works published in this anthology will help make comprehensible the value and meaning behind these questions.

Translated by Medeinė Tribinevičius

The Cane
(As told to me by my good friend)

Jonas Biliūnas

Today the farmstead of my birth stands on a hill in the barren, sandy, windswept lands not far from the Šventoji River. Forests can be found only far to the north of the land, and only tiny pine saplings dot the east and the west. As I recall, not that long ago the entire farmstead was buried in deep, rich forest. Beyond these forests and stretching amongst scattered quagmires to the very banks of the Šventoji were the splendid pastures, shaded by oak trees, belonging to the people. The fields are no less splendid today, but the forests that once girdled them are long gone. They disappeared like the fairy tales we forget as we grow up, but which continue to inhabit our memory like distant, seductive images.

Those beautiful forests were the property of 'our lord'.

Don't laugh at me for saying 'our lord'. I, too, could never understand why my father called that lord 'our lord' even though he lived far away from us – two miles away. Later I understood that he collected a tithe from my parents and that's why my father, according to tradition, called him that. He must have had good reason to call him thus because for years the lord exploited the people of our farmstead, claiming rights to their pastures and forests. A forester had been assigned to guard the forests; he lived adjacent to our farmstead at the very edge of the forest in large, dilapidated quarters. The forester took pleasure in reporting on us to the lord, and my father, who lived closest, was often called upon to hear out the lord's grumblings.

There's one incident I will never forget...

One day the lord came to our farmstead to hunt; a large party of guests accompanied him and they took many deer, rabbits and birds. Their large bounty of game was laid out on the road near the forester's cottage. Uninvited, we young parasites swarmed in from all sides, picking our noses and gaping at the game and the gentry. The gentlemen were seated in their carriages, preparing to travel home. My father, who'd been working his harrows near the pile of wood, was also on his way to have a look. As he walked over, he overheard the forester lodging a complaint to the lord about the villagers' use of the pastures. Frightened, he hid behind the barn.

'Get me one of the peasants!' the lord bellowed from his carriage.

The forester told him that my father was nearby.

Hearing that he was the object of discussion and aware that there was no way for him to extricate himself, my father emerged from behind the barn. A hundred steps away he removed his hat and bowed deeply. Frightened and miserable, he rushed over to kiss the lord's hand. The lord, with a voice not his own, began screeching at my father, threatening to send him and the entire village to beg in the street. With pale lips and a palpitating heart I witnessed this scene, noting the forester's face beaming with satisfaction. Some of the guests watched with pity, and others with disdain. After he concluded his rant, and paying no heed to my father's excuses, the lord whipped his horses and rattled off.

Father, hatless, stood for a few moments. Then he called me over. Agitated and trembling, he instructed: 'Run over to the river to see whether it's true that the shepherd is grazing his livestock on the lord's lands.'

I rushed over with my friends and found the animals grazing ever so peacefully in their own fields, while the shepherds taunted the village dunce. I returned home and described everything to my father. Shaking his head he sat in silence.

But my mother, hearing that the shepherds were innocent, said accusingly: 'Didn't I tell you? Like master, like servant. Any reason to stab you in the back.'

'Don't be angry, mother. Our lord is a good man,' father said, laughing softly and sadly as he often did.

'Enough is enough,' mother snapped. 'Have you forgotten how he exploits the people? Have you forgotten the cane?'

I must admit that although she never said a bad word against the lords, my mother had no warm feelings for them. She often remembered the old days, telling us about events from the distant past, her voice sorrowful as she described the suffering of the serfs under their masters. As usual, father tried to apologise for the lords to mother, but he did this so timidly and then laughed so sadly that his voice betrayed resignation, not truth and conviction. But father's apologies for the lords sometimes annoyed mother and that's when she would remind him: 'Enough already, father. Have you forgotten the cane?'

Father would not respond to this; he would only laugh sadly and, picking up the Book, he would read aloud to us about the life of Christ. For a long time I had no idea which cane mother was referring to and why father would always laugh so sadly whenever he defended the lords. But finally one day he took it upon himself to tell us the story.

Along with the forester, there was a man, one Dumbrauckas, who lived with him in the same quarters. He was a tall man, old, completely grey and alone, with no family. He had never been married but he was father to an adult son; that son lived somewhere deep in Russia and he visited his father infrequently. They said that once upon a time Dumbrauckas had been very wealthy but that he had lost all his wealth and property in a game of cards. How much of this was true, it's hard to say. Only this is known: in my father's memory he had become overseer under our lord.

After serfdom was abolished, Dumbrauckas lost his position and thus inexplicably came to live on our homestead with the forester. He lived there for many years, rarely venturing outside, spending all his time inside his room. He would either pace the room or sit at his little table at the window. As small children, seeing from a distance his grey head in the window, always in the same spot, we imagined some strange, incomprehensible and not necessarily benevolent creature, and we were afraid to get too close. Perhaps Dumbrauckas might have even died in that nest of his at the forester's if it hadn't been for unusual circumstances.

It must be said that our lord's power and wealth were on the decline. The lovely forests surrounding our homestead had been bought up by Jews. The people had cut down the forest, transported the logs to the Šventoji and floated them down the river. All that remained were clearings littered with stray branches. On a hot summer's day some fool from our village, while carting hay along the scarred lands, suddenly felt the urge to smoke. As he lit his pipe, the dry branches went up in flames. In an instant a fire was raging and the clearings were crackling... The entire homestead would have been destroyed if the villagers hadn't banded together with pitchforks and rakes. After two hours all that lay alongside the homestead was a wide expanse of flat land, blackened and smelling of charred wood. The village later bought up this land from the lord for a trifle.

In this way, the lord's power ended along with the forests. The village no longer needed to fear his threats. The forester was now expendable. Appropriately, the house he lived in collapsed. Water poured in through the roof, the winds whistled through the walls. And one fine day the forester disappeared without a trace. Dumbrauckas had to move somewhere as well. I don't know if it was his idea or my parents' suggestion, but Dumbrauckas moved into the living room of our house. He brought with him his little table, a few books, and his cow. Nothing else.

And as before, Dumbrauckas spent his time pacing the expanse of the living room, or sitting at his table by the window. He lived with us for two years and – in my opinion, very unexpectedly – became my teacher. He placed the largest Polish book possible into my hands, stood next to me and ordered me to read. He would stand there all day, and all day I would read. And so it went all summer and all winter long. I had great difficulty with the Polish language:

24

I lisped and there were many words I could not pronounce. But my teacher was ruthless. He obliged me to exercise my tongue in all sorts of directions, to repeat the same word up to a hundred times – I would break out in a sweat and my eyes would flood with tears as a result. I would see Dumbrauckas's fingers quivering – that's how badly he wanted to box my ears or punch me in the nose. I got to know those hands quite well! They were the hands of an overseer – hard as steel. But when I heard he was leaving us – no one knew why – I became sad; I pitied him. That was in the autumn. An unfamiliar 'gentleman' arrived and drove him away.

As Dumbrauckas said his goodbyes, he left me his desk, and because my father was an old man, he left him his old applewood cane.

'For you Joseph, I leave my cane as a keepsake,' said Dumbrauckas to my father.

'Thank you, sir,' answered my father, visibly moved. 'I wonder if we shall ever meet again?'

My father held the cane for a long time after Dumbrauckas left. As he turned it in his hands, he smiled sadly.

Then he raised his eyes and asked us unexpectedly:

'Do you children know what this cane reminds me of?'

We all looked up.

'It was long ago,' my father began in an emotional voice. 'Long, long ago. Your mother and I were still young, most of you were not yet here on this earth – only Michael had been born. We were afflicted by many great misfortunes that year. Bread was scarce and the fields and pastures were dry. And we worked not just for our own benefit, but also for the lord's. We had to walk two miles to get to work – all the way to Burbiskis. I drove the oxen to Burbiskis one autumn to plough the fallow land. I couldn't take much with me: I packed some bread and salt for myself and a few handfuls of old chaff for the oxen. We had nothing else. And I had to work for three days. As I was ploughing I ran out of feed for the oxen. I had no way to get more. There was nowhere for the oxen to graze – it was forbidden. My oxen were exhausted. They were barely dragging their feet. And one more day of ploughing remained! I stopped the oxen for lunch, sat down at the edge of the field and ate the dried bread and salt that I had pulled out of my basket. My oxen watched longingly as I ate. I felt so sorry for them that I had to stop eating. Nothing but crumbs remained in my basket. I fed them to the oxen and looked around: a few feet away I spied several piles of recently raked clover belonging to the lord.

'And a terrible thought came into my head. Yes, as it might sometimes happen to you young people today. I work for the lord, so why can't I feed the lord's oxen some of his own grass?

'I got up, went over to the pile and took a small handful of clover. I brought this over to the oxen and fed them by hand. The oxen happily devoured it. Watching them made me feel better. But then I suddenly felt someone strike my back, oh so painfully, with a hard object. I staggered and collapsed. My oxen jumped and almost ran off with the plough. Dazed, I raised my eyes: standing on top of me was Dumbrauckas with a cane in his hand. "You dog! Thief! Thief!" yelled Dumbrauckas, who walloped me in the back with his stick.

'Seeing that I wasn't moving, he helped me up from the ground with his arm, then he kicked me, knocking me down yet again. As I came around, I opened my eyes and saw my oxen standing nearby, their heads turned to watch me. Half-dead, I staggered home and lay in bed for three weeks.'

My father was silent. We sat in our places, stock-still. No one uttered a word. Only my sister, with tears in her eyes, asked: 'Father, was this the same Dumbrauckas who lived at our house?'

'The same one,' answered father. 'But you mustn't be angry with him. During the uprisings the Cossacks beat him so badly that for three months he lay soaking in his own blood...'

'Do you know, children, which cane he used to beat me?' asked father, now smiling. 'This one!'

We all shuddered, our eyes wide. Father raised his hand and showed us the cane, the one Dumbrauckas had left him as a keepsake.

My oldest brother approached father and grabbed the cane from his hands. He turned it again and again, as if considering something in his mind, then he threw it onto the lumber pile, saying with a barely audible voice. 'Let's burn it, father!'

'No, no, children,' answered father pleasantly. 'Let this cane remain amongst you. When you look at it, remember that even your parents had once been punished. As you remember, don't be angry that your mother and I sometimes hit you with a switch. We did it for your own good.... Perhaps our lord beat us for our own good?'

'Enough, father, enough,' mother ended the conversation. 'It might be this very cane that caused your illness. This is not how we teach our children.'

Father smiled sadly, and taking up his book, he settled down to read.

As far as I know, my brothers still have the cane. It remains on the shelf in the granary. And nobody touches it.

April 25, 1906

First published in Jonas Biliūnas, *Lazda; Ubagas; Svečiai*; *Brisiaus galas*, Vilnius: Lietuvos ūkininkas (1906).

Translated by Jūra Avižienis from Jonas Biliūnas, *Liūdna pasaka: kūrybos rinktinė*, Vilnius: Baltos lankos (1995).

Jonas Biliūnas (1879–1907) was a prose writer, poet and publicist. Over his short life, he remained faithful to his left-wing worldview and explored working class life in his literary works. His creative legacy reveals a solidarity with the oppressed and their tragic fate. In his short stories and short novels he emphasises moral self-determination, guilt and feelings of responsibility.

The Herring

Vincas Krėvė

I

It was the middle of Lent, turning to spring. The days were warm and sunny; the snow was melting and the hilltops were losing their snow cover. Rivulets coursed through the valleys, roads and furrowed fields; with a roar they told the story of spring, announcing it was just around the corner.

'Ladies, do you have any herring, chickens or eggs?' Kušlius asked, rapping on the window one day.

He was an old Jew with a long, bushy, red beard that went right up to his eyes. His hair was all grey, his beard only partly so, but this half-greyness couldn't hide the hair colour of his birth. He was shortsighted and couldn't even see what was under his feet. That's why he used his cane to feel his way like a blind man; he was especially careful when carrying eggs.

'Why don't you get yourself some eyeglasses?' the people asked him on many occasions.

'Eyeglasses? Where would I get money for eyeglasses?' he'd say with a heavy sigh.

The village children must have caused him much suffering. Their favourite prank was to stick something under Kušlius's feet to trip him. How funny to see him fall to his knees! But Kušlius would anticipate their tricks and was on guard whenever he saw the children playing or the farm hands nearby.

'Why are you so unkind to an old man?' he would ask

reproachfully, using his cane to push aside the stick or the stone that had been intended to trip him. 'Would you be happy if I fell and killed myself?'

But he never held a grudge; perhaps his heart had grown accustomed to this kind of ridicule.

Whether it was winter or summer, he dressed always the same, and would walk among the farmsteads carrying his basket and his bag – a veritable store on his shoulders. There wasn't a farmstead he wouldn't visit.

Now he was standing at Gerdvilius's window, listening with his ear pressed against the glass to hear what the women were saying.

'Do you have boar's liver?' teased the shepherd. He was seated on a bench outside the window whilst making a fishing net. But Kušlius, used to hearing such jibes, didn't take his words to heart. He waited a moment. When he didn't get a response, he knocked on the window a second time.

'Do you need soap, needles, matches or herring?'

'Come in, come in. We'll see.' Mrs. Gerdvilius invited him into the cottage after conferring with her daughter-in-law, who was leaning over the cradle nursing her child.

As Kušlius made his way through the yard to the porch, the shepherd dashed over to the oven, pulled out the thickest stick from under it and placed it in the doorway.

'Remove that stick! Remove that stick!' Mrs. Gerdvilius scolded. 'Do you want to get an old man killed? You shameless boy!'

'He doesn't matter – he hasn't been baptised!' jeered the shepherd and sat down by the window. 'These pranks are nothing compared to what we used to do to him when I worked in Šilakiemis.'

Monica, Gerdvilius's daughter, a girl of about fifteen, leaned her bundle of flax against the wall and, jumping up quickly – Kušlius was already walking into the porch – she grabbed the stick and threw it into the fire.

'You wicked boy! I'll give you such a beating. Then you'll know!' she berated the shepherd, before returning to her place by the flax.

'You don't dare. Are you aching to become Kušlius's daughter-in-law? Is that why you're standing up for him?' The shepherd taunted her.

'Beast! Gloating like a dog with two tails.'

'Whatever were you doing there in Šilakiemis – there will be none of that here,' Mrs. Gerdvilius scolded him as well. 'Only scamps make fun of old men. Don't laugh. You'll be old yourself one day. It's a sin against God to make fun of old age. God won't let you live to see your own golden years.'

'It's hardly a sin against God to laugh at a Jew,' Marcela, the hired servant, chimed in. 'After all, they tortured our Lord and put him to death.'

And now Kušlius, sighing, walked heavily across the threshold. He seemed exhausted.

'Blessed be the Lord,' he said, not taking off his cap.

'Forever and ever, amen,' answered only Mrs. Gerdvilius.

Having come inside, Kušlius moved closer to the window. He removed the pack that contained his merchandise from his shoulders and placed it all on the table. He put the egg basket under the bench after checking the spot with his cane. He placed the bucket of herring at his side on the bench, pulling off the ragged cover to reveal the fish.

'Come, take some herring,' he invited the women, placing the smallest ones at the top of the bucket. 'How many do you need? Two? Three?'

Mrs. Gerdvilius stepped away from the stove, smoothed her dress, and went over to the bench. She stuck her hand in the bucket and chose the herring that looked best to her.

'My, oh my, you've taken the very best ones. Who will buy the little ones?' Kušlius murmured.

'Come now. They'll take the little ones, if that's all there is.'

Mrs. Gerdvilius chose five herring and placed them on the bench.

'How many eggs do you want for these herring?' she asked Kušlius.

Kušlius picked up the herring and examined them, turning them, lifting them up and down, weighing them in his hands.

'How many eggs? Eggs are cheap these days, and you took the choice herring. Look, they're as plump and juicy as chickens. He showed the herring to Mrs. Gerdvilius.

'Don't shove them in my face. I'm not blind. I can see. These herring are as thin as rails.'

'These are good rails! I never ate better ones in my whole life. Fine. Give me fifteen. Agreed?'

'Not a chance, you infidel! You expect me to pay that much for these rails! Take your herring. Keep them.'

She picked up the herring from the bench and threw them back in the bucket; then she turned and went back to the stove where she had left her spindle board on a small bench.

'Well, how much will you give me? Tell me how much.' Kušlius yelled as he pulled out the very same herring from the bucket and put them back on the bench.

Mrs. Gerdvilius wiped her hands on her apron and sat down at her spinning wheel.

'If you'll take eight,' she offered to Kušlius, 'then I'll do it.'

'Eight eggs for these five herring?' Kušlius was astounded. 'Would my worst enemy have it so good! I paid more for them myself. How about fourteen?'

'No. Take nine if you want. Not a penny more.'

Bringing her spindle board upright, she pulled it close to her, lubricated it with a bit of spit on her hands and began spinning as if she had forgotten the herring.

'How about a baker's dozen?' Kušlius asked. 'That's the best I can do. On my life, that's the best,' Kušlius swore, but he did not put the herring back into the bucket.

'Ten is my last offer. Not a single egg more.'

'If only the herring were quality herring,' said her daughter-in-law, coming to her defence. She had finished nursing her baby and swaddled him. Walking to her spinning wheel, she glanced at the herring on the bench. 'Tiny, skimpy, like roaches.'

'On my life, I swear that they cost me more than what you're offering.'

31

Kušlius put the herring back in the bucket, threw his portable store over his shoulders, attached the basket with eggs to the corner of the bag and, sighing heavily, he made his way towards the door.

'How about twelve?' he asked, stopping in the doorway.

'Ten, I said. No more. Don't waste my time haggling. I'm not a child.'

'I can't do it. God knows, I can't.'

'If you can't do it, then don't,' the daughter-in-law blurted.

Out in the yard Kušlius went over to the window and asked one last time:

'Missus, how about eleven?'

'And still he bothers me. I said ten.'

Kušlius stood thinking for a moment: should he go home or go back? But how could he not go back – there would be profit either way: five or six cents, maybe even ten.

Kušlius went back to the cottage, returned his wares to the same spot and unpacked the herring.

'All right, bring me your eggs and take the herring,' he shouted, placing them on the bench.

Mrs. Gerdvilius, resting the spindle board against the wall, took a bowl for the herring down from the shelf.

'Which herring are you giving me? Do you take me for a fool? I will not take such herring!' Mrs. Gerdvilius was angry, sorting through the herring on the bench. These much smaller ones had been chosen by Kušlius.

'Which herring do you want?' Kušlius shouted. 'This is best herring I've seen in my life.'

'Take them, take them, I don't need herring like that.' She pushed them back into his hands. 'Just look! He gave me the worst ones!'

'For ten eggs you want the finest herring,' Kušlius grumbled and switched two of the herring for better ones. 'These are better ones. Take them and bring me my eggs.'

Mrs. Gerdvilius sat by her spinning wheel, refusing to look at the herring.

'I don't want them. If you can't give me good ones, keep them all.'

The Jew was looking through the herring in the bucket again. Selecting them, smelling them, he replaced two more.

'Will you take these, Missus? I don't have time. Why are you wasting my time?' Angry, the Jew yelled. 'Here, take the ones you picked out last time.'

Mrs. Gerdvilius noticed that he had now selected the best ones for her.

'Marcela, take the herring from him,' she ordered her servant as she carried her bowl to the porch to the cupboard where the eggs were kept.

Marcela, without getting up from her spinning, reached for a lid used to cover up pots of hot stew and protect them from flies and placed the herring on it.

When Mrs. Gerdvilius brought the eggs, Kušlius looked each one over, lifting them up to the sun, shaking them and placing them next to his ear.

'What kind of eggs did you give me?' This time it was Kušlius's turn to be demanding. 'Who has ever seen such eggs? I wouldn't even get two cents for them.'

'If you don't like them, don't take them. I'll sell them in Merkinė.' Mrs. Gerdvilius retorted. 'Marcela, give him back his herring.'

'My, oh my. Why so hasty?' Kušlius's voice was now softer and more obliging; he placed the eggs in his basket. 'Just give me some fried potato. I haven't had a thing to eat today.'

'Monica, give him some potato.' Mrs. Gerdvilius turned to her daughter.

Monica brought a handful of potatoes and placed them on the table. Kušlius peeled them and ate two, then a third. The rest he put into his pockets.

While the Jew was peeling and eating the potatoes, Marcela pulled out of his bucket one, two, then three herring – so slyly that nobody seemed to notice when she pulled them out and hid them behind the spindle board. But the shepherd did. As she was hiding the herring he winked at her, roaring with laughter.

'What are you splitting your sides about?' Monica looked at him. 'He's laughing so hard he's howling.'

'He's laughing at an old man. He's laughing at the old man's hardship,' Kušlius lamented as he devoured his potato. 'It's cruel to laugh at someone's suffering.'

Marcela glanced at the shepherd and also had a laugh. Realising that he had seen everything, she winked at him to ask him to be quiet.

Kušlius put the remaining potatoes in his pocket and explained: 'I'm bringing them home to my wife. She's very sick.' He then tied up his sack, threw his bag over his shoulders and sighed deeply. 'Missus, do you have a chicken to sell me? A chicken or a rooster?'

'No. Nobody's selling chickens these days.'

'My wife is sick; she needs a chicken, but there is no chicken.' Kušlius sought the women's sympathy. He picked up his bags and went towards the door. The old man sighed, for his load was heavy; he was barely dragging his feet along, and yet he had to wade through the slippery muck. He was wet, muddy up to his knees. And back at home was an old lady who was sick, alone and without anyone to help her.

'Oh, if only my enemies had a life as easy as mine,' Kušlius exhaled noisily as he trudged along.

As soon as he crossed the threshold, the shepherd and Marcela burst out laughing.

'You curs, what prank did you play on him?' Mrs. Gerdvilius asked. 'Did you steal his entire day's wages? With a sick wife. Don't you fear God?'

'The devil take him!' Trying hard not to laugh, Marcela justified herself. 'It's not the first time they've cheated one of us.'

'It's their job. We'll see what the priest says when you go to confess.'

Marcela fell dead silent at the thought of the priest. It occurred to her that perhaps Kušlius and his family might actually be starving. She remembered how hungrily he had devoured the fried potato.

'You'll be laughing, the both of you, when you meet St. Peter with herring in your mouth, begging Kušlius to take them back from you,' Monica threatened.

'That will be the day when I beg for a Jew's apology,' the shepherd shot back. 'Will there be Jews up there with us Catholics?'

'When you end up in hell, you'll find all kinds there: Jews, Catholics, gentry, and ordinary folk.'

'What a laugh! Since when is it a sin to cheat a Jew?' Marcela was certain of her righteousness. 'They tortured our Lord to death and hung him on a cross.'

'Oh, girl,' Mrs. Gerdvilius replied. 'We torture our dear Lord every day. We torture him and hang him on the cross. And he always forgives us.'

II

Marcela dreamed that she had arrived in heaven. It was beautiful, like the church in Pivašiūnai. Everywhere candles and lanterns burned. The Lord God himself, grey-haired with a long beard, sat high on the altar, surrounded by angels. Some were tiny, like those in the painting of the Virgin Mary in Merkinė, flying high and low circling around God, while others were bigger, with long robes and large wings. Kneeling at the altar, their hands were clasped in prayer as if they were young priests or clerics worshipping God.

Everyone in heaven was dead. Marcela could not see one living soul. Her throat tightened at the sudden thought that she might have died and that's why she had ended up here. But she could not remember when she had died. She didn't have much time to wonder because more and more dead people starting pushing and shoving to get through the narrow gates where she was standing. They drove her into a corner, pressing her against a wall. There were as many dead people in heaven as in Merkinė church during the indulgences of St. Roch. Men, women, gentry, priests and ordinary folk, they were all well-dressed, as if they had been buried recently.

The gentlemen and the ladies were seated behind the grates, closer to God; seeing this, Marcela sighed: 'My Lord, even in heaven the gentry are better off!'

Marcela saw many of her acquaintances; some had been long dead, some had died only last year. There was Peter Lukošiūnas, her godfather, for whom she had worked for five years as a shepherd and as a servant. She also spotted Mrs. Vakšas, her godmother, who'd given her a silk scarf when Marcela had made her first confession. Sure, the scarf was no longer new – a tiny hole peeked through at the very centre – but Marcela still wore it when she attended the more important rites. She saw many others whom she barely remembered.

Marcela stood near the gates, pressed against the wall, and had a look around. Kneeling behind the gates was her own dear, old mother. With a pang she felt a longing for her mother so keen, so strong, that her heart seemed to be gripped by pliers. Now she would have a chance to talk with her, to pour out her heart, tell her of her woes like she used to when her mother was still alive and Marcela would visit her every holiday.

Marcela elbowed her way with determination to where her mother was kneeling; pushing, shoving, stepping on toes, getting there any way she could. The souls were furious and cursed her. But she paid no attention and pushed herself forward.

When she had made her way to the very centre of heaven and her mother was within reach – just a few steps remained – an angel stopped her. He was dressed in white with a red sash embroidered in gold across his shoulder; in his hands he held a large, golden sceptre.

The angel reprimanded her: 'What are you doing here pushing your way in like a boorish lout. You're disturbing the souls' worship of their Lord God!' He looked her up and down and added, 'You came here all filthy and you're rubbing your dirt onto the souls' white robes!'

Marcela looked at herself: she was filthy indeed. She was wearing her everyday dress and the blouse she had not changed in over two weeks. She was humiliated, afraid even, and averted her eyes. But the angel stared at her ever more angrily.

'Why did you bring those herring into the House of God?' he asked, 'Are you trying to make the place stink? Give me those fish. I'll throw them out.'

Marcela looked down; there were herring in her hands, the very ones that she'd stolen from Kušlius's bucket. She had no clue how she'd gotten them and how she'd brought them here. She remembered only that she had already eaten them, and this made her even more frightened. Now Marcela felt the brine from the herring dripping from her fingers onto her dress. She stretched out her hands all the more quickly to give the angel her herring. The angel called over another smaller angel and said:

'Take these herring and throw them out. We have our own food here in heaven; we have no need for earthly food. No need for herring here.'

The smaller angel was reaching for the herring when an angry voice was heard from behind heaven's gates:

'Give me back my herring! That's the fish she stole from me!'

Horror-struck, Marcela recognised Kušlius's voice. She noted that all the souls were moving away from her, and even God, sitting up high, was scowling. Marcela was afraid to raise her eyes, but she saw his fury from the corner of her eye. And that brazen Kušlius was still yelling at her from behind the gates. She'll pull out his beard, she'll even ask the shepherd to set the dogs on him! Doesn't he deserve it? He should have told her privately, asking her to pay him for it, but not here in heaven, in plain view for God and the angels to see.

'Is there no justice even in heaven? Why won't she return my herring? Even here the poor Jew is oppressed.' Kušlius wouldn't stop.

'You're a thief and yet you've come to heaven? Bringing stolen goods into the House of God?' The angel accused her, but Marcela was silent and dumbstruck – that's how frightened she was. 'You have nothing to say for yourself, no explanation for your actions? Let's go see God. Let him punish you as you deserve!'

The angel took her by the hand, and led her across the entirety of heaven, straight to God's throne by the altar. Marcela was so humiliated she wanted to disappear. All the others were moving aside as if she had scabies, jeering, throwing insults at her.

'Thief! She stole herring from the Jew,' Marcela heard as she passed by.

This is how the souls accompanied her with their angry glances. Most difficult for Marcela was that the angel was taking her past the very spot where her mother was praying. Although Marcela did not raise her eyes she felt her mother look at her dolefully. This look made her turn red as a Guelder Rose. Or at least she thought she was blushing.

'Did you steal Kušlius's herring?' God asked Marcela as she kneeled before his throne.

Marcela was silent as a deaf mute. She covered her eyes with her hand and quivered like an aspen leaf. God was silent waiting for Marcela to speak. When he received no answer, he turned to the angels and ordered: 'Take her to hell and give her to the devils. Let them torture her for eternity.'

The minute God said this, the angels darted toward Marcela and, without giving her a second to catch her breath, they pushed her out of heaven and locked the gates behind her.

It was dark, gloomy and frightening outside the gates of heaven. The gates had barely clicked shut when she was surrounded by devils. They had horns and tails; flames burned in their throats like fire in a furnace. They were climbing over one another to get to Marcela. The most horrifying one of all was already poking his pitchfork at her. At the sight of this Marcela grabbed onto the gates to heaven and shrieked at the top of her voice and woke up.

Marcela sat up in her bed, drenched in sweat and quivering as if burning with fever.

Her first thought was to jump out of bed and run to Kušlius, confess and beg his forgiveness. But she saw out of her window that it was night, dark, and Merkinė, where Kušlius lived, was far! How would she find him this time of night? And what's more, people would think she'd lost her mind...

Marcela sat in bed for a long time, cross-legged, fearfully looking out of the window from time to time to make sure a horned devil wasn't climbing in.

Finally, she made the sign of the cross over her bed, the floor, the walls on all four sides as well as the windows and the door. She made the sign of the cross over everything, and then she jumped up out of bed and walked over to Mrs. Gerdvilius's bed where she fumbled around looking for Mrs. Gerdvilius's dress. She found it and, with hands shaking out of fear of waking anyone, she turned the pockets inside out looking for the key to the cupboard.

She opened the doors carefully so that nobody would hear and went out into the porch. There, in the dark, with the utmost care, stopping every so often to listen and make sure that nobody had awoken, she unlocked the cupboard looking for the bowl where she knew the eggs were kept.

She found one and stuck her hand in – it was a bowl of fresh milk. Then she stuck her hand into another bowl – her fingers felt sour cream; and then another – it was barley. Finally she found the eggs. She took six, locked the door to the cupboard and buried the eggs in the sand pile in a corner of the porch; the pile had been there since the autumn and they kept it so that there would be something to scatter onto the swept floor in the winter.

After she hid the eggs Marcela went back into the cottage, as carefully as before. She returned the key to where she'd found it, lay down in her bed and peacefully fell asleep.

The next morning, Mrs. Gerdvilius was confused why the doors to the cupboard and porch had milky fingerprints – her own dress did too. Had she been sleepwalking?

She searched all the dishes and found some eggs missing. She blamed the shepherd. He defended himself, swearing that he had nothing to do with it, but Mrs. Gerdvilius would not believe him.

Marcela heard everything and kept quiet. Now every evening she checks the sand pile to make sure the eggs are still there and she impatiently awaits her day off when she will bring them over to Kušlius and pay him back for the herring…

Then she will no longer fear that that God will again order her to be thrown out of heaven for stealing!

First published in Vincas Krėvė, *Šiaudinej pastogėj*, Tilže: Lituania (1921).

Translated by Jūra Avižienis from Vincas Krėvė, *Šiaudinej pastogėj*, Vilnius: Baltos lankos (1998).

Vincas Krėvė (1882–1954) is the godfather of modern Lithuanian fiction. He wrote many long works of fiction as well as the play *Šarunas* (1911), and the short novel *Pratjekabuda* (1913). He worked for many years on the epic *Sons of Heaven and Earth* (*Dangaus ir žemės sūnūs*, 1949) and established himself in Lithuanian literature with his rich and colourful short stories depicting the influence of a traditional, pre-Christian worldview on the mentality of village inhabitants. His work has had a significant impact on the development of the Lithuanian short story. He was a professor at Vytautas Magnus University in Kaunas and harboured political ambitions throughout his life. He played a controversial role in the loss of Lithuanian statehood when he was the prime minister of the first Soviet government. Later he emigrated to the United States where he worked as a professor at the University of Pennsylvania until the end of his life.

The Light of Your Face

Antanas Vaičiulaitis

When Theresa lifted her head from the bed it was dark in the homestead. The wind murmured in the leaves of the oak tree, which brushed the roof. The wooden lever of the well creaked uncomfortably in the yard and the ash-grey cow mooed: its voice quickly dissipated in the storm, while inside the room a brisk and lively fire crackled. An ember fell through the slots, rolled down over the ashes and glittered on the dirt floor. The woman looked at the spark and recalled how she was forced to lie in bed because of sharp pains and tremendous exhaustion, which made her sight dim. But she was still alive! And to her, the spool of wool on the spindle and that little piece of sourdough bread in the tub in the corner seemed like new and distant things, things she had seen in childhood.

She lowered her legs to the floor. Shuffling, she went to the fireplace. Her head was spinning. Her chest was empty and heavy. A pot hissed, puffed and bubbled. She raised the lid, which rattled quietly. Busying herself around the fire, the old woman raked the wood chips that constantly twisted and scattered into a pile. It was peaceful here, though a blustery wind blew and rattled the roof; it was so strong that it was as if it wanted to split the earth's crust down the middle and fling the heavy clouds about like a shawl.

Grandmother threw the sweepings into the flames. She was warmed up now and was satisfied like someone who had completed a useful task. She wiped the table with her apron and looked at the geraniums.

'So!' she said loudly. She scratched at the hardened, cracked soil in the vase and nodded her head: 'They'll certainly dry out.'

When she returned to the flowers with a cup of water, the geese squawked in the yard. Someone stamped their legs on the porch and banged their shoes against the doorstep. Maybe it's Vincas, the woman thought.

The water sloshed and ran out of the cup, hiding in the cracks, popping in pale bubbles. Yes, she missed Vincas. He had been gone for a week already. Oh, those forests, those forests! And only he understood her and defended her from her daughter's words.

The door screeched plaintively. Smiling, Theresa slowly turned her head, and having turned around, she almost shrieked. She caught the cup on the vase and it fell on the dirt floor and smashed.

Tall and slender, her daughter stood there saying nothing. She unwrapped her shawl. Her hair fell on her temples. She was angry. Good Lord! She was always angry and hard! Why do you hate me so, you, who I carried in my womb, she exclaimed in her mind.

Agnė stood there and didn't say a word.

Frightened, the old woman knelt down by the shards. Her eyes swam. She fumbled around with shaking fingers, raked up the pieces but could not grasp anything. She hunched her shoulders as if she were afraid of being hit.

Agnė still stood there.

'It's wilting,' Theresa spoke.

'Without you mother, it would never be tidy in here! I've said that many times.'

'My little Agnė!'

'My little Agnė, my little Agnė! You'd laze about better in bed.'

The old woman, kneeling and stooped over, raised her eyes at her daughter: 'My dear, why do you hate me so much?' she said.

She sat on her heels and wiped a tear from her wrinkled face with her sleeve.

'What isn't there to hate?' Agnė said rudely. 'Just don't get underfoot.'

'I won't be here long.'

'Mama, no one's keeping you here.'

Theresa rose, grasping onto the table, feeling weak and tired. She was jealous of the roof over her head! And gasping, so small and weak, she went to sit in the hallway between the barrels. It was cold there. The wind whipped about even more severely. It blew with full force and travelled from one end of the earth to the other. Yes, Vincas will return and find her here. She will complain to him, yes, she will complain. He will defend her. He will give that daughter of hers a good scolding. Rats scurried on the storey above, scratching and squeaking. The children, three boys, charged into the farmhouse. They hadn't noticed her. But once inside the homestead, after clattering around for a few minutes, they began to ask:

'Where's grandmother?'

'Did she go out somewhere?' Agnė replied.

'Uh-huh.'

Opening the door she spoke sharply, mocking her: 'You're going to have to wait a long time before Vincas comes back.'

Theresa didn't reply.

Then her daughter spoke again: 'Well, are you there? Why aren't you saying anything!'

Receiving no reply, she lit a match. The faint light flickered on the barrels and on the thick beams of the ceiling and that black opening leading up into the attic. Pale and looking out in front of her with eyes full of dread, the old woman squirmed as though she wanted to disappear completely. The flame rose a little, flared brightly and then went out.

A sharp voice spoke from out of the darkness.

'Sit there if you like. But you should know Vincas isn't coming today or tomorrow. He informed me through Francis from Stakniškės that he still has to finish up in the Didžiagirė birch forest and then he has go out to the Šikšnine forest. You understand?'

And she slammed the door. In the hut, the children were quiet. The old woman hid there for another good hour and then said to herself: 'Didžiagirė…' She got up and went into the room, pulled a gnarled cane out of the corner and wrapped herself in a shawl. The little ones looked at her in the dark, afraid to utter a word. She turned around at the threshold and said: 'Goodbye, children.'

No one answered her; only little Joseph started to cry.

It was brighter outside. In the west, far off near the edge of the valley, stretched a black cloud; the sky glistened through it and reddened in a plaintive and tearful way. Two ravens darted through the yard against the wind. They flew diagonally, climbing up and then rolling downwards and cawing. Now and again the storm hurled them backwards and the both of them stroked forward slowly, persistently, like a person swimming through water.

For a short while the old woman took shelter near the dovetailed corner joint of the cottage, afraid to go into the wind. Leaning on her cane for support she then opened the gate. A raucous blow hit her in the chest. She almost fell backwards. With her head thrust out, she descended down the slope. The river loomed below. It was wide now, flooding the meadows. Lanterns were already lit in the village. Ducks clambered onto the shore. They bowed to the side, talking and looking ashamed that they were coming back so late. Going past the old woman they cackled, pulled their heads back and bobbed their beaks up and down. 'Didžiagirė, Didžiagirė,' the woman repeated. She could not see the forest in front of her. It was black, totally mixed in with the clouds. It was only from a flickering lantern off in the distance that she understood where the white of the birch forest should come into view. There were puddles on the path, clouded and muddy like dirty sheets. Mud splashed out from under her clogs. So that she wouldn't step into a rut or hole she, keeping her eyes glued on the path, fumbled about in front of her with her cane – the way the blind do when they walk by themselves. Out there, once again, the windows glowed.

And she thought about the people who were now sitting in their cottages. They were eating dinner. Children were squealing with delight while outside the wind whistled through the corner joints. The dogs lay in their doghouses, noses tucked between their paws, and the sparrows chirped and rested in their attics. All of them had their own homes. She stopped and bent over while gasping for breath. She coughed in that same hacking, whistling way as children suffering from whooping cough would do. When the attack subsided, she wiped her eyes and looked on in amazement. For one thing, the darkness was thicker. No, there was something there. She looked around fearfully, as if asking herself: where am I now? She wanted to see something familiar, be it a tree or a cross or at the very least the earth beneath her feet. She did not find anything familiar. But I was born and raised here, she thought. Eighty years. And now…

She shook her head and felt as if she were lost, as if she were in the wilderness. She imagined that there was nothing around her: go north or go south, you won't find even one bonfire or a single animal or human being… except that one standing right in front of you. Theresa saw how he bent over, raised the lapels of his jacket and struck matches, trying to light his pipe. The sudden light flickered on his chin and nose, and then died out.

He managed to light his pipe.

Then he said: 'I look at you, grandmother, and I am amazed.'

Theresa sighed. Yes, here was a good man. He spoke so slowly, as if he felt sorry for you.

'Where are you going in such rainy weather?'

'To my son-in-law's.'

The passer-by was quiet for a while, as if he were meditating.

Then he said: 'But you have a very bad cough.'

Theresa didn't know what to say. She whispered timidly: 'He's in Didžiagirė… He's working there…'

'I know, I know, there was a fire there in the summer.' Then he added: 'However, at your age I wouldn't be going alone at night and in such a storm. Are you really in that much of a hurry?'

She was ashamed. Yes, perhaps she had been too rash. However for years her daughter had been like a knife. Just think: I carried her in my body, and I suffered while giving birth to her. 'This is what's left of my life,' she complained. 'Did I think about this when I was young…'

'Anyway, it's on the way for both of us,' the man said, redirecting the conversation.

And they continued on their way. It had become completely dark.

Occasionally tiny sparks flashed from his pipe and died out right away. When now and again the storm died down one could hear the muffled murmuring of the river down below. The willows groaned and whistled. There was nothing else around. They were both alone in the night; the meadows were without grass and without crops. Theresa talked of her troubles and all those long years of hers full of work and worry. And old age! The sharp pains, the cough and death always loitering... And no shelter... The man listened attentively. He spoke good and well-worn words that struck her right in the heart.

It roared against them even more.

'Here's the forest,' the traveller said. 'Grandmother, you should go to the oak with the top broken off... Do you know it?'

How could she not! It was only at first that she had gotten so muddled that she had felt lost.

'And from there you go along the path to the left...'

'I know, I'm familiar with everything here...'

'Goodbye. I need to travel along the edge of the forest.'

And the two of them parted company.

In the forest Theresa sighed. She felt like she was in a home of some sort there. The wind howled and tore at the treetops. But below there was none of that fury. Only occasionally did a small whirlwind break through. It would bump into her and disappear once again. The trees rustled and roared so loudly that the old woman experienced terror and longing. She thought that all the beasts in the vast forest were now slumbering in their dens and listening to the voice of the fir and linden trees, which has existed for centuries and would never subside. And the birds were crouched in their nests, beaks nestled under their wings, huddling together and occasionally chirping in their sleep.

Only she alone had to walk. And stopping, she thought: I have never been so weak before. The cane in her hand trembled as if someone were shaking it. She already wanted to lean against a tree and to press her head against that branch-rich linden in order to rest. Rest for a long time, until the storm quieted down, until the firs stopped waving in the wind and dawn came, so calm and good.

'No, you have to find Vincas,' she said loudly. 'If you rest here you will never ever get there.'

Her voice was so weak, so trembling between the din of the firs and hornbeams. The woman coughed, as though gathering courage. Raising her cane, she fumbled for the path. There were roots sticking out in front of her that had been worn down on one end.

'I would have stumbled,' the old woman said to herself and was joyful that she had averted disaster.

She moved as fast as she could. It was so difficult, so very difficult to drag her feet. And how nimble, how quick she had been as a small child. And when she had grown up she scurried around like a titmouse. She would pass George, her husband, in all the races when he was courting her. What fair, curly hair he had. And his words: 'My little Theresa, my little deer...' If there were no clouds, the stars would twinkle high above in the sky. And Pleiades would shimmer... And then they had children. They died, all of them died... just that one was left. Like a viper. Goodness gracious, all of my sons and my daughter lay in the ground, just that one is alive, she thought. Will I ever see my little ones, I, a sinner... And what about my husband?

A bird shrieked overhead. Theresa gripped her cane tightly with both of her hands.

'That's a jay,' she said, waiting for a little while.

She did not want to walk at all. Her heart beat slower and slower. It palpitated wearily, as if for the last time.

'But the crossroads should be coming up soon,' the old woman thought.

She shook her head watchfully, while at the same time she moved her cane from side to side: 'I've been toiling for so long already...'

She glanced upwards. The sky was black.

'What time is it now?'

No stars were twinkling up above, nor had the moon risen. Maybe it was still early, or maybe it was already midnight, when the evil spirits...

She laughed to herself: 'They probably don't need an old woman like me. All right, Theresa, get going. Don't sit here like a bump on a log.'

A puddle lay in front of her. She needed to make her way along the shrubs to get around it. A blackthorn got caught on her dress. A thorn scratched her hand and it smarted a little. She understood from the murmuring of the trees that she had ended up in a fir grove. The firs, sagging down to the ground, always frightened her. It seemed like there was a beast, a person or some kind of spirit hiding under their branches.

Theresa hurried. Jabbing at the path with her cane, she tread as fast as she was able. She felt how her hair crept out from underneath her kerchief and fell into her eyes. Ach, even her hair was not braided nicely... It was warm, as if she had entered into a cottage where they were baking bread. Something shone in her temples, as though something blurry had suddenly become clear – whatever it was that should be appearing through the mist. And the old woman now imagined that she was trudging toward a day that would soon shine forth from beyond this darkness, shine so brightly and peacefully. Just another step, then another... And she pattered and bowed forward like that woodpecker who pecks at tree bark. As if someone were calling her, quietly but at the same time powerfully calling her to herself. Her shawl was slipping down onto her neck.

She thought that she needed to arrive on time.

'It's not good for me to be late and to run around at night,' she said quickly.

Then she was quiet for a while.

'I'm from a good home, after all,' she said. 'There's not a lot of land, but to roam around like this...'

And she stopped and looked around. In her eyes it was brighter. She understood: 'There's the birch forest over there.' Theresa looked around and was amazed: 'Good Lord, how white those trunks are.'

No, she didn't see those trunks. But nearby her, she saw a grey wall. The trees rustled their song, the one that is grand and eternal. The old woman listened, and it felt so good to rest here and listen to the ebb and flow wafting in from the lagoons and waters so far away. She touched the trunk of a birch tree.

'How soft its bark is, like the palm of a child,' Theresa whispered.

Her knees bent and her head hung towards the grey earth. And her eyes started to close. However, between the rows of off-white birches, she saw something dark looming. Theresa approached. There were branches – a large pile of them, as big as a granary. The woman leaned her cane against the pile, rubbed her hands together and slowly snuggled up into it.

'What's this?' she said, astonished.

She found a hole so spacious and deep that a whole person could crawl inside. And it was warm in there and comfortable for the old woman. She reclined her head on a thick branch, rearranged some twigs underneath her head and whispered to herself quietly, as if she were afraid to wake someone: 'I am finally home.'

She thought that she wanted to remember something, but she couldn't. Outside, around the pile, the wind was blowing – loudly at first before softening to a mere squeak. And the trees continued to sough and sough.

And she thought for a long time, a very long time.

'What's that?' she whispered and wondered.

She saw meadows so green and in them flowers blossomed elegantly. Over there her entire family were coming through the grass – George and all of her children, all of them who had died. They strode together hand in hand and she felt that they were so far away. And once again she saw, as if she were walking there herself, having given her hand to George. And she felt so good, so good...

Her head hung down onto her shoulder. Her hands were folded on her chest, as if she were praying.

'It's me... me, George... My children... we are all here,' she murmured and fell asleep.

And she never woke again.

First published in Antanas Vaičiulaitis, *Pelkių takas*, Kaunas: Žinija (1939).

Translated by Jayde Will from *Tavo veido šviesa*, Vilnius: Vaga (1989).

Antanas Vaičiulaitis (1906–1992) was a prose writer, poet, translator and diplomat. He taught at Kaunas Vytautas Magnus University and worked at the Lithuanian embassy in Rome, but on the eve of the Second World War he emigrated to the United States. In the inter-war period he became known in Lithuania as an erudite writer who had a deep knowledge of modern Western European literature and who rejected naturalism and chose, instead, an impressionist narrative style. With his the prize-winning poetic novel *Valentina* (1936), in which he related a story of a radiant, unrequited and tragic love, he confirmed his place in modern Lithuanian literature. After he emigrated to the United States he taught at Scranton University and worked at the Voice of America.

The Red Slippers

Jurgis Savickis

Look at what spring does to people! It drives them mad. Take me, for instance. I'm getting on in years, but the minute I let my guard down, some demon brings my frozen blood back to life, making it boil. It's as if I were a young man, donning my student's cap for the first time. What audacity! And one is tempted to take all kinds of risks, which at the time seem so brave, so logical and so necessary. But, in reality, people think that you are trying to make them laugh. Because you are young.

Take today, for instance – Sunday. Instead of heading to the chemist's where my wife and doctor have sent me because the veins in my calves are swollen, I find myself walking down Kaunas Street, tailing a woman unfamiliar to me, indeed a complete stranger, dressed in a suit. She is one of those Sunday 'widows'. I really should be getting to church. My choice is the cathedral; that's where I go on Sundays because it's more formal. And the priest's sermons are better structured. Afterwards, as usual, there's Sunday breakfast and supper at home. Breakfast is somewhat more formal; supper is simpler. I'm devout. This pleases me. But I'm not doctrinaire. I'm open to differing opinions. I'm generally considered a happy person. I sometimes even venture out alone for a good time. Of course I'm referring to cultural amusements. And, getting back to the ladies, I have never taken advantage of any 'opportunities'. I'm a married man.

But my wife is away and I'm home alone, free. No, not wickedly free. But I do find the city enticing today. Like a child is enticed by a toy. Even though normally I'm very respectable. In fact, I'm a professional of rather high rank. It's hard to believe! Because right now nobody can see inside my soul. On the surface, I'm quite proper. I'm the departmental assistant director – no more, no less. And at this moment, looking at my suit and tie, you'd say I was dressed in my Sunday best like everybody else.

I'm sensible and practical. I survey the street with a fresh perspective. It's as if I suddenly find myself back in Paris in the old days – a quiet, empty Parisian street on a typical Sunday afternoon in summer. I haven't been thinking about Paris lately, not even the Sorbonne where I went to university. Thinking about Paris doesn't seem to be part of my job description these days. I have many responsibilities at the office; I'm known for my professional thoroughness. I deal with my people as necessary, often requiring my staff to work overtime. I sometimes think that without me the state apparatus couldn't function. But the government employees do not complain. They understand that I give them work that is interesting.

But today this former Sorbonne alumnus is in Paris – even though in front of me there is only a 'Sobor', an orthodox cathedral left behind for us by the Russians, an atrocity in brick. I see that the 'widow' is having a chat with an automobile owner. There aren't many cars in our little city, even if we are the 'temporary capital', so we know almost every one of them by sight. They don't chat for long and the car rattles away. Left alone, she stares at the store ceiling for a long time.

A grey, stylish skirt pleasantly outlines the curves of her bottom as she whooshes along. Her lovely-shaped legs are fitted out in delicious stockings. What could be more beautiful than a woman's attractive legs, so tempting that they might lead to your demise! If you were so inclined. She is tall in stature and has a not unintelligent profile. Two silver foxes rest heavily on her shoulders. Now she'll probably buy herself a hunk of bread and go home to eat breakfast.

Hello! She doesn't say a word but pronounces this with her eyes. But still I can almost hear it. She's probably already noticed that I'm searching for 'Paris' and am a bit unhinged. Who was that? Do

I know her? A client? She acted with such ease and dignity. I'm not sure now if I haven't met her at the club or the ministry at some point. But she's walking away. With nothing better to do, I trudge off slowly, hobbling on my legs swollen at the calves. I don't say anything to her or even smile. I walk by all flushed like someone cursed by God. Even the woman is left flustered because of me. She also turns and hurriedly disappears. Who was she? Might she be a lady of negotiable affections?

There are people who mistreat these kinds of ladies. They don't pay up or they intentionally hurt them in some way. And they're rude on top of it all. Not me. I'm polite to everyone. Men like that should be beaten; under no circumstances do they deserve clemency. Some are even members of high society. Beat them, I say, with whatever is handy – canes or charred sticks pulled from the hearth. Those fat-cheeked, pampered men! They come home kissing their wives' dainty little hands. Of course I'm not that kind of man.

The goddess is gone. Here I am becoming sentimental and preaching sermons to myself. The religious Sunday air is getting the better of me. I don't procure my medicine. All the pharmacies are closed. I return home but with so many thoughts that I could write a short story. I've lost my bearings. But it's not as if I'm going to the ministry today.

All the women are dressed to the nines because it's spring. Everything is brighter, fresher. It's as if everything in this community has been regulated to make it just so easy to live. It won't rain today. The young people have left the city by whatever means available, mostly by bike, but some on foot. Bright-eyed and bushy-tailed, yelling at the tops of their lungs in jubilation. The day will be redeemed for us all. And for some the day will redeem the rest of their lives.

Such is the mood today and such are the women. Some, it appears, weren't able to get out of town. Or perhaps they're waiting for their escorts. But today they all command quiet smiles. And their hairstyles are more carefully done because it's Sunday. They are refreshed and enjoying their clothing caressing their bodies; they are all so happy and interesting. And they all know how to reveal what is revealable and are even more aware of what should not be revealed. It must be their entire subject of study in school, this eternal coquetry.

Home alone. Because my wife has gone abroad, as is to be expected in our newly-forming high society. 'I need to get away from domestic life for a bit,' she said, even though we live a very harmonious life together. But one requires one's amusements. Besides, she said, she needed to do some shopping. After all, as we all know, money is easier spent abroad. And during her trip she might even manage to miss me. But where and for what reason she herself probably cannot not yet anticipate. As often happens with women, at some point along the way she will meet a lady similar to herself and then her itinerary will finally be determined. After she returns I will continue to pound the pavement to work as always, and she, along with other Kaunas ladies, will organise charitable teas which must be referred to as 'five o'clocks'. And we will both be successful. And soon I will grow old. I cannot say that there is much passion in Kaunas. By the time I get old I will have reached the post of general secretary, which is much more important than assistant director or even director. Indeed, it's almost as important as minister. Although I have connections in politically conservative circles, I have little interest in politics. I am not aiming to become a minister and have no desire to end up there. At least that's my plan.

So how did this happen that suddenly I, too, am travelling abroad? The ministry is sending me to Lausanne to an international conference on social issues. I can see that the conference has been well organised and well attended, with guests from the Far East, India and elsewhere.

How pleasant it is to travel. Nobody knows you, and you get to journey along foreign roads like some Lord Fairfax or Van Housen. However, that spring bee from Kaunas is still buzzing in my bonnet.

Perhaps this is my farewell to youth? Who will finish whom? It's a tournament. What a contest. A majestic contest, watched by everyone. As I stagger forward, I look deep into the eyes of the women in the Mitropa railway carriage. I intentionally taunt the men.

I choose either a light-coloured rose or a sweet little flower to pin onto the lapel of my spring jacket. This is the prerogative of those who have reached 40 and then some. I'm travelling alone. Young, rich and adventurous. But privately I think that even if I were to stay where I am until I retire, even only as assistant director, I would be satisfied. There are fewer worries when you know your job. I have no debts and more than enough money. I don't own an estate either because I never tried to make a claim after the land reforms were carried out in the Republic. By contrast, those *confrères* of mine lost their minds trying to administer their little estates while spinning around in their chairs and talking on the phone as they worked at the ministry.

Every one of my colleagues, to a man, is eating crow at home. They never go out; they have no peace, all because of those estates of theirs. They're spoiled and careless! And they keep sinking deeper into debt. They don't love the land, nor do they work it themselves. Oh no! I say either work the land or don't bother anyone. At least I sometimes have free time to thumb through a book. I help out my older sister, a teacher who stayed on the farm. Let her live out her old age on our land. A while ago I bought her a Dutch tile stove. I don't ask anything of her. The farm is practically hers. The topic of to whom it belongs never comes up between us. What's the point? Besides, everything is so clear. Each one of us can trace our heritage back to the farm, even if we all avoid this fact and pretend otherwise. I don't have children. I get along with my wife. What more do I need?

When I returned to my hotel today after the conference hall I found myself intrigued by the women at the conference, and even those back at the hotel. Despite it being midnight, I had decided to walk back to my hotel. I felt happy and carefree.

And it was during a conference outing that I came to the conclusion that it was these expeditions that were of the greatest concern to the conference participants – along with eating. The bigger the conference, the greater such nonsense. They are in all likelihood the main purpose of such gatherings. And the women were kindly disposed towards introductions and friendly interactions. Sporting their newly-tailored outfits and smiling, they appeared to be in the same happy state that I was enjoying. After all, we all appear 'not quite the same' when travelling.

During the opening ceremonies one particular young lady dominated the corridors. A journalist of some sort, she was bringing around a guest book for all the participants to sign. I told her I only write poetry in ladies' albums.

'Ah bien! En ce cas – poésie!'

'But doesn't it seem to you, Miss, that it's a bit outdated… *Un petite peu démodé?'*

Beside my name I drew an anchor. In other words, 'hope'.

This made my lady even happier. She soon forgot my promised 'poems'. She grabbed onto the anchor I threw out to her.

'More, more!'

'What do you mean?'

'You forgot your country.'

'Lituanie,' I wrote. But feigning patriotism, I added the name in Lithuanian: 'Lietuva'.

'If you are so witty, sir, please include your motto. Your motto!'

'But I don't live by a motto.'

As I glanced down at the official papers in my attaché case, I thought about copying into the album our 'Vytis', the national herald, which in essence is very beautiful and powerful. But the throng of guests carried me away from the guest book.

Some people have all the luck! But the conference must go on.

It's a good thing I didn't draw it. I wouldn't want a repeat of what happened two years ago in Vienna, at the Prater, when I inscribed into a book of important guests a laurel leaf with two ribbons held by two doves. Under one of them, as required, I signed my name. Under the other ribbon appeared the signature 'Mme Deveikis'. It was by lucky coincidence that I ran into her while travelling abroad and it appeared to me a very patriotic gesture to embrace my fellow pilgrim.

I returned home and had barely opened the door when I was

greeted by my wife's extremely curious face.

'So how was your dinner with Mrs. Deveikis?'

I was astounded by her feminine intuition.

'What are the two doves for?'

'It's a local tradition!'

A stolen glance revealed that my journalist was examining me. And so? I could read in her glance: 'so respectable and yet not so respectable...' It was just a momentary examination. But such tiny glimpses often hold great meaning in life and usually have lasting repercussions. But she had already disappeared among the guests. I was able to memorise her image in my mind's eye. With hair like waves of the sea, combed and pinned to one side and tinged red, her movements and speech revealed her to be as hot-blooded as an Arabian horse. I don't regret using a word like 'horse'. That's her! The hot-blooded one. After all, Lithuania is an agrarian country!

Just then, one of the Swiss delegates, a man who looked like a stump with a belly – a celebrity in the world of international social issues, which is perhaps why he has such a long and heavy beard – noticed my interest in the conference organiser:

'That's our famous poet.'

How poetic everything is here today.

Later that evening he danced on the stage. The Swiss guests, it turns out, were country people, lovers of folklore who danced their predestined dances. Elsewhere, other groups of people sang. There was clapping, drinking and talking – and more talking. All these speeches were whetting the congressional appetite.

If I wanted, I could grab one of these naughty ladies and together the two of us could sneak off to a park somewhere or to a little restaurant; we would understand one another perfectly.

I've never been a poet – besides writing up legal cases, I can barely compose a single line. I have trouble writing letters, even to relatives: 'I weigh 80 kilos, and my wife has gone to Siauliai.' It's only with my sister, the widow who has devoted herself to raising two orphans, that I'm more open, and the two of us converse through letters quite pleasantly. My sister respects my wife; they visit one another quite often. And although they have very different interests this doesn't seem to hinder their relations.

I will not ask that young woman out, nor will I chat her up – even though I could learn much about contemporary Swiss poetry and she shows her willingness to teach me by smiling at me during other people's lectures!

What would you do with her, you old wolf? You'd regret it later. Let her circle the fire and drag down someone else with her bohemian customs. Because I am so decent, my thoughts turn to my wife who is perhaps not quite as youthful as I am.

The conference members were invited for a boat ride on Lake Léman for the purpose of more thorough sociological study and to admire the night-time fireworks display. I excuse myself and head to bed. This is to be expected of a well-bred citizen, the backbone of the entire reawakening homeland. I'll leave the evening studies for the others.

But really, how can a person of such an age, when he is not yet old but no longer young, willingly refuse the town's fireworks and adornments? After all, adornments and fireworks are the meaning of life. And what an evening! Women's eyes flashing like lightning. Everywhere I turned a brunette with a ruddy face kept handing me steins of beer for the road; right before midnight, just before the club closed, she also made clear her womanly congeniality.

Back on the street I run into a charming Japanese woman from our conference. She's delicate, with attractive and feminine facial features, and of course she has eyes stretched upwards like delicate ribbons. How kind and naïve are those Japanese women! Walking alone in the street this time of night! But a Mexican woman and a New Zealander catch up to her. The three women must be hurrying back to the hotel. They smile like brothers. Meeting them would be beneficial to me: I could enrich my knowledge of the world. It would be pleasant to become acquainted with such a nice and charming Japanese woman and to exchange opinions, even if it's well past one in the morning. Where are they all going? I don't know. We're all scattered throughout the city's hotels. I bow to them gallantly – it turns out we are all staying at the same hotel. All of us. I allow the Japanese woman to go first with her clever, ever-smiling and child-like eyes. How clever those Japanese women must all be, all of them, just like this one. For, as you can see, they can control a man with the allure of the domestic, with their loyalty, submissiveness and feminine charms, of which she seems to have inexhaustible reserves.

I'm back home at the hotel. My head is swimming. It's calm, like after a big party. It feels as if you've just finished watching a bold, old-fashioned cancan. I wrap bandages around my leg, which is swollen and in a sorry shape. I apply a compress. I might be able to fall asleep. I set my shoes outside my door, the shoes that have carried me through so many of the streets of this foreign city during the day.

But to set your shoes outside your door in such a big-city hotel, where people have all come together for whatever reason and do not know one another, is not such an easy task. Do they want to know one another and are they intentionally looking for a way to meet one another? If only their train ticket wasn't obliging them to check out the next morning.

All the shoes are lined up. Even the women have thick alpine shoes. How can women wear such clogs in summertime in the city? They must be on an expedition. Over there, a couple's shoes, look respectable. But opposite my room, a pair of red slippers! Unique, elegant and with pointy toes, they are neatly placed. In other words, they belong to a serious woman who has her act together.

They must be the Japanese woman's!

If I were to go to her room, she, dressed in her silk pyjamas decorated with large, white ibises, would hardly be surprised; she wouldn't scream hysterically. Or maybe it would be worse. She'd start screaming in the entirely incomprehensible language of the Samurai. On the other hand, she is very dignified, without preconceptions; she would examine a person calmly.

Renseignement? She would ask.

She's still awake. You can call her – on the phone.

And what if she's asleep, what innocence!

I slap myself on the forehead. The shoes I am leaving in the hall to be shined fall from my hands. I go to bed. But I can't forget the Japanese woman. All night I dream of devils poking me with their pitchforks. They're the very same specialists who in their civilian lives work as close as they can to the forge. Surely, I must have inhaled or eaten something.

The next morning I am again thinking about legs – this time, mine. They hurt. I have bags under my eyes. I miss my wife. Where is she? She should come here. She would understand. But can a woman ever learn? A man alone on a business trip, working... I stop myself at 'working'. And she isn't 'old' in the least. What was I thinking? She would look elegant compared to the others.

I linger with a few others in the elegant lobby. We stall, unsure of how to start the day. Conference attendees are everywhere. How many of us are there? Everyone is preparing; they all look extremely busy. One is a blunt-faced woman, as though she was flattened by God when she was being moulded out of clay. She's flat and short, and with her meaty nose she looks rather like a man. She has broad shoulders and very short legs but admirably styled hair which gives her a lot of femininity.

I saw her earlier at the conference. But now I can't remember what country she's from. She is preparing intensely for the day, poring over the local and national papers, even some sort of textbook and a school notebook full of many notes and remarks. There's not a man in sight. Have they gone into the city or are they not up yet? It's only the ladies. As I was leaving home I promised myself that I would follow the conference proceedings diligently. And here I am paying close attention to the actions of these women, and to their work. One never knows where inspiration may hit.

A waiter brings a glass of water to another lady, seated in the lounge, for her morning medicines. She is remarkably pale, but stylish and tall. She, too, is poring over her morning correspondence. She appears to be signing cheques. She is so tough, much more like a man. Does she have a heart? She smiles at the waiter, but in a very official manner.

Could one of these two ladies be the owner of the red slippers? No. I wouldn't want them to be.

The blunt-faced woman is wearing sensible, masculine shoes, and the other, the lean one signing the cheques, keeps adjusting the strap of her purse across her chest; it keeps sliding down because of her boniness. A real Englishwoman. She orders tea with milk, as is expected of a good Englishwoman. Her face, one can see, once had a more prominent jaw. Was it an automobile accident or did she scrape her face skiing on a sudden descent? Quite a bit of blood must have been lost in the snow. And all this because she wanted to lose weight or because she took up the in-vogue sport of skiing despite the fact that her legs were unsteady. She probably no longer participates in sport. Her face looks tired, even if it was nicely repaired in the operation. She's quite elegant, even if flat-chested. Not bad at all. Could she be my Cinderella with the magic slippers? No, she wears different shoes. Comfortable and plain. She probably has no idea what else to seek in life. Englishly sad. Although a conversation with her would probably be scintillating. No! It's not her.

The Japanese woman enters the room. Tall and fair, she smiles at everyone. Like yesterday, she is accompanied by the New Zealander and the Mexican. How pleasant for me! I dash across the floor to greet her. What do I care what the others think?

'*Bonjour*,' and 'How are you?' endlessly. Oh, what loyal eyes that woman has. Our acquaintance pleases me greatly. The Japanese woman truly intrigues me. And she is interested to learn more about me as well.

'You see, Madame, how easy it is to reach the world of the Far East!' I say to the woman, convincing her of my super-human powers.

New Zealand and Mexico get lost so as not to get in our way; they go into town for some shopping. After we've discussed the geographies of Lithuania and Japan, the traditions of home and family as well as politics (we talk quickly and without any particular order), my lady also decides to go into town for some shopping. But I cannot go with her. To walk from store to store with a woman – how demeaning.

But the shoes! The whole time I was convinced without even looking. It was her! Alas no, she's hitting the town in very stylish shoes, but they are not at all red. Not at all my Cinderella, that fair princess.

My slipper fetish makes me feverish every time I think about those mystical slippers, like a detective of some sort. I must find my Cinderella.

I remain in the lounge. The room is half empty. The second day of the conference has begun. Another woman! This one is clutching her newspaper as if she doesn't have any other work to do. She even takes a bite to eat from time to time as she reads. She has a tailored suit, which is very stylish. Two foxes on her shoulders for this generously proportioned lady of the morning. But her face cannot be seen. With a confident beat and tempo, I approach this interesting woman holding the morning newspaper, who is undoubtedly interested in politics.

Ah! The red slippers!

How can it be? It's her.

Finally.

What divine legs. Shoes are shoes; that's not what interests me. But what is finer than a woman's legs beautifully displayed! Beautiful! I am satisfied with my research. We might be in a city but spring has intruded into every store window display and has left its mark on every metre of the place.

Oh, those red slippers. I am pleased with my keen senses. I rub my hands in delight. A reward for a job well done! I feel like a detective who has finally apprehended his criminal. I head off to look for a newspaper like the one she's reading. For me, an important conference delegate, this is crucial. The ends justify the means.

I embark on the newspaper hunt with some diligence. The lady, noticing a strange man tramping about annoyingly, casts her newspaper aside and looks up coldly, exasperated. She is a very beautiful woman. For a few minutes I stand there speechless, my mouth agape:

It is my wife. The woman speaks: 'I finally found you...'
She drops her newspaper to the floor.
'It's you? I thought you were the Japanese woman.'
'Japanese? I've always said that conferences are not good for your health.'
'But how did you get here?'
'Just like this.'
Her words make no sense to me.
'You're tired, my conference delegate.'
She comes closer. I am very happy to see her.
'What Japanese woman are you talking about? Japanese? Do I look Japanese?'
'No, I thought... it was the shoes.'
She appraises her shoes.
'Do you like my shoes? I'm surprised at how gallant you've become. You would never notice my shoes back in Kaunas, even if I were to buy a dozen pairs.'
'But they're... so unusual.'
'Really? You think they're unusual? Nothing unusual about them.' This bit of news delights her. Turning about, she admires them as she lifts up her fair legs. I grow abashed.
'There are people here... be more considerate.'
'What people? I'm showing you my stockings. And my purchases. Every decent man should concern himself with his wife's legs. And her purchases.'
'Your legs belong to you!'
'Even so. Not to the people.'
My wife speaks at length about the benefits of buying things abroad. I don't argue with her. I keep thinking about the lady with the red slippers. My ears were ringing with a real *chanson sans paroles*, but I could just as well be watching a tragic comedy.
'How did you get here?'
'In the usual way: I hailed a taxi and came over.'
'But I mean, here, to Lausanne.'
'Also in the usual way. Second-class train from Leipzig. I wish

63

I'd flown.'

She is toying with me. I realise I will also have to switch to a more frivolous and relaxed tone, as is more suitable for a tourist travelling abroad. One mustn't be too serious with women.

'But back home you said you wanted to travel elsewhere.'

'Oh, Alfred... A life without Alfred is no life for me.'

'But how did you find out I was in Lausanne?'

'Sometimes the ministry reveals secrets about incredibly important events. And they inform the concerned wives of their functionaries when they have left for a conference. You only need to be a little clever. Everyone sends their regards. No need to hurry back. It seems you've gotten on their nerves.'

'And how did you know this was my hotel?' I am still disconcerted.

'That was sheer coincidence.'

'And the shoes?'

'Of course it's a bit risky to set out your shoes right in front of your husband's room. Just be happy it wasn't two pairs.'

First published in Jurgis Savickis, *Raudoni batukai*, Brooklyn, N.Y.: Gabija (1951).

Translated by Jūra Avižienis from Jurgis Savickis, *Vasaros kaitros*, Vilnius: Baltos lankos (1997).

Jurgis Savickis (1890–1952) was a prose writer and diplomat who, after the First World War, resided in Denmark and represented Lithuania diplomatically in Scandinavia. He went on to become a high level official in Lithuania's Ministry of Foreign Affairs, and, in 1939–1940, was delegated as representative to the League of Nations in Geneva. When Lithuania was occupied by the Soviet Union he moved to France, where he had acquired property, and began farming. Over the course of his writing career his narrative style changed from lyricism to expressionism.

Christmas Eve

Antanas Vienuolis

The pharmacist's assistant Martin Gudelis was working on Christmas Eve at Kalpokas Pharmacy. On duty with him was the night guard and the clerk, Jonas.

The clock had already struck nine. It was well below zero outside. The streets were emptying. Only the occasional hunched human form would trudge by crunching through the snow, or a random sleigh would whoosh past the pharmacy's frozen shop windows before everything would fall silent again. Inside the pharmacy it was so still that you could hear the clock ticking in the supervisor's office and Jonas sniffling in the dispensary.

Gudelis was seated at his desk, and, resting his chin on his palm, he was considering whether there could possibly be a profession in the world more demanding than that of the pharmacist...

'Be it Christmas Eve, Christmas, New Year's Day or Easter,' he thought, 'you sit like a dog chained to his kennel and can't relax even for a minute. Look at me now: why would anybody in their right mind come to the pharmacy on this holy night?'

His thoughts were interrupted by the ringing of the telephone.

'That's Christmas Eve for you, you sap,' he mumbled to himself before walking over to the phone with little enthusiasm.

'Kalpokas Pharmacy. How may I help you?'

'What is your name, please?' He heard a pleasant female voice coming from the telephone receiver.

Thrilled, flushed and flustered, Gudelis answered. 'Me? Jonas.'

'Jonas? Thank you. Ha, ha, ha, ha,' chuckled the sweet voice.

'And you, miss? What's your name?' Gudelis took his turn.

'Me? Louisa. Ha, ha, ha, ha. Louisa and Jonas. A lovely couple, like Matthew and Barbara. Ha, ha, ha, ha.'

Gudelis heard a crackle in the receiver followed by silence.

'What a pleasant voice. Could it be Aldona enticing me? Too bad she hung up so quickly.' Gudelis pitied himself and returned to his desk to daydream...

The municipal clock tower struck ten. Upstairs at the supervisor's, guests and children were singing a Christmas carol, accompanied by the piano. Gudelis stood up, paced the pharmacy a few times, then stopped at the frozen window. He admired the tropical brush and palm trees painted on the window by frost. Upstairs, the supervisor's children and guests sang:

Let the trumpets play, let us sing the songs,
Let us celebrate and rejoice...

As the carol ended, Gudelis grew pensive once again. This time he was not thinking about the challenges of his profession, but rather about how even Kalpokas had once been like him, serving as assistant to the pharmacist, toiling during the night shift, working from morning to night. But Kalpokas went on to have his own pharmacy, a beautiful wife, children, a splendid apartment – and look how happy he is now. Is he any lesser than Kalpokas? Gudelis suddenly felt warm and happy because he felt an infinite power inside himself. Standing in front of the mirror he began to admire himself.

He was especially pleased at the thought that nobody would come to the pharmacy on this holy night, that he would get a good night's sleep and he would be free all day tomorrow. He would meet some friends and pay a visit to Miss Aldona, who for quite some time had enthralled him, heart and soul. After twirling his moustache, spinning around on one leg and smiling at himself, he saw his lovely white teeth in the mirror. He became so giddy that he didn't even notice that he was now belting out a Christmas carol, projecting his bass voice with such power that the bottles rattled on the shelves...

'Jonas, Jonas,' he suddenly shouted, startled by his own voice. 'It's time to close up the pharmacy.'

A sleepy Jonas stumbled out from the dispensary. After he bolted the pharmacy door and made a bed for the assistant in the office, he lay his own mattress down behind the display and immediately began to snore. Having locked the display and turned out the lights, Gudelis also lay down, but his dreams and his joy, that illusory joy which sometimes overtakes a man just before it ushers in some misfortune or unpleasantness, gave him no peace. But who doesn't dream on Christmas Eve? And here, as if deliberately, was the Christmas star peeking in through the window, flickering, flirting and promising future love, happiness, wealth – whatever his heart desired...

And so Gudelis dreamed that somewhere beyond the Caucasus lives a wealthy, old pharmacist, an expatriate Lithuanian with an only daughter. Somehow Gudelis manages to get a job at the pharmacist's shop and the pharmacist's daughter falls in love with him, and soon he becomes the happy manager and owner of the pharmacy. Right now he likes Miss Aldona, but who is this Aldona anyway? Like all other Lithuanian girls with some education, she is vain, proud and dreams of having only a doctor or engineer for a husband. If she were to marry me she would only suffer and complain; she wouldn't be happy and she would ruin my life. I'm better off finding myself a different girl, even if she's not a true-blooded Lithuanian bride, but a girl brought up to marry a man, not a doctor or engineer. Besides, there's the uncertainty of Aldona's dowry. But here everything is as it should be: the girl is an intellectual and well-positioned in society, and of course, there's the pharmacy. And her parents would be happy having married off their daughter to such a loyal husband. To tell the truth, at the moment he is not yet a pharmacist and is penniless. But he is nonetheless young, attractive, energetic and appealing to women. And with a little bit of money it wouldn't be too hard to acquire the qualification of a certified pharmacist.

In his dream he was just about to seat his young wife and himself into a first-class couchette on their way to Moscow University to attend some lectures when the pharmacy bell rang all of a sudden. Gudelis listened attentively. Jonas didn't get up either.

A minute later the bell interrupted the anxious silence in the pharmacy once again. Jonas groaned, angrily he cleared his throat and, cursing to himself, shuffled over barefoot to answer the door. Having let someone in, he barked a few words at them and slowly approached the office, knocked on the door with his knuckles and said coldly: 'Get up. They're here.'

'They can wait,' Gudelis replied, irritated. He lay for a while longer and then got up.

When he entered the pharmacy he saw standing by the door a timid, sixteen- or seventeen-year old ragamuffin of a young man who was shivering all over and holding out an arm bandaged in rags.

'What do you want?' Gudelis asked angrily.

'Sir,' the youth stammered, stepping cautiously toward the counter, 'a few days ago I stabbed my finger with an awl and now my finger and my entire arm are swollen, my head aches, and I'm trembling with cold. Please, sir, some sort of tincture for my headache and the sweating.'

'Show me your arm!'

The youth unwrapped the bandages on his arm and Gudelis could see even from a distance that it was swollen and red up to the elbow.

'Where were you all day? Why haven't you gone to see a doctor?'

The youth was silent as he regarded his arm, then he met Gudelis's eyes and explained:

'I had to finish off a job during the day. My supervisor wouldn't let me go, and now the hospitals are closed. No doctor will see me.'

'The hospitals are closed, no doctor will see me,' mocked Gudelis. 'But you're perfectly happy knocking at the pharmacy door – at midnight, no less! Don't you know that the pharmacy's closed at night as well? There's no reason for you to be banging about the pharmacy in the middle of the night. Get yourself to a doctor at once.'

'Just some tincture for my headache and sweating. Tomorrow's a holiday. It's Christmas...'

'No tinctures,' said the irritated master of medicinal mixology, who did not allow him to finish. 'You don't need tinctures, you need surgery! Your arm will have to be amputated up to the shoulder. Can't you see that gangrene has set in! Go and see a doctor at once because soon it will be too late.'

The youth was stunned. Eyes wide, he held his aching arm in his healthy one, crying out in misery.

'Get to a doctor at once! Why are you standing here?' Gudelis snapped.

The wretched young man wanted to say something more, but seeing an irritable, dishevelled Jonas approaching him, he wrapped his arm up in the rags and left.

Jonas locked the doors and returned to his spot behind the display and, as if nothing had happened, he fell onto his mattress.

Gudelis heard something out in the street like the howl of a dog or the wind whistling. He pricked up his ears. But at that moment a thought disturbed his heart: human beings are granted beauty and responsibility. And this incomprehensible, innate instinct caused a change of heart: he understood that he had done wrong, he understood that he had behaved less than admirably and that he had not been compassionate, that he had blasphemed against a man's greatest duty. Besides, he knew that the youth was truly in danger, that the only medicine for gangrene was to rub the arm with iodine as soon as possible, apply a compress, and immediately transport the poor wretch to the hospital...

'Jonas! Jonas!' He shouted, running from his office. 'Run as fast as you can. Find that young man and bring him back here.'

'The young man? Which young man? Why?' Jonas was surprised.

'Jonas, my brother, I'll give you a rouble tomorrow. Just find the young man and bring him back here.'

The promise of the rouble was more effective on Jonas than brotherly love. Jonas collected himself, got up, threw on his furs and swiftly left the pharmacy. Outside the door he looked around and stealthily ran to one side street and peered around, then he crossed onto the other side of the street – to the other side street – and returned quickly, explaining that the youth was nowhere to be seen.

'Jonas, you'll find him ringing the bell at the hospital door. Run and fetch him. The doctor won't be in and the village doctor's assistant went with his wife yesterday to visit his in-laws. Who will take him in?'

This time the obedient Jonas ran all the way to the hospital.

Losing his patience and greatly concerned, Gudelis himself went out into the street. It was below freezing. The two ends of the avenue were flanked by two rows of lamps; not a living soul could be seen in the streets. In the distance, on the outskirts of the city, a steam engine screeched as if it were lost and a million stars looked down upon the earth from the heavens.

'No, he's not there.' Jonas returned, gasping for breath, reporting the same news. 'I asked the night guard. He said that a girl had passed by a few minutes ago, but not a young man.'

They waited a few moments and looked around. Then they both returned to the pharmacy. It was only when Gudelis was back inside his office that Jonas managed to catch his breath and piped up from behind the display:

'I feel sorry for the child. Of course, who will take him in tonight?' He thought for a moment and added, 'One of my friends, a cobbler, died from an injury like that to his finger.'

Gudelis hoped that the young man, finding no luck elsewhere, would be forced to return to the pharmacy, and so he picked up a first aid book and read up about gangrene and how to treat it.

But an hour passed, and then another, but the young man didn't ring the bell.

Gudelis had just lain down on his mattress when a sleigh stopped in front of the pharmacy and the night bell rang in the dispensary. Gudelis jumped up and before Jonas could get out of his bed, he ran to open the door. A military officer and his lady sauntered into the pharmacy. They requested a variety of perfumes, eau de colognes, soaps and powders. Gudelis couldn't refuse to wait on them for fear that tomorrow the military officer might complain to his supervisor, so he waited patiently as the mystery lady selected her cosmetics; he even went down to the basement to retrieve some mineral water without saying a word.

After the military officer left, he went to bed.

Gudelis no longer expected the youth to return, but he knew that he would not be able to fall asleep again, so he lay there fully clothed with only a blanket to cover himself, burrowing his head underneath to block out Jonas's snores.

He heard the clock strike three, then four; a few times he heard someone walk past the pharmacy, footsteps crunching in the snow. But eventually he fell asleep. He didn't hear the bell, but he could make out Jonas's words from the other side of the office door: 'Get up. He's here.'

Gudelis got up instantly, quickly dressed and with a pounding heart entered the pharmacy. At the door stood the same timid young man reaching out his bandaged, aching arm, trembling...

'My dear brother, my dear brother.' Gudelis rushed over to the young man and putting his arm around his shoulders he led him to his office. 'I didn't sleep a wink all night waiting for you... You're cold, tired and it's all because of me... My dear brother...'

'Just a tincture for my headache and the sweating,' the young man sobbed.

'I'll give you anything, anything, just calm yourself, warm yourself, don't shiver so. Here, sit by the stove. Jonas, bring him some iodine and cotton wool. More cotton wool, more. You can see he's frozen.'

Gudelis rubbed his arm in iodine and wrapped it in cotton, but the more he rubbed it, the more inflamed it became.

'Jonas, quick, make me a compress. Hurry! What are you gawping at?'

And while Jonas made the compress, Gudelis kissed the young man's head and pressed it against his chest.

'Just some tincture for my headache and the sweating,' murmured the boy with blue lips.

'I'll give you anything. Anything. Look. I'm just about to call the municipal hospital. I've called the ambulance. The doctor is coming. They'll examine you at the hospital, lay you in a warm bed, feed you.

They'll heal your arm. Stop shivering. Stop shivering.'

'Jonas, he's fading!' Gudelis shouted. With all his might he pressed the young man to himself.

'Jonas, get to the phone at once and call the municipal hospital!'

Ring, ring... Jonas dials.

Ring, ring, ring...

Gudelis jerked awake, and jumped out of bed.

Ring, ring, ring... The phone rang incessantly. In the darkness Gudelis grabbed the phone, placed the receiver to his ear, and shivering, inquired: 'Kalpokas Pharmacy. How may I help you?'

'Pharmacy? What do you mean pharmacy? To hell with the pharmacy! I need the City Club!'

'Jonas, what kind of night duty do you keep that you don't hear people ringing the pharmacy bell?' Gudelis interrogated his assistant. 'You sleep and our customers can't reach us...'

'What do you mean sleeping? I wasn't sleeping! The phone did ring, but nobody came to the pharmacy. What do you mean I didn't hear! Anyway, we're not required to answer the phone.'

'Are you saying that nobody came to the pharmacy?'

'Of course not! A few people walked by the shop, but nobody stopped. What do you mean I've been sleeping? I hear everything. My good sir, you must have been dreaming.'

Gudelis was silent. He lit the lantern and sat there until morning.

When the employees and the supervisor came to the pharmacy and wished him a Merry Christmas, good fortune, good health, and all the best, he just mumbled, averting his eyes and feeling the words burning his heart.

He left the pharmacy with a heavy heart. Nothing could cheer him up, not the Christmas holiday, not the bright winter morning, not the sun newly risen over the forest, not the light smoke rising from the chimneys through the rays of the sun and up into the sky, his eyes were no longer dazzled by the trees covered in hoarfrost that looked as though they were cast in metal... He looked around him; the people seemed unhappy, gloomy and, like him, unsatisfied. When he returned home, he took no joy in his decorated room or the deliciously prepared foods on the table. He drank a glass of tea, curled up on the sofa and for the first time in his life he thought deeply...

***

Today Mr. Gudelis owns his own pharmacy. He has a beautiful wife, children, a splendid apartment, but he does not enjoy even an iota of the happiness that he once so envied in his supervisor Kalpokas.

Every year, when his children are playing around the Christmas tree and his beautiful and happy wife is passing out expensive gifts to them all, Gudelis remembers that fateful Christmas Eve. And though he participates in the family celebrations, he feels no joy; he feels estranged, out of place. At the first opportunity he disappears into his office and looks out of his window at the Christmas star shining in the night sky. And he desperately wishes he could invite his little family to his tastefully decorated office to show them the Christmas star in the sky and to describe to them in his native language something of his youth, to tell them about that young man and the events of that Christmas Eve. But he knows that neither his children nor his wife will understand. He sleeps poorly at night. He dreams of that young man and of Jonas, long since deceased, tapping his knuckles on his bedroom door or calling on the phone. When he gets up, he paces through the rooms and sits in his office before his wife calms him, reminding him that if he keeps eating so many sweet foods, then of course he won't be able to fall asleep.

1912

First published Antanas Vienuolis, *Raštai*, Kaunas: Švyturys (1920).

Translated by Jūra Avižienis from Antanas Vienuolis, *Grįžo*, Vilnius: Lithuanian Writers' Union Publishers (2011).

Antanas Vienuolis (1882–1957) was one of the leading Lithuanian prose writers of the last century. He wrote his first two books of short stories and legends, *The Eternal Violinist* (1908) and *The Cursed Monks* (1910), while living in the Caucasus. These works gained him national recognition. He lived in Georgia for a number of years where he worked as a pharmacist; he also studied pharmaceutics in Moscow. His later novels, written after he returned to Lithuania (where he continued to work as a pharmacist in Anykšciai), include *A Female Guest from the North* (*Viešnia iš šiaures*, 1933), the historical novel *Crossroads* (*Kryžkelės*, 1933), and the short story collection *Sleepless Nights* (*Nemigo naktys*, 1937). The books he wrote after the Second World War were written according to the rules of socialist realism and under the guidance of a Communist Party censor in the hopes of securing the release of his son from the Soviet Gulag. Despite this turn of events, his reputation as one of Lithuania's most important prose writers had already been secured.

Forest of the Gods
(two excerpts)

Balys Sruoga

XLVIII

Construction Fever

There's a law of nature known from ancient times: it's extremely easy to steal from construction sites. It's difficult to say whether or not the SS authorities were aware of this law, but in any case they observed it: they built, and they stole, on a very grand scale.

For five years thousands of people worked at constructing Stutthof Camp, yet even at the end it was far from finished. Even the most essential of the camp's facilities were never completed. The crematorium, the gas chamber, the bathhouse, the laundry, the kitchen – all were squeezed into inadequate and unsuitable buildings.

Take the crematorium, for example. The incinerator in the crematorium could accommodate only a few corpses at a time; it was completely unsuited to such a large enterprise. There were always corpses in reserve… But then the corpses could afford to wait their turn, they weren't pressed for time. The disgusting part was that the crematorium was made of wood, crummy boards thrown together. In this same building, next to the warehouse where they stored the corpses, the crematorium's workers had a food locker where they kept bread, sausages and ham. They even rigged up a moonshine still on the sly. The moonshine was a necessity for them as a defence against the stench of the corpses; the authorities turned a blind eye to the still. One time the crematorium workers got blitzed, and while cooking up a batch of moonshine in the kitchenette they burned down the entire crematorium. The excess corpses were quite rank but they were still suitable for the incinerator. The remnants of the food, on the other hand, no longer passed muster, even with the crematorium specialists.

The gas chamber was also deficient. Clothing was piled inside to be deloused, but many of the pale grey beasties clung to woollen fabrics and survived to wreak fresh havoc. And when the necessity arose to poison humans with gas it was a truly difficult task. Closing people in the chamber wasn't hard; they'd be herded in, packed tight, locked up and that was it. But releasing the gas into the chamber was terribly difficult. SS men wearing gas masks had to clamber onto the barrack's roof and toss the gas canisters through the chimney into the incinerator. From the incinerator, the gas drifted quite lazily into the chamber, in no hurry to fulfil its assignment. The chimney itself had to be hermetically sealed so the fumes wouldn't escape and go to waste. After enough time had elapsed, the fumes had to be dispersed – and the SS had to mount the roof again like cats in heat. In short, the situation was complicated.

The authorities had been concerned with this inefficient state of affairs for a long time. Back in 1943, they started erecting a gigantic one-storey building in a peat bog. The building covered a huge expanse. It was to accommodate the gas chamber, the bathhouse, the kitchen, the food larder, the laundry, the office and many other facilities. Thousands of people worked on the site, but construction progressed slowly: there was always something lacking. The missing stuff would finally arrive, but by then the building material already on the site suddenly vanished. And try to find it! The devils who'd stolen it didn't leave a trace. So the authorities struggled, swearing at the bricks and bricklayers alike.

At last a new gas chamber was successfully built, designed for both disinfecting clothing and despatching people. Several cartloads of clothes were loaded in the chamber for a trial run. The doors were locked, the furnaces ignited. The firemen barely had time to sit down and have a chat when – whooosh! – the whole chamber filled with smoke! The clothes burst into flames and left behind only a stench.

The new kitchen didn't fare much better. Everything had been almost completely fitted; a sewage system had been installed along with central heating, waterworks and new built-in boilers. All that needed to be finished was the glass for the windowpanes plus a few other small items. But when the winter of 1944-45 set in, 500 metres of piping shattered, as well as a few hundred faucets. Someone forgot to drain the pipes. And in wartime, where were they going to get so many new pipes and taps?

Three halls of enormous size were also begun. Officially it was claimed that they were to be used to cut timber in the future, but actually they were intended to house a factory for airplane parts. They were erected right next to the prisoners' barracks: if the enemy planes had decided to bomb, they would have had to incinerate the prisoners. But it never came to that. The halls were finished, expensive machinery was hauled inside for assembly, everything stood in readiness – when the roof fell in with a terrific crash and crushed the new machines.

With so many big projects going on, large quantities of building material were stashed in warehouses. This German building material had a peculiar property: it could melt away into thin air. Building material vanished every day. In time, the shortage of such materials became critical. Clearly someone was swiping the stuff, but how could they find the culprit? Some SS stock clerks were sent to the front, but this move didn't replace the missing material. The authorities wracked their brains but they still couldn't come up with a practical solution. They decided at last that there was nothing left to do: the warehouses had to be burnt.

And burn they did! A pretty sight to behold. While they were burning, however, it became evident that for some mysterious reason ammunition and other explosive materials had been hidden there. And when these started exploding there was no question of getting near enough to put out the fire. So the warehouses burned clean to the ground.

If warehouses could be so ignorant and irresponsible, how could anyone be surprised that, shortly after the warehouse inferno, the entire construction division went up in smoke, with all its plans and blueprints, all its ledgers and inventories? Ammunition exploded in this fire, too – it was as though all hell had broken loose! The cause of the fire was never discovered. It was determined that the construction division's fire had begun in the furnaces, but the premises were empty at the time. No one was held responsible!

The bathhouse didn't manage to burn, but it also remained unfinished.

The camp did have a sort of bathhouse, with intermittent, tepid showers capable of accommodating about a thousand, or in desperate cases two thousand people. At the end of 1944, when about 40,000 people lived in the camp, the little bathhouse was approximately as useful as a dead canary...

The prisoners took matters into their own hands. They organised bathhouses in all of the blocks – simple ones like those found in the countryside. And they rigged up bathhouses in all the barracks, no worse than the authorised ones. They improvised furnaces, laid pipes, installed faucets and anything else that was needed. And the authorities turned their backs on all this, though occasionally they'd come around, interrogate, swear a little...

'Where did you scarecrows get these pipes?'

'They were sent from home in packages... in the mail...'

'Oh, and the bricks were sent from home in the mail?'

'Oh sure, captain, sir, from home, in packages...'

'*Blöde Sauhund!*' Mayer howled. He knew perfectly well that the building material had been taken from DAW government warehouses. But according to the laws of camp life, this wasn't theft – it was organisation.

For purposes of organisation, there was another excellent source: the SS canteen's depots. Here the SS kept portable treasures, life's little essentials: sheets, blankets, pillowcases, towels, underwear, overcoats, furs, soap, razors, utensils, tools and so on. The depots' stocks were frequently renewed with confiscated prisoners' goods, those that no one had organised on the way to the depot. With thousands upon thousands of prisoners arriving, treasures accumulated.

The SS and Gestapo would rip off certain valuables from the newcomers and haul the rest of the booty to the depot. Furthermore, various camps in Lithuania, Latvia and Estonia were being evacuated and a large share of their treasures landed in the depots. On the day fifteen typewriters were brought in from Riga, seven of them vanished without a trace. Of eight sewing machines shipped in, only two remained. The SS members who evacuated Riga tried to create an inventory for the goods they'd brought in, but this proved to be impossible: only garbage remained to be listed. At this depot it was possible at times to organise silver and gold spoons as well as rings and watches, plus bolts of English cloth for suits!

The senior depot sentry, a German SS, had a weakness for sugar moonshine, so he frequently needed to organise sacks of sugar. This snake guzzled moonshine like milk and slipped some to the other SS men. They tried to hide the fact they were swilling it; they reported for duty equally drunk. But the snake wouldn't give prisoners even a drop. Prisoners had to organise varnish from the DAW carpenters' workshops. This stuff made a wonderful, very thick liqueur. For the drunks, it was doubly convenient – you'd get loaded and satisfy your hunger as well.

A tremendous amount of varnish disappeared from the carpenters' workshop, but it could still be justified somehow. The situation in the hospital was worse. The authorities, naturally, tried to spoil the alcohol by pouring gasoline and other filth in it, but the camp had wonderful chemists: they'd convert this foul filth into fragrant nectar.

'Are they taking alcohol baths? What the hell!' the authorities cursed, checking the alcohol accounts. But there was nothing they could do.

In the SS depots stills of sugar moonshine bubbled away. The one and only brewmaster was my dear friend Jonas, the Prot from Biržai. He cooked and cooked that sugar, but he didn't bring me any; he swore that the snake of a stock clerk wouldn't even let him taste his own brew. And he told the truth. Only very rarely did he return from the brewery smashed – no more than twice a week. Otherwise he was as sober as a judge. You can't get much from a barrel with a straw!

And Jonas didn't stink too much of moonshine; just a touch, a little bit. You could smell him from about three metres away, upwind. Occasionally, some official would want to have a chat with him. The official would shout for Jonas to come closer. He would step to within five metres of the official. The official would move closer but, like a goat, Jonas would step backwards.

'Wait, you dirty mutt. Where are you going?' says the official.

'According to the laws in effect, a prisoner must keep a five metre distance from an official,' explains my dear friend, the Prot from Biržai.

'Not five, three,' the official retorts.

'Yes, you're right. But five metres are better than three. Five metres show the authorities greater respect!' And again Jonas steps back.

Try guessing what he reeks of!

XLIX

The Grim Reaper's Shelter

The concentration camp was a very complex death mill. Every individual crossing over its threshold was actually already condemned to die – sooner or later. Frequent starvation, beatings, long hours of hard labour, nights of no rest, parasites, bad air – sooner or later they did their job, if some other disaster didn't do it first, or if someone didn't get it into his head to finish you off himself.

In such an atmosphere the cruel psyche of the camp resident matures. Thrust into a brutal environment, the instinct for survival takes over; a person scarcely has a chance to notice how he is drawn into a state of primal fear, how little by little he becomes an organically functional piece of the horror. He already views the dreadful and drastic measures he takes to do battle with the Grim Reaper as mere expedients. His ethical sense grows dull; abominable acts no longer seem so loathsome. His only desire is to live. He'll violate his kin, snatch his last crumb of bread, shove a pal into the Grim Reaper's embrace so that if by doing so he might himself remain alive! This hideous situation becomes the norm: once you've stepped on this treadmill, it's nearly impossible to get off. It's hard to rediscover the golden mean, hard to tell the difference between self-preservation and ruthless injury to a friend.

Oh, if only all the prisoners would understand each other and quit brutalising, beating and robbing each other – there'd be more food for everyone, the work wouldn't be so backbreaking and daily life wouldn't be such hell! It's easy to say: if. What's there to do when none of this exists, when the one or two hundred who comprehend this situation are completely helpless to change the environment, to overcome the predatory instinct that seems essential to staying alive.

In these savage struggles for survival, some drown others; breaking through to the top, they give full rein to the predatory instinct and no longer bother to pause on their way; they have more than they need to keep living. The others, the ones with no luck, unable to break through to the surface at any price, sink down in the dregs and die. You slip in the constant skirmish for life – no one extends a helping hand to lift you up. The brawlers behind you may yank you to the ground and stamp you flat, then stride or slog over you without a second look, staring all around in an idiotic terror. They feel no remorse. There's nothing for a conscience to do, no need for one, no time to fret. Today you fell – I'll fall tomorrow; what's the difference? No one will bat an eye for me, either. Perhaps the most horrifying thing that camp does to a person is this inexorable erosion of every trace of what people call conscience, humaneness, simple respect.

One good thing about these surroundings is that the fear of death vanishes completely. With death a threat at every step, a person gets so used to the prospect that it becomes insignificant, trash underfoot. Death loses every vestige of nobility or tragedy. Lyricism is out of the question.

If they kill you – so they kill you; if they hang you – so they hang you. What's the big deal?

People die in camp without anxiety. They don't make death into a catastrophe. They're certainly not sorry to leave this earth. It's all the same to them.

The minute they're dead, they're disrobed, a number is written on their naked chests and their personal belongings are immediately stolen. The corpses are stacked just like cordwood in a shed near the hospital. The shed is tiny and the corpses don't all fit. The extras are dumped on the ground next to the hospital. No one inquires about the cause of death, no one inspects the bodies. Only the corpse's teeth are examined. If someone hasn't managed to steal the gold already, an SS man extracts it with rusty pliers. He turns a fraction of the gold in to the treasury; the rest he keeps for himself.

A transport wagon arrives drawn by a dozen prisoners. The transport workers pile the corpses into a big black coffin. The coffin was built to accommodate three corpses, but five or six are stuffed into it. The lid doesn't even close. Black and blue arms and legs, withered like twigs, stick out of the coffin; they flutter to the rhythms of the swaying wagon and wave as if beckoning passers-by. When there's even more corpses, the coffin is dispensed with; corpses are simply piled in the wagon like slaughtered pigs bound for the butcher. One is thrown next to another; one is tossed on top. Sometimes they're covered with a ratty gunnysack; sometimes nobody bothers. It makes no difference to the corpse, and for those of us who are still alive, it's neither here nor there. What's the difference?

The wagons head for the crematorium adjacent to the hospital's windows. Day and night the crematorium belches rosy and pale yellow smoke over the camp. This smoke isn't especially palatable. In fact it's rank, truly rancid – a weird stink like frying rubber.

It's a heavy smell, the smell of human meat grilling. Very heavy, day in and day out!

Near the crematorium, the corpses are heaped in a warehouse. After the moonshine brewers burned down the warehouse, the corpses had to be unloaded into a massive heap right in the yard, which was very inconvenient.

The crematorium's incinerator was adapted for liquid fuel and the corpses burned for about two hours. In 1944 there was no liquid fuel to be found, so coke was used instead. In a coke fire the corpses burned for about six hours. At this slower rate, there was no way that the crematorium could ever manage to burn all the corpses, but there was no material left to build another one. The corpses couldn't be buried either, because the camp stood on a swamp. Water stagnated near the surface, just two shovelfuls down. After a downpour a buried corpse would rise up out of the ground and would have to be dealt with all over again.

The crematorium workers always took the top layer of corpses, the most recent additions, to the incinerator. So the bottom layers rotted. If it weren't for the repugnant reek, a rotted corpse would have been more convenient to stick in the incinerator. As soon as a fresh corpse was fed into the furnace, it immediately raised up its arms and legs, as if consciously warding off another corpse from entering the oven. But of course it could not be incinerated alone; others had to be shoved in, too. The uncooperative corpses caused a lot of grief: their flailing legs and arms had to be wrestled down before their neighbour could be jostled in. Decayed corpses didn't thrash, but that smell of theirs was horrendous.

In December of 1944 and January of 1945, quite a sizeable daily surplus of corpses would accumulate – up to one and a half thousand or more. Every day two to three hundred people died. The crematorium was helpless to deal with them all. The chimney fractured from overwork and threatened to collapse from being kept so hot without respite. The dead, waiting so patiently to be burnt, were silent but hardly unnoticeable. When the weather was cold it wasn't so bad, but when a thaw set in the camp's mood grew foul. The stink of the corpses crept into every corner. Even boiled potatoes had a questionable flavour. Worst of all, this feckless smell had the temerity to permeate certain official abodes. Consequently it was determined that a serious battle with the corpses must be undertaken. The authorities deliberated at length but couldn't come up with anything better than to order prisoners to dig holes in the forest, dump in the corpses, douse them with tar and burn them.

Corpses smouldered slowly in these ditches. More tar had to be frequently applied and the prisoners had to play the chef, using a pitchfork to flip the corpses like hamburgers until they were cooked to a turn. In daylight this sight was dramatic enough but at night it became an operatic spectacle!

So the little corpses smoke and smoulder, shrouding the whole camp with the fumes of frying rubber. The stokers jump around the pit with pitchforks like devils tussling with witches on Walpurgis Night![1]

Serious problems cropped up here, too. As soon as night descended alien airplanes would begin to circle the camp. They didn't actually toss bombs at the corpses but their buzzing was still unpleasant: you never knew – would they drop a bomb or were they just harassing us? Or maybe the beasts were photographing everything? It's impossible to extinguish corpses quickly and besides, tar can't be wasted! But due to these intimidating airplanes night work had to be halted. The burnings could only continue by day. Winter days are short. The population explosion of corpses carried on.

The corpse situation hadn't always been so disastrous in the camp. From August to October of 1944, there were 50,000 to 60,000 prisoners in the camp, but daily deaths numbered between just three and fifteen. There were even days when no one died. No fresh corpses! The authorities were displeased with this meagre showing, naturally: how can capital invested in a crematorium remain inactive?! So the authorities manufactured corpses by artificial methods. They'd take a truck or two filled with the aged, the sick, the crippled and other weaklings, and then 'Rat-tat-tat-tat!' – there's your corpses! The Jews, who had grown quite numerous in camp at this time, were

1 During the Medieval and Renaissance period Walpurgis Night was an occasion when witches congregated to celebrate the coming of spring.

heavily relied on for this project.

They weren't always shot – bullets are made of metal after all, significantly more valuable than a corpse. The authorities more frequently resorted to gas. Of course, those being herded into the trucks were not told where they were being taken; they were lulled by an announcement that they were on their way to jobs where the food would be better. But they soon realised in what direction the gears of fate were grinding. They refused to board the truck, they wouldn't enter the chamber; the SS had to manhandle them to get them under control.

The SS had an especially difficult time with the old jewesses. They had to be lifted into the wagon – they refused to climb aboard themselves – and then lifted out of the wagon again. Most annoying was that once they were seated in the wagon, they shouted and screamed so that the whole camp resounded: '*Wir sind auch Menschen*! We are people too!' The SS, it seems, was of a different mind, however. Not once did the shrieks of the jewesses convince them.

The jewesses seated in the wagons weren't the only ones who shrieked. Those left behind on the other side of the electric fence also yelled – daughters, sisters, mothers. They all shouted and screamed – some louder, some softer. SS nerves had experienced everything, but even they couldn't tolerate this screeching for long. The SS ran out of the jewesses' block. The prisoners, of course, had no place to run. The prisoners listened and ruminated. What they underwent while listening was their personal affair. There's no reason for outsiders to butt in.

To stop the jewesses from ravaging any more SS nerves with their shrieks, a new means for coping with them was conceived. The jewesses would be herded on foot to a small train, so they'd believe they really were being taken to work. Next to the train stood a husky commandant's official wearing a railroader's uniform. He invited them most politely:

'Please take a seat on the train, dear ladies!'

Once the jewesses were stuffed into the train, the doors were locked. As soon as the train began moving, gas was released into the cars.

This method was used only once – nothing was gained by it. The jewesses, sensing the fumes, started screeching inside the train, too. They hammered against the doors and knocked on the windows; they frightened the civilian residents along the way.

These hastily created corpses weren't considered officially deceased.

The officially deceased were marked with the letter T in the record books – for *Tot*, dead – and were crossed off the list of the living. Those who voluntarily hung themselves got the emblem FT – *Freitod*, suicide. Others were noted with an Ex – *Exekution* – performed in accordance with some Gestapo court decision.

The corpses that had been rushed off to death in special trucks, trains and chambers were denoted in the books by the initials S.B. This must be read, Lord save me, not as Sruoga, Balys, but *Sonder Behandlung* – special treatment. Those unfamiliar with the Gestapo's special language might make what they wished of this delicate title!

Sometimes a grieving woman would show up at the gates of the camp, wishing to possess at least the ashes of an only son, a dear brother, a beloved husband. This wish was always complied with. Money was demanded for the ashes, urn, packing and postage – this came to about 230 marks. The authorities would then give an order to scoop out a couple of kilograms of ash from the common pile of ashes, which were mailed to the grieving woman. Of course the authentic ashes of an individual were never sent out; this was impossible. Everyone's ashes got mixed in the furnace. And by the time a request for ashes arrived, the dearly beloved had long since been strewn the devil knows where. How would you gather him up? But you don't want to upset the woman. Isn't it the same for her? Ashes are ashes.

Ashes were frequently requisitioned. To get 200 marks for a few leftover kilograms of ashes wasn't a bad deal, but there had to be corpses!

1945

86

First published in Balys Sruoga, *Dievų miškas*, Chicago: Terra (1957).

Translated by Aušrinė Byla.

Balys Sruoga (1896–1947) was a poet, symbolist, dramatist, critic, essayist, translator and one of the most colourful figures of inter-war Lithuanian cultural life. A professor at Vytautas Magnus University, he was the founder of the country's first university theatre department and created the tradition of theatre criticism in Lithuania. His own dramatic works most often examined historical themes, delving into the decline of the political might of the Grand Duchy. During the Second World War he was arrested and incarcerated in Stutthof Concentration Camp, along with several other academics, for anti-Nazi resistance. This experience was the basis for his non-fiction work *Forest of the Gods* (*Dievų miškas*, written in 1945 and published in 1957), which, due to the interference of Soviet censors, was only published almost ten years after the author's death.

No One's to Blame

Romualdas Lankauskas

The woman was truly beautiful and her children, a fair-haired boy and a graceful girl, were like their mother – cheerful and glowing with good health and a youthfulness that had not yet reached its end, although she must have been about thirty-five, if not more. Her husband was obviously much older – a small man with a tired face, yet nimble, good-humoured and full of the joy of life, which he wanted to share with everyone. I quickly became friends with Benedict. He was open and talkative.

'It's great here, isn't it?' he asked me, arranging his fishing poles. 'And what peace!'

'The lake is wonderful, but still, it's not the sea,' I said. 'Nothing compares with the sea.'

The house where we were spending our holiday stood on a hill. The lake sparkled below – a blue jewel in a ring of green trees.

'No, don't say that,' said Benedict as he sharpened his fishing hooks. 'Of course, Palanga is a nice resort, but I don't like it. Too many people, too much noise. You can only really relax beside this lake. This is already our third year holidaying here. And the perch! Good Lord! Early yesterday morning, I caught three. And one weighed more than a kilogram.'

'You don't say,' I doubted.

'You don't believe me? Then ask my wife. I'll call her.'

He shouted.

A window opened and a woman's beautiful face appeared.

'Good day,' I greeted her, bowing my head.

The woman smiled at me.

'You'll be spending your holiday with us?'

'Yes, I've already made arrangements for a room with the landlady.'

'Will you stay long?'

'Perhaps the entire month, if the weather is nice.'

'Lucia, he doesn't believe that I caught three perch yesterday, each about a kilogram,' Benedict said in a slightly offended tone.

'Yes, he caught them,' the woman assured me. 'Benedict catches something every day. I'm tired of cleaning them. I give the smaller ones to the cat.'

'You see, and you didn't want to believe me,' Benedict said triumphantly. 'So get your fishing poles and let's go to the lake. I'll show you a spot where there's perch aplenty. You won't catch anything if you don't know where to look. At first, I'd come home with very little. But now, I'm thoroughly convinced there are many fish in this lake.'

'So what if there are a lot of fish,' the woman shrugged her shoulders. 'I'm bored. We must go to Palanga next year.'

'Lucia, you know that the doctor advised me not to go to the sea.' Benedict turned to me and said: 'You see, I've been sick with TB. I worked very hard, I was exhausted, and I caught that cursed disease. I was afraid I might kick the bucket, but I was treated at the sanatorium and recovered somehow. I feel reasonably well now. The air is good here among the pine trees. My lungs will get better and I'll be able to go back to work.'

'Lord, but it's boring here,' the woman sighed. 'You won't be able to tolerate it for long. What are you going to do when you grow tired of fishing?'

'I'll go sailing. It's my favourite sport.'

'Ah, sailing,' she smiled. 'Perhaps you'll take me along.'

I remained silent, disconcerted by her request.

'Of course he will,' Benedict said cheerfully, 'if you fry him some fish. He'll go fishing with me and won't come back empty-handed.'

We walked to the lake, carrying our fishing poles, cans full of worms and nets to hold the fish in the water. As we walked down the hill, I felt the woman's eyes following me. I was tempted to turn around but didn't, and I quickly began pushing Benedict's rowing boat into the water. There was a wet rope on the bottom, coiled like a snake; one end was tied to a heavy stone. Benedict used it as an anchor.

I rowed and Benedict sat on the bench opposite me, his bare feet thrust forward, his old pants rolled at the ankles, talking about himself, his wife and his children. You couldn't help but think he was one of those rare people fortunate to have a happy family. Many would undoubtedly have envied him.

We rowed out to the other side of the lake for here, according to Benedict, was the kingdom of the perch. We dropped anchor, cast our fishing lines, and before long, my bobber submerged. I pulled out a small perch.

'*Perca fluviatilis*,' I said.

'What?' Benedict didn't understand.

'It's the Latin name for perch.'

Benedict laughed.

'You must be a naturalist, since you know the Latin names.'

'Yes, you're right.'

'I may be uneducated, but the fish like me better,' he chuckled as he pulled out large perches and mullet. Meanwhile, I had to satisfy myself with rather puny specimens. 'But, don't be discouraged. Tomorrow we'll get up at sunrise and catch some roaches... What is the Latin name?'

'*Rutilus rutilus*.'

'Indeed, we'll catch some roaches and then we'll get the perch.'

'From your lips to God's ear,' I said.

The next morning, Benedict woke me very early (the sun had not yet risen) and by six o'clock we were on the lake, which was covered in a greyish mist. The morning was foggy and very quiet. Not even the smallest wavelet disturbed the surface of the lake and only once in a while did a fish hunting its prey splash in the reeds or a duck screech upon awakening. The air was filled with the scent of water. I washed my sleepy face and then suddenly I felt the first demure rays of sunlight. In my heart I felt at peace and contented. Beyond the noise of the city, beyond the heat and humidity, I was once again where I wanted to be, a place where you could feel the wonder, the mystery and the infinite vitality of nature from which we sometimes so foolishly distance ourselves, drowning in the smoke of diesel and tobacco, losing ourselves amid stone walls and strange and indifferent people. My efforts at fishing were not as successful as Benedict's, whose fishing pole had already twice curved down and twice I saw and heard a heavy perch, flat as a slab of silver, fall into the bottom of the boat. I had snagged a large perch myself – both of my bobbers had shot like bullets toward the bottom – but I was unable to pull it out; it escaped right at the side of the boat and dived into the depths. Benedict tried very hard to console me, for I was very upset, and pointed out the mistakes I had made.

Perhaps I misunderstood his instructions that morning because I didn't catch anything. The roaches died and I threw them back into the water. I sat in the boat in a sour mood.

Benedict pointed the tip of his fishing pole at the largest of the perch.

'This handsome predator is yours,' he said.

'No, keep it for yourself.'

'I said it's yours, and not another word. I'll tell my wife to cook it for your dinner.'

Benedict's family was already up by the time we reached the shore. The children were playing in the orchard. His wife, seated in a wicker chair, was embroidering a silk handkerchief. She wore a dress with a deep neckline and I noticed that she was wearing lipstick and had done her hair differently. Now she looked even more beautiful, and Benedict's homely and unhealthy countenance was much more conspicuous. His face was a matt grey, like the faces of those seriously afflicted with tuberculosis.

The woman looked at the fish with disgust.

'I'll have to struggle with those perch again. Cleaning them is miserable: my hair smells of fish and my hands look like they belong to a laundress.'

'I'll help you,' I said

'Do you know how?' She laughed and rose from her seat. 'Very well, bring the fish behind the barn. That's where I clean them.'

Benedict went up for a nap.

There was a board in the grass behind the barn. It was covered with fish scales. I placed the perches on the board. The woman brought a knife and fork. She knelt down beside me.

'Pierce the tail with the fork and hold it firmly.'

Fish scales flew in all directions and her strong, bare arms worked so close to mine that I wanted to touch them and feel the softness of her skin. A gold wedding ring glittered on her finger and she wore another with a precious stone. She smelled of expensive perfume and even the acrid smell of the fish did not smother its aroma. On one occasion she leaned against my shoulder and it smouldered for a long time as if it were sunburned.

She then threw the cleaned perch into a bowl, looked at her scale-covered hands, took off her apron and asked me if I could see what had fallen into her eye. Her eyes were large, blue and clear as lake water. My fingers trembled when I touched her eyebrow.

'I don't see anything,' I said.

'Oh, it's all right now,' and she gave me an enigmatic and curious smile. 'Thank you. It must have been a midge. When I've cooked the fish, I'll bring it to you.'

She walked away, stepping carefully with her bare, suntanned and strong legs. The cat was devouring fish innards in the grass. I decided to go for a swim and then for a ride in the sailboat that the village yacht club had let me use.

The wind had picked up and the boat leaned dangerously to the side when a squall rose in the middle of the lake; I nearly capsized when I tried to turn it around. I would have died of shame if the young men had run from the yacht club to help me and found me floundering beside the boat. Nevertheless, I made it safely to the shore, fastened the boat to a post at the pier and hurried back for dinner. I was ravenously hungry.

Benedict's wife brought me a fatty fried perch and some freshly boiled potatoes. I tasted it and licked my lips.

'Delicious.'

'I can't even look at fish.'

She stood and watched me eating for a while, then left the room humming a melody. Benedict's wife – what a woman! Why had I not met her while she was single? I would've proposed instantly.

I don't exactly remember when it happened, it must have been Saturday. The landlady went to the market, Benedict went to the village to buy some hooks and lead weights, and the boy and girl ran off to play with the yacht-club guard's children.

It was drizzling outside. I was reading in my room. Benedict's wife, that beautiful and lovely woman, knocked on the door and asked if I could put up a rope up in the barn so she could hang the laundry. If it weren't for the unexpected rain she would have hung up the washing outside. But it didn't look like the rain would stop any time soon.

'I hope I'm not disturbing you, Leonard.'

'Not at all,' I said. 'I'm happy to be of service.'

I put the book, an interesting work on the habits of bugs and beetles, to one side. I took the rope from her hands, found some nails and a hammer and went to the barn to look for a suitable place to drive in the nails. The acrid smell of freshly mown hay filled the barn. I stretched the rope from one wooden wall to the other.

She brought in a basket of laundry and began hanging it. I stood nearby, giddy from the smell of hay and her closeness. Suddenly, she burst out laughing, she laughed long and loudly, and then, as though bereft of strength, she collapsed onto the hay and stretched out her strong brown legs. Her dress slid upward. I saw her round, tanned knees and in that instant I saw nothing but them and a hot mist covered my eyes.

I turned around and practically ran out of the barn. Her laughter rang in my ears for a long time. Soaked through, I walked aimlessly in the rain. Finally, I went to the yacht club, sat on a bench and stared at the surface of the water, grey and stippled by the falling rain. A profound sadness overwhelmed me.

After that hot and rainy afternoon, she no longer spoke to me. She would greet me coldly, yet politely, on her way to her morning ablutions by the lake. Benedict and I would fish all day and now I fried the catch myself. Often we heard the rumble of a motor on the lake; a red motorboat would speed past us. A large, corpulent man in a green shirt sat at the wheel. That motorboat belonged to the chairman of the co-operative; he dashed about the lake like a madman, throwing out jigs and setting his bobbers baited with small live fish with which he always caught large pike.

I didn't like him, I don't know why. But Benedict found some common interests to talk about and even invited him for dinner. Benedict's wife began to smile again – not at me but at the chairman of the co-operative, who spoke charmingly and was very deferential.

At that time the blueberries in the forest on the other side of the lake had ripened. Every day the women and children would return with full baskets.

'We should pick some berries too,' said Benedict's wife.

She was washing her legs in the lake. Benedict and I had just returned from fishing and were winding up our fishing poles. The chairman of the co-operative was tinkering with the motor on his boat. He raised his head.

'If you like, I can take you to the other side of the lake.'

The woman glowed with pleasure.

'When?'

'Right now. I'll just fill the tank with gasoline,' he said, scratching his broad hairy chest.

'What are you waiting for?' said Benedict. 'Call the children and go.'

They cast off. The children were thrilled but the rumble of the motor soon engulfed their cheerful voices. The boat lunged forward and took off, spraying white foam in its wake. It soon disappeared from view. Benedict went off to clean his perch. He whistled as he walked up the hill.

If I had kept a diary I would be able to read in it now, more or less, the following intermittent entries:

Wednesday. Benedict's wife returned in the evening with a basket full of blueberries; the children had gathered mushrooms. When she cooked them, the whole house was filled with their aroma.

Thursday. They went berry picking again. Today, Benedict

94

seemed out of sorts for some reason. He didn't joke with me and he didn't catch much while fishing; he let go of two large perch.

Saturday. This afternoon I went sailing, wanting to practise turning about in a strong wind. At the north end of the lake, beyond the peninsula, I passed the chairman of the co-operative and Benedict's wife sitting in the red motorboat. She pretended not to see me. In the evening, Benedict walked in the yard for a long time and smoked many cigarettes, although he had told me he quit smoking when he became ill with TB.

Sunday. The beautiful woman is blooming like a flower. She went berry picking again today. She and the chairman of the co-operative can be seen on the lake with increasing frequency. It's as though Benedict doesn't exist.

Tuesday. Benedict no longer goes out fishing. His face has become completely grey. He looked very ill and appeared to not have slept well.

Wednesday. In the early morning, Benedict rowed out onto the lake alone. He didn't wake me. Before noon, someone noticed his empty boat drifting on the lake.

All efforts to find Benedict were unsuccessful. Members of the yacht club looked for him, as did the fishermen and the chairman of the co-operative in his fast motorboat. Benedict disappeared without a trace. Presumably, he fell out of his boat and drowned. No one's to blame. He should have been more careful. After all, the lake is so deep! Maybe he didn't know how to swim.

That's what people said at the lakeside, consoling his weeping wife. She sobbed and sobbed, wringing her hands, and the wind carried her cries into the distance. I went down there to that spot on the shore where Benedict's boat was floating and, looking into the bottom of the boat, I saw neither the rope nor the heavy stone he used as an anchor when fishing for those big perch.

Translated by Ada Valaitis from Romualdas Lankauskas, *Pilka šviesa*, Vilnius: Vaga (1968).

Romualdas Lankauskas (born 1932) is a prose writer, dramatist, translator and painter as well as one of the founders of Soviet-era abstract Lithuanian art. In the 1970s and 1980s he became known as the master of the laconic short story, writing against the cultural groove of the Soviet era. His works explored forbidden themes, putting him at odds with the wardens of Soviet ideology. Throughout his career he composed over thirty short story collections, novels and travel essays. He founded the Lithuanian PEN centre in 1989.

A Cry in the Full Moon

Juozas Aputis

He was not always alone in the day. Indeed, if he were running a fever he would sit alone in the shade on a rickety bench at noon; at that time his hunched back was nearly parallel to the ground and he would hold one hand outstretched to grasp a cane so that he would not fall flat on his face. He would sometimes free his hands by leaning his chin on the cane and then this small-town Quasimodo would resemble a wooden sculpture that was splitting and being eaten away by the elements.

He could remain motionless for a terrifyingly long time, and he even wore a hollow into the bench. He would gaze, with his blue, ever-dry eyes, out into the courtyard at the well that the inhabitants of the neighbouring homes often went to for water. Usually it was the women. Drinking them in with his sometimes blank, sometimes bitter eyes, the hunchback would follow every drop of water splashing over the well-curb. If a stream poured over the edge he did not of course jump off the bench but instead, irritated, would move his neck (from which his long, angular face grew in a peculiar way) back and forth, and his mouth would open. He was certainly not short of water; though he walked with difficulty, he could still reach the lake encircling the town. Besides, people often left water in the bucket chained to the well. As he watched the water flowing over the well-curb, one might suppose that the hunchback thought about something beautiful, something real, something that he had been lacking from the time he was in the crib and which all these people possessed, whistling in their carefree way, coming and going, coming and going.

The worst thing for him was when the young women – which the small town, with its many summer visitors as well as the natives, did not lack – would bend over to pull up a bucket full of water and their legs – beautiful or un-beautiful, still holding for the hunchback the foreshadowing of some sort of secret – would be shamelessly revealed. He would feel the cold crawl up from somewhere in the earth through the torn soles of his shoes, rising up through his wizened, bony legs, squeezing under his loosely clasped belt, and then would begin to creep higher, gently and pleasantly adhering to his large hump and rushing out though his eyes. There were also those women who leaned heavily over the well-curb on purpose – it is truly a womanly foolishness to take eternal joy in that which others do not possess and to feel a pleasant tickling near their hearts understanding that those others see her and perhaps even desire her a little bit. This type of hunchback-teaser bent over for a long time, dawdling over the bucket, and the man on the bench would hear how his cane would pierce through the compressed earth as he pressed down with his chin. Even worse was when that stout-legged heartbreaker, having poured the water into her bucket and without fail having released a cold stream of water over the well-curb as though it was nothing, would turn to the hunchback and greet him:

'Good morning! You're up early…'

And then she walked away, staggering a little from the weight of the bucket but still managing to move properly that part of her body that a hunchback does not have and which the woman knew would elicit desire. After the woman had already gone some distance the man would slowly lift his cap – having not managed it in time after being stunned by the beautiful and rarely heard voice – and would smile openly, revealing his yellowed teeth.

Then he would be left almost alone, the townspeople having dispersed – some to the fields, some to catch fish, some driving off on the dirt road to the larger town to look for more fashionable cloth for a jacket or a dress before returning with a full basket of lovely rye or wheat bread in tow. Quite a few non-locals wandered by and they would draw up exorbitant quantities of water, banging the bucket on the cement edges of the well-curb. After pouring the water into their own oily buckets, they would then carry them over and dump the water into the hissing radiators of their autos before rushing off in a cloud of dust. There were others who were of more interest to him. These people would climb out of shiny automobiles and walk the streets of the town with their hands in their pockets, looking at the newly built houses and the red-brick school. The hunchback, having on occasion heard a fragment of news on the radio at the town snack bar, understood this pageantry – this was actually the white-shirted visitors' job. Sometimes he would pretend he was slinking away somewhere purposefully and would pause and carefully look at those very powerful people climbing back into their automobiles and careering further along the wide roads of the homeland.

Sundays were most pleasant for him, when the women from the countryside flocked to the market in front of the church. He was acquainted with all of the market women, and when he paid for his purchases he could consequently praise each and every one very convincingly because he really knew which woman pressed the best cheese and which one would never bring a huge block of butter dyed with carrot juice to sell. He would be the last to leave the market, feeling great pleasure and satisfaction, and would head to the town square, but rather than going straight along the street, he would go in a roundabout way, passing alongside the lake from whose centre a purple-hued island peak, overgrown with bent grass, protruded. Every summer during the haying season he would buy a rake; the rake-maker knew this and he would carve and polish one beautifully for the hunchback. There were about fifteen of those rakes piled up in the attic, if not more, but he bought a new one every year. It was more interesting to live like this.

In the summer he had yet another pleasant little undertaking. After escorting those wayfaring vehicles into the distance with his eyes and having allowed to enter before him the spryer, healthier and more hungry, he would calmly enter the town snack bar before resting his chin on the table edge. He would then rifle about through the crumbs in his pockets for a long time until he found a metal coin of some sort. Then he would make his way slowly towards the counter; the portly woman behind it, who had known him for a long time, would offer to serve him out of turn, but he would turn his head to look at those standing in queue, lower his voice and say: 'No, no. I'll stand, I have time. These people are in a hurry.'

And he would stand at the end of the queue, and when he reached the counter he would take a coffee and a small bun. On some days he did not have enough money and on others he did and was given change. He would sit on a chair in the very furthest corner of the snack bar and, using all his strength, he would try to lean back far enough that there would be sufficient space for a glass between his chin and the table. The snack bar was full of people he knew, and when they ran out of room they would sit at his table, eating and drinking, not really paying any notice to the hunchback. And he felt good; he loved all those people and for this reason he could not say no to a drink when it was offered. The first time someone offered him something to drink, he carefully studied the person who pushed the glass towards him; later, he no longer studied them, understanding that they offered out of goodness and love to him, a fellow inhabitant of the town without whom nothing would be quite the same and much would be lost. Having drunk a couple of glasses he would grin, opening his mouth even wider than when the woman by the well wished him a good morning, and his stiff body, which had never walked upright, would warm up and he would let loose with all sorts of things – things for which he would later be sorry and angry with himself to such an extent that they would sometimes even keep him from daring to enter the square for a few days. He would wedge his feet against the cross of the table legs and lean his chair back, shouting at those sitting with him at the table: 'Look, I'm vertical too, I'm vertical too! Ha, ha!'

But there was rarely a time that, after saying those words, he did not proceed to crash down to the floor, chair and all. Though only the very drunk and those who were not regulars at the snack bar laughed, he would lose his wits and get caught up in the commotion. He would hop back up and sit on the chair again before kicking up his feet once more. When he finally managed to push himself up, the man would hang his head, the muscles of his wrinkled nape, overgrown with grey hair, straining from the horizontal state of his back as he twisted his head to the side, wanting to look at the ceiling. When he eventually achieved the desired position, he would swallow the saliva accumulating in his mouth from the strain on his muscles and would shout once again: 'Didn't I tell you! I'm vertical too…'

Then he would let his body collapse back down, rest his chin on the table, take his cane in his hand and leave. Perhaps it was for this reason that when he stepped outside he felt an unburdening before overwhelming regret set in. He would then go over to the fence, overgrown with peonies, where the patrons of the snack bar who had had too much to drink would make themselves at home. The hunchback would find work here. The men who had left the snack bar and crawled into the grass and peonies thought they were already home and so would remove their footwear by the fence before stretching out and sticking their bare feet through its gaps. The hunchback would collect their shoes and put them back on the their dirty feet, tying up their laces while chattering away, chiding the men, shaking them and telling them to go home. And then one day this beautiful sight was witnessed by some people passing through the broad fields, and the town council tore down the fence. The peonies were quickly trampled on, no refuge remained for the drunks and the hunchback no longer had anywhere to do his penance, and so he stopped mentioning verticality even though the villagers had become very used to it and continued to feed him drinks and ask him to remember the good old days.

Night-time belonged to him. When everything settled down and the people closed their doors or dispersed on the last buses, he would once again go out into the square, only now he did not sit on the bench but made his way slowly to the well, grasping the edge of the well-curb with his hand or else resting his chin against it as he stood rooted there. Here and there the lights in the windows went out as the day's life began to die. On nights with a full moon you could see him, illuminated by the dim light, lonelier than in the day, looking over the edge of the well-curb in the direction of the hill fort and the large lake. The hunchback would listen, his ears perking up like some sort of animal, and it seemed that all those hidden, unknown things that surround us flowed into his hump. Gazing into the night with his shiny, moonlight eyes, the hunchback felt that there, in the town square by the well, he was useful not only to the well and the sleeping people, but to the trees, lakes and other things. He felt how his life-breath pulsated alongside and around the love-torn life surrounding him and returned once again into his hump. That night a miracle happened: the humpbacked man raised his free hand, the one that was not grasping the well-curb, and gestured towards the lake, and out there splashed a huge fish and he waved back at her while a bat flapped by the well, flying low. That night he turned his hand towards a lit window and a woman with bared breasts came into view; she then undressed entirely and gazed at herself for a long time in a large mirror.

An inexplicable feeling riveted the man to the well, and an unattainable yearning clambered up onto his hump. The man now saw himself clearly in the light of day, his singularity and his superiority. He had something others, drowning in their small daily joys and sorrows, did not: he felt everything deeper than they did, everything that surrounded them on that full-moon night, all that eternity and infinity. And he felt sad for his own sublimeness.

The naked woman passed by the small window once more and he thought to himself that a woman's body hides everything within itself – the lakes, the hill forts, the wells. Like two flints, the original woman and man ignited everything on earth – life and death, godliness and hell, spiritual heights and declines.

The woman passed by the window and went to turn out the light. She extinguished it quickly and what remained on the other side of the window was only the woman's spirit, which longed for the symbol of womanliness.

Just then, behind him, he heard the voices of another woman and a man. Suddenly a woman ran out into the yard. She cried quietly and then began to sob violently. Between her sobs you could hear the chirping of crickets. A cold drop of water fell from the well lid and into the bottom of the well. The woman's sobs were now resembling an unending moan. A terrible woman's moan in the full-moon night, her sobs reverberating around the whole world reminding everyone that a person, having created and idealised something, will also destroy it in the most brutal way. A man's angry and cruel words spilled out into the yard, following the woman's sobbing.

One more cold drop of water fell to the bottom of the well and the hunchback could no longer keep hold of his protective field, and he returned instantly to this world. Hurrying, dragging his feet and stumbling against the fence, he rushed into the yard from where the sobbing was emanating. The woman was nowhere to be seen and all that could be heard was sobbing coming from under the apple tree. A man stood on the gravel path – dishevelled hair, half naked, eyes bulging. The hunchback recognised him; not too long ago the man had urged him to 'make yourself vertical' in the snack bar.

The hunchback stopped in front of the man, transferred his cane to his left hand and weakly raised his right hand upwards.

'Hey, hey, hey!' he stuttered raising his head and moving closer. 'Hey, hey, hey…'

Then he passed by the man and ran towards the apple tree where the sobs were emanating from. There stood a woman dressed only in a shirt, which was torn, and he took a good, long look at her face – it was the same woman who had greeted him the other morning and then walked away so skilfully.

'Hey… hey… hey…'

The hunchback wanted to say something more but not a word left his lips. The woman suddenly stopped crying.

'What are you doing here?'

He felt anger in her voice, that horridness eternally hidden in the relations between men and women, and he wanted to scream like he was crazy, for this woman had stopped crying only out of hatred for him and not for hatred of that other man, the one who shook and hit her, who idealised her and then vilely debased her. But not a sound came out of his gaping mouth. The hunchback quickly stumbled out through the gate and raced back into his own moonlit square, stretching out and feeling something crack under his hump. In the time it took him to reach the well he twice repeated:

'Life is brutal.'

'Life is brutal.'

He then grasped the edge of the well-curb with one hand like a little hawk and with his other hand held onto the handle. When he had hauled the bucket back up he pulled it out using his mouth, grasping the lip of the bucket with his teeth. Water splashed all over his tattered shoes and soiled trousers and poured mercilessly onto the grass. The water appeared bluish in the moonlight. In this way he drew up three buckets of bluish water.

Translated by Medeinė Tribinevičius from Juozas Aputis, *Gegužė ant nulūžusio beržo*, Vilnius: Vaga (1986).

Juozas Aputis (1936–2010) was one of the most important short story writers in Lithuania. He also created memorable short novels. His work is distinctive in the context of Lithuanian literature of his period for its focus on the decay and changes in traditional village culture. Through his writing he conferred onto the Lithuanian novel a large dose of existential anxiety, enriched the Lithuanian short story form and expanded the bounds of psychological narrative. His short story collections *Wild boars run on the horizon* (*Horizonte bėga šernai*, 1970) and *Returning through evening fields* (*Sugrįžimas vakarėjančiais laukais*, 1977), are classics of the short story genre.

The Earth is Always Alive

Icchokas Meras

The setting sun, red as a fire, peered into the pit from the other bank but no longer saw a single living person, though he, alive and well, stood near a long, uneven ditch that skirted the gravel pit, while his accomplices, the whole group of them, roamed about, dividing up the clothes and possessions left behind by the executed.

Standing with his legs apart, as before, with the same glassy eyes as when he fired the last shot a short hour ago, he scanned the naked corpses lying strewn in the ditch. His eyes, together with the black abyss of the barrel of his automatic, quietly traced a circle. The metal butt pressed firmly beneath his heart. He knew that it was over, that there would be no more today, but he still didn't want to release the metal clenched tightly in his palms, the metal which, in his hands, had the capacity for murder.

Having scanned the ditch he reluctantly squinted at the red sun suspended in the sky. He then opened his eyes wide and looked at the group tussling over the pile of possessions. His glance stopped and pierced each of them separately. For a moment he forgot the haul and saw only life. His eyes glittered like glass for he wanted to pull the trigger and start shooting again, even shooting at the group below. The index finger of his right hand bent and then pressed the trigger half way...

'If I released several rounds, I'd lay them all flat,' he said and laughed heartily. 'Not a single one would be left alive, I'd shoot them all.' He imagined how they would fall with their hands outstretched, curling up with faces grimaced in pain, how the streams of blood would soak into the yellow, almost transparent sand to leave dark, quickly drying stripes.

Holding the index finger of his right hand still, he turned and looked again at the naked dead bodies lying in the ditch.

'If they all rose right now I could shoot them again,' he mused.

He caressed the barrel of the automatic and burned his hand. It was still hot.

He swore several times and only then heard a whisper rising from the ditch:

'Mama, mama, mama...'

And then:

'Open your eyes, open your eyes.'

The young girl gently stroked her mother's hair, but her mother did not move. The mother lay with her head lowered, her legs curled up, her lips were a pale blue. Only her hands were as before, behind her back, fingers tightly entwined as though even now she was still clutching her daughter and shielding the child with her own young body.

The girl caressed her mother's cheek. She tried to pry open her mother's eyes with her tiny fingers, but the woman's cheeks were getting cold and her eyelids, heavy as those of a wooden doll, would close again.

'Open your eyes, open your eyes.'

He was delighted. He spread his legs wide again and, no longer feeling any pain in his right hand, he grasped the automatic, placed his index finger on the trigger and held the butt firmly against his chest.

The girl was unable to communicate with her mother. She stood up and climbed out of the ditch. The girl was already grown up. She was three years old. And she had the courage to ask for help because her mother wasn't listening and did not open her eyes.

She extended her left hand and said to the man:

'Come... Open my mother's eyes.'

She was pale, this grown-up, three-year-old person. She was naked like the rest. Only two red stains smouldered in this whiteness:

her long hair, red as a fire, that covered almost her entire face, and the large, red apple in her right hand.

The man who was standing at the ready, didn't know that the girl's apple had once been white. A white summer apple with two tiny incisions – the marks of two milk teeth. The girl had carried that large white apple all this way and had not once let go of it. She had the time to leave the two tiny incisions in the skin of the apple when everyone was lined up by the rim of the ditch and when her mother had pushed her behind her back. The apple had turned red after it had rested on her mother's chest.

'Come... Open my mother's eyes.'

The girl extended her left hand.

He stood still. Then the girl extended her right hand, which held the red apple. She wanted to give him the apple so that he would come and open her mother's eyes.

He was delighted. His chin quivered with satisfaction. He was delighted – one had risen from the ditch. He had been ready for a long time and the index finger of his right hand slowly, slowly pulled the trigger. He savoured every minute and did not want to lose it. But perhaps he had waited too long, had extended the moment too far, the moment between life and death. And when he felt the resistance of the trigger, when all that was needed was to pull harder in a final sudden movement, his eyes were dazzled. The girl's hair was fire-red and it blinded him like the red setting sun.

He closed his eyes and when he opened them he felt that he really was looking at the sun. He closed his eyes again and now he saw the red apple.

'Come... Open my mother's eyes. I'll give you the apple.'

He looked at the girl and again saw the sun, then the girl and the apple, the apple, the girl... Three circles red as a fire. Larger, smaller, larger.

He no longer knew where to aim, where to shoot, and the black abyss of the barrel traced wide, fitful arcs.

Finally, he fired.

'Come... Open my mother's eyes.'

Evidently, he had fired at the sun.

He fired again.

'Come...'

At the apple?

'No, I must fire at the largest of the red circles,' he thought. 'If I fire at the sun, then surely I will hit that red hair.'

He fired one round after another.

The group dividing up the clothes of the executed fell into disarray. Someone moaned. They all dropped to the ground behind the piles of clothes.

'Stop, have you gone mad!' they screamed.

But he kept shooting at the largest of the red circles.

'Stop, we'll kill you!' they shouted.

He changed the clip and kept shooting.

Then no one was shouting anymore, and many barrels turned toward him spitting fire and bullets.

He collapsed to his knees and then fell. As he was falling, he grasped the burning barrel, but his hand no longer felt pain. His eyes bulged but they were still glassy only there was a redness under the glassiness, as though the red summer apple had painted them.

The group hastily packed the things into wagons and left.

And then the gravediggers came to the gravel pit. Young men and old – gravediggers. The shovels did not appear heavy. The sand in the gravel pit was packed evenly. But these men walked, dragging their feet, heads lowered.

They were not gravediggers. They had been ordered to be gravediggers.

Among them were a father and son. The father was a short, bent man with grizzled hair and half-closed eyes. The son was tall with wide blue eyes and thick, fair hair that always fell onto his face because of his bowed head. Both were called Ignas. The grandson, who had not yet arrived in this world, was Ignas too.

The son looked at the ditch through a shield of drooping hair and said:

'Father, how can the earth endure this?'

The father was silent.

The son kicked a clump of earth that had fallen from the edge of the gravel pit.

'You see,' he said again to his father, 'the earth is dead. It is earth and nothing else. You can kick it, stomp on it, soak it with blood. The earth is dead. It doesn't care.'

'No, son,' replied the father. 'The earth is alive. You're young and you don't understand.'

'No!' said the son. 'Just look. They dug a pit, shot them and left. We came to cover it up. We will cover it. Yet, the earth is silent. It is dead, it doesn't care. You can kick it, stomp on it, soak it with blood.'

'That's not true!' said the father and gave his son a stern look. 'The earth is alive, you'll see for yourself.'

The men were ordered to cover the ditch so that no traces were left, but instead they pushed the earth, trying to form a grave. It was a long grave, stretching across the entire length of the gravel pit. They had not planned it, but each man did the same thing.

'You see?' the father said, thinking about the grave.

So what, if the men didn't do what they had been told to do? The son didn't understand. He was still young.

They were both digging at the spot where the girl was lying. The shooter who had been shot was sprawled nearby.

'Bury the girl,' said the father to his son.

The son put down his shovel, picked the girl up in his arms and carefully lowered her into the ditch. His eyes were half closed like his father's so that he would not see too much. He would have closed his eyes altogether but he had to bury the girl.

After that they continued digging, avoiding the shooter as if they hadn't seen him, even though he lay right next to the ditch. His head was hanging down on top of the executed people, his hands clenched in the sand and his legs were stretched straight out. His bulging, glassy eyes still glittered. He didn't want to be dead.

His trousers were green and contrasted starkly with the white sand.

'He's in the way,' said the father. 'Let's push him over.'

The son raised his shovel and was ready to push the green legs into the ditch, but his hands froze. How could he throw this green thing next to that pale girl with the red hair and the red apple?

'Wait,' the father said, thinking that his son had not understood him.

He did not push his shovel under the man's legs to throw him into the ditch, but instead pushed it under his back. The only way they could lift him was out of the ditch. The son looked at his father and his eyes were radiant with joy. He also pushed his shovel under the man's back. They spat on their palms and threw the green-clad man out of the ditch.

The other men gathered around, coming from the right and from the left. They were silent, but looking at the father and son, they all had the same thought. They lifted the shooter with their shovels and carried him out of the gravel pit.

On the other side, just past the road, there was a steep slope. Below that lay a gully that always teemed with crows. It was the city garbage dump. At the edge of the slope the men swung their burden and threw it into the gully below.

On the way back, the father said to the younger Ignas:

'The earth is alive, it is always alive.'

The son looked at his father's half-closed eyes that had seen many things and bowed his head. They resumed their digging and finally a long grave, neatly formed by work-hardened hands, extended along the length of the gravel pit.

Translated by Ada Valaitis from Icchokas Meras, *Stotelė vidukelėj*, Vilnius: Lithuanian Writers' Union Publishers (2004).

Icchokas Meras (born 1934) lost his parents in the Holocaust and was rescued and raised by a Lithuanian woman. He became famous after the publication of his novels *A Stalemate Lasts But a Minute* (*Lygiosios trunka akimirką*, 1963) and *What the World Rests On* (*Ant ko laikosi pasaulis*, 1965) in which he tells narratives of the

Holocaust and examines Lithuanian-Jewish relations using romantic ballads, parables, and mythological narrative forms. Meras later works – the novels *Striptease, or Paris-Rome-Paris* (*Striptizas arba Paryžius-Roma-Paryžius*, 1976) and *Sara* (2008) – appeared after the author moved to Israel and reflect a surreal narrative style, which is unusual in Lithuanian prose.

Lady Stocka

Antanas Ramonas

Lady Jadvyga Stocka possessed a manor estate with five hundred registered souls in the Kaunas Governorate. She was married to Kazimir Stockis, who was much older than her and a former chamberlain. Lord Stockis liked vodka with cherries, fatty food and hunting. The wooden manor house with four columns, that back then were green and built during the times of Stanisław August, stood on the high, beautiful shores of the Virvytė river. On the southern side, alongside the terraces, there was a small park with maple and linden trees. A moss-covered Apollo Belvedere sculpture stood in an oval flower bed opposite the grand entrance. The enormous manor gardens also stretched along a slope on the right side, next to the park, gradually disappearing into the undergrowth of hazelnut trees and osier shrubs near the shore.

Lady Stocka was descended from the minor gentry. Her father, Kristof Saudargas, had many daughters and many debts, but what he had the most of was haughtiness. Jadvyga, who was the youngest, was lucky. She was taken in by a rich aunt when she was still a child. Jadvyga learned good manners, how to speak fluent Polish and a little French, to sew a little and to play around on the piano a bit. Her aunt would spend the winter in Vilnius where her husband had a house on Rūdninkų Street. It was there that Jadvyga became acquainted with a distant relative of her aunt's husband, the old-fashioned Lord Stockis, who still wore a *kontush* and red shoes. He seemed ridiculous to her, but when he proposed Miss Jadvyga agreed – of course only after taking the council of her aunt. What else could she do, a girl without a dowry? And she departed to Lord Stockis' secluded manor estate in Samogitia.

Life ran its course at the Brėvikiai Estate; to be more precise, it stood still like pond water, as if there had been no Napoleonic wars and no uprisings that had laid waste to the entire region. The peasants performed their required tasks and Lord Stockis hunted, drank, played cards, and on Sundays and during holidays he went to church diligently where he would fall asleep on the *prie-dieu* after the first chords from the organ. Lord Stockis smelled of tobacco, vodka and dog. The young madam ordered fashion magazines from Paris, made efforts to play the piano, which Lord Stockis, though he sighed about it because of the expense, ultimately did buy, and visited the neighbours. But the neighbours, of course, were no different than Lord Stockis: they talked about the profits of the breweries, hunting and the beastly peasants. Lady Stocka understood nothing and kept quiet, smiling melancholically. The piano was out of tune and a tuner had to be called from Kaunas. Lord Stockis never could understand such trivial matters, but after being nagged by his wife one day he brought home Joshke the Jew, who played the fiddle at the village inn in Šiaudine. The Jew turned a few things, slid a finger across the keys, accepted a silver half-rouble and left; the piano remained in the same state it started out in. The magazines from Paris would arrive, Lady Jadvyga would flip through them in bed in the morning, admiring the dresses and hats before sighing: who will sew things like that here? She played the ramshackle piano less and less, and she rarely sewed anymore. She just walked through the park and gardens reading the same French novel. She filled out and her curves became more evident. But what could she do, for life was so boring, so monotonous.

And suddenly, having lived ten years in what was appeared to be a happy marriage, Lord Stockis had a stroke and died. All the concerns of the manor estate, which had been so distant for her, suddenly sat squarely upon the rounded shoulders of Lady Stocka. She toiled as best she could, but the servants mocked her, the peasants didn't listen and the bailiff got drunk. The widow wrote a tearful letter to her aunt. The wise aunt responded quickly with her advice and Lady Jadvyga, as was her character, listened to it without hesitation and found herself a warden named Bučis-Bučinskas, who was a minor noble. The minor noble happened to be resourceful, cunning and knew how to speak well.

Soon the affairs of Brėvikai Manor and of Bučis-Bučinskas improved. Lady Stocka could once again flip through magazines in the morning and walk through the park and garden reading her endless French novel. But she felt alone, sad and bored and she needed some sort of live, soft creature. She could not stand the smell of dogs, which reminded her of Lord Stockis; thus she took a servant, a seventeen-year-old orphan named Annika. She had the type of simple beauty that is possessed by the beautiful, inconspicuous flowers in the forest. She had timid blue eyes, and was gentle, supple and well kept. She glowed of youth and had the scent of that unique aroma of a blossom opening up early in the morning for the first time. Lady Jadvyga was amused by the girl's naivety; her attentiveness soothed her ladyship's false sense of pride.

After some time Lady Jadvyga, on this occasion not asking for the advice of her aunt, got another servant, a worker on the estate named Nicodemas. While Pan Stockis was alive Nicodemas would drive him around and he helped to look after the horses. He had been in Kaunas and often visited Raseiniai with Pan Stockis. He had a strong, handsome body, hair as black as a raven's wings and a fiery, piercing glance. Everything somehow just happened when Lady Stocka was preparing to go to Šiaudine while Nicodemas bridled the horse with the movements of a spoiled servant. She stood nearby and looked on, and Nicodemas, without an ounce of shame, brazenly ran his eye over the Lady's curves and murmured nonchalantly: 'In a minute, my Lady, in a minute', and, as he had seen done before, helped her get into the light, two-wheeled buggy. A hot wave went through all of Lady Stocka's body from the touch of his strong, rough hand. Upon sitting down she suddenly blushed, then she got angry at herself, then she got angry at Nicodemas – that scoundrel! – and she shouted in a shrill, studied tone: 'Drive, you fool!' That night Lady Stocka only fell asleep just before dawn. The June nightingales flapped incessantly on the shores of the Virvytė River, the silver moon gazed at the flattened mist, while Lady Stocka tossed and turned in bed, feeling the touch of Nicodemas's strong fingers on her elbow.

Lady Stocka was ill for three days and a week later Nicodemas became her servant. He quickly understood what was expected of him, and this young and strong creature filled Lady Stocka's monotonous night hours. Lady Stocka was rejuvenated; she was no longer plagued by headaches, she floated through the rooms with her hips swaying, and the sleepy manor estate echoed with her voice: 'Nicodemas!' Of course, Nicodemas became even more insolent. He didn't do anything anymore. He shouted at the servants of the manor; he walked through the forest, accompanied by Lord Stockis' beloved dog Mirta, wearing Lord Stockis's hunting boots and with an English double-barrelled shotgun on his shoulder. Annika's attentiveness was no longer soothing and her naivety began to grate. Lady Stocka shouted at her more and more often; the young girl suffered without complaint and was the same gentle and obedient girl. Her quiet humility infuriated Lady Stocka even more – she was helpless against that gentleness, quiet and hard as a diamond. She did not want to get rid of her but instead wanted to teach her a lesson. For what reason she did not know herself, and she did not think twice about it. She just simply wanted to and that was that.

Lady Stocka had heard about Lord Granovskis, who had a small estate somewhere at the edge of the Vilnius Governorate. Lord Granovskis, for whom money was no object, would buy young and refined female serfs. There were many anecdotes – funny, indecent and horrifying – that circulated concerning his passion. It would be wonderful to be able to sell him a servant girl! But she did not want to leave everything at the manor, leave Nicodemas, to do so. And how could she take him along? In any case, she would still need to stay with her very observant aunt in Vilnius, without raising suspicion and rumours while trying to get to know the Don Juan of Liučicai Manor. She had to think everything over carefully and wait for winter.

But again, for the third time in Lady Stocka's life, everything unexpectedly worked itself out. Nicodemas always entered into the Lady's quarters with ease, and one day upon entering into her rooms Lady Stocka heard the rustling of clothes, quick steps and the sound of a chair being overturned. She opened the door. Nicodemas held the blushing chambermaid in his arms. With her head tilted back she pounded both of her hands into Nicodemas' chest and quickly whispered 'I'll tell her Ladyship, I'll tell her Ladyship.' Annika was the first to see Lady Jadvyga and she screamed, tore herself out of from Nicodemas's embrace and ran away. Nicodemas, not missing a beat, twisted the aristocratic moustache that he had grown: 'She was holding onto my neck, she wouldn't let me go.' Lady Stocka opened her mouth to rebuke him, but Nicodemas pressed his lips up against hers. 'It's daytime now, it's daytime, someone will see us,' she just managed to mumble but Nicodemas, as always, didn't ask.

Hot, and with glazed, tired eyes, Lady Jadvyga fixed her hair in front of the mirror and suddenly remembered the flushed cheeks of the chambermaid – soft and radiant – and understood that she had stopped being seventeen a long time ago. She understood that Nicodemas would get what he desired and that he saw both of them clearly, and her hands started to shake. In the evening she requested that the estate blacksmith come to her and she ordered him to make four rings and fasten them to the floor.

'Where?' the blacksmith asked, smoothing out his hat in his hands.

'Here, you mongrel!' she shouted. 'Here!'

'When?' the unperturbed Samogitian asked again.

'Right away, you imbecile, right away!'

She was unable to sit still and went out into the park. It was already well past midday; the sunlight fell through the leaves and somewhere far from the flood-meadow of the Virvytė workers were raking hay and singing. The day cooled but its furious envy, glowing like an ember, did not. She returned to the manor; she wandered through the rooms, picking things up and setting them down again.

She tried to play the piano but it was as though her surroundings had conspired against her. Each small thing – the vase on the table, the drapes through which flooded the heavy golden light of the evening sun – talked about her shame. She needed to do something, to be engaged in something.

She ordered that the estate's floggers, Woodpile and Skinner, be brought to her.

'Cut two armfuls of switches. Be sure they aren't too thick.'

'Yes, my most enlightened Lady, we know our work. Last year, after Pentecost…' said Woodpile, his way of speaking involving cutting off the ends of his own words.

'Soak them in brine tonight. Just make sure they are thin.'

'Yes, your most enlightened Ladyship, we know of a place, there, where Griciukas…' said Woodpile, once again cutting himself short.

She sent them away and calmed down. Tomorrow, tomorrow. I need to wait until tomorrow. The blacksmith came and fastened the rings to the floor and then evening came. Annika made the bed, and helped her lady undress.

'It's fine, Annika, it's fine. Go, go to bed, get some rest.' Lady Jadvyga's voice was soft; it was only her eyes that glimmered. She thought that she would not be able to fall asleep and had ordered poppy milk to be brought up to her, but she fell asleep almost at once. In the morning she awoke fresh and happy; she ate with an appetite and ventured out to enjoy the refreshing morning air of the park and garden. She looked in on the dogs belonging to the late Lord Stockis, something she had never done before.

'Don't feed them today,' she told Matthew, 'I said, don't feed them,' she repeated angrily as she saw his mouth open wide in disbelief. She returned to her room. She checked the rings to see whether they were firmly secured, if they were good, and ordered that all of the carpets be removed and that the picture of the Virgin Mary of the Gates of Dawn be taken down. Then she ordered Annika be brought to her. Woodpile and Skinner were already waiting.

Lady Stocka sat in the armchair. The maiden turned pale at the sight of the floggers.

'My Lady, my most enlightened Lady, my good and generous Lady,' she whispered.

'Tie her up!'

They lay the girl down on the floor and, putting her arms and legs through the rings, tied her up. Lady Stocka, grabbing Woodpile and Skinner by the sleeves, placed them opposite one another.

'My most enlightened Lady, we...' Woodpile began, but Lady Stocka pulled him so hard that he nearly fell down. The maiden lay there with her head turned uncomfortably to the side and tears poured silently from her bulging, bewildered eyes, rolling down her cheeks and lips, and quietly trickling onto the floor.

'Flog her!'

Woodpile and Skinner took turns flogging her with the switches.

'Not so quickly! Morons! Slowly, slowly, but firmly, firmly, now again. Yes, exactly, exactly!

The maiden's body shuddered and she moaned softly. Lady Jadvyga watched in a hunched-over position with pursed lips. Bloodstains appeared on the linen blouse, the switches whistled, the shirt was in tatters, the girl's groans subsided and now she only whimpered from time to time like a suffering beast. Lady Stocka wiped the blood that had splashed on her.

'Stop!' she exclaimed quietly. She rang the bell. A horrified servant girl from the manor appeared in the doorway. 'Bring her something to drink. Bring wine!' she yelled after her.

'Drink, drink. Don't be afraid, drink, my love, for strength.'

She looked hungrily at the girl's dry lips, which were parched from pain. Afterwards she ordered them to pull the blouse up, exposing her back and neck. The room was filled with the salty smell of blood. Skinner and Woodpile waved their switches half-heartedly. The girl didn't moan anymore and stopped shuddering.

Without being instructed to, Skinner and Woodpile lowered their arms. Lady Stocka looked at the bloody, unrecognisable corpse. The late June sun had already set. The dew fell on the park and in the garden and a mist rose from the flood-meadows.

'Take her away...' Lady Stocka ordered in a tired voice.

Woodpile and Skinner brought a linen sheet, wrapped the girl in it, and then went outside through the park, turning in the direction of the dog kennel. The kennel was further away from the other buildings of the estate, at the very end of the park. The dogs, who hadn't been fed all day, howled and whined. Matthew came out and stared first at Woodpile and then Skinner.

'Her Ladyship ordered us to, her Ladyship said...' Woodpile started.

'Put it on the ground,' Matthew said. 'I said, put it down and go. Go.'

'Her Ladyship ordered us to...' Woodpile began once again.

'I said go. Go, man.'

Woodpile looked at Skinner, but he looked past him and was silent. Woodpile, not saying a word, trudged up to the estate through the park, with Skinner following behind. Matthew looked around and called to a page named Francis. Having seen the horrified face of the boy, he admonished him: 'What are you afraid of? There's a person in there.'

Annika was buried under the old wild pear tree on the shores of the Virvytė River. Lady Jadvyga Stocka, née Saudargaitė, poisoned herself in the jail of Kaunas Fortress. The next summer, a year after Annika's death, Brėvikiai Manor caught fire. Bučys-Bučinskas ran around tearing his hair out, as if it was his property that was burning. The peasants who had been herded out of the buildings watched the blazing estate quietly and indifferently. The fire, which was being poorly controlled, spread to the barns, granary and stable. Everything burned to the ground. The heirs to the estate didn't rebuild it. As the years passed the park became overgrown with bushes and the garden grew wild. It was only from the terraces on the slopes of the Virvytė River that you could tell that someone had once lived there.

Translated by Jayde Will from Antanas Ramonas, *Lapkričio saulė*, Vilnius: Vaga (1989).

Antanas Ramonas (1947–1993) was one of the most subtle and lyrical prose writers in Lithuania in the 1980s and 1990s. His work includes essay-style short stories and elegiac urban prose that uses historical themes. His short-story collections *North Wind* (*Šiaures vėjas,* 1984) and *November Sun* (*Lapkričio saulė*, 1989), and the short novel *The White Clouds of Last Summer* (*Balti praėjusios vasaros debesys*, 1991), tell the stories of artistic spirits who pay no mind to the ideological and career advancement concerns that were prevalent in the Soviet Union. By depicting the aimless lives of these characters the author evokes a cultural shift in the late Soviet period, one that is most clearly expressed through the rise of the individual who displayed a conscious effort to reject the stifling pressures of Soviet ideology, which had penetrated into all aspects of everyday life.

Handless

Ričardas Gavelis

For Gražina B.

Winter in that land lasted eight months. Four were left for the other seasons. But the river never froze completely. As if alive, its current had to breathe air and be able to see the world. It surrendered to no frost; it was invincible, as if it were the current of the lives of all the people who had been relocated to its banks. Tens, hundreds, thousands could perish. But there was no power that could destroy every single one of them.

A solitary raft of rough logs floated down the river. It made its way forward slowly, as if it were dead tired. Driven by the cold, wild animals stopped on the riverbank and followed it with fearful glances. But the raft did not care about them, it was looking for people. And still there were no people.

The raft was bare. Only by looking extremely carefully could you make out something pale and crooked on the middle log – perhaps a small frozen animal, a sign, or maybe just an unclear mirage, the reflection of the boundless snows.

***

The desire came on suddenly. It took over not only his soul but also his entire body like a disease that had secretly lurked inside for a long time and awaited its hour of triumph. Vytautas Handless thought about why it had happened just now. Perhaps his retirement was to blame, endless spare time and a sweet kind of vacuum that had enveloped his life in a few weeks. Both his daughters concerned themselves with the separate apartments they had longed for, and when he went to linger by Ona's grave he could find nothing to say to her. He could not explain anything or describe the unquenchable desire that was oppressing him. Smoking by her grave, which was encircled by a chain, he awaited some sign – a ghostlike reply from Ona. But no sign came. The dead tend to be silent; they don't speak even in dreams.

For eight years now he had been writing her a letter every week and reading it out loud every Saturday in the empty living room. He wrote about everything: the scent of the lilacs, the neighbour's hook nose, the contours of the clouds, the St. Bernard that he had wanted all his life but had never had except in his imagination. He would tell Ona everything, though sometimes it occurred to him that he would write to her a good deal more in these letters than he would have admitted to her had she been alive. He would confess to her his sadness and frailty; had she been alive, he would never have revealed such things. Without any shyness he would tell her all his quirks and little peculiarities: that all his life he'd been desperately afraid of fish; that he read relatives' letters only in the bathroom; that he swore by all that was holy that his childhood friend Martin's soul had been reincarnated in the neighbour's cat. He didn't even hide the fact that he had been unfaithful to her twice. He almost came to believe that he could tell her absolutely everything in the letters.

But he never forgot that it wasn't really so. He couldn't find it in himself to write about what was perhaps the most important thing – that lost period of four years. He never spoke of it to her or to anyone else – not even when every year Alexis came on the fifth of March and the two of them would light a candle by the portraits drawn from memory. Even then he didn't speak of it. Alexis, who worked at the theatre, would complain that it had been simpler at the old theatre, but who the hell could understand the caprices of current fashion. Vytautas Handless spoke of the shortage of parts, the outdated machinery and the hysterical director of the artel[1*]. One might say that they communicated in code, thinking and wanting to say something entirely different. They never spoke about the most important thing, the reason why they actually got together here; they never spoke, otherwise they would have been forced to remember that only the two of them had survived out of the entire twenty-six.

'The message, the message is the most important thing,' Bruno kept repeating with his eyes shut. 'I'd make up the kind of message so the whole world would drop everything and come running to us. But I have nothing to write with and nothing to write it on.'

The men's heads drooped to the ground, although they were light as feathers. All their faces looked the same, and their eyes were the same, revealing the effort to force out at least one idea.

And the clouds kept floating and floating in the same direction, as if showing them the way, if not to freedom then at least to life.

To speak would have meant to remember at once that which had been forgotten only with the greatest effort, that which had been exiled from the memory, chained and thrown into the deepest hole, perhaps the abyss. It would have forced them to see again that rambling, brown stump like a bull's head that had gripped his hand with its teeth, the frost and the blizzard – or first the blizzard and then the frost – and the men repeatedly falling into the snow banks, their faces all the same, all equally ashen and expressionless, quite unlike the ones that Alexis had drawn with a blunt pencil, though once upon a time they had really looked like that: Valius, Zenka from Kaunas, the two foreigners, Francis, and all the others. They had stood in a circle around the thin, solitary candle on the table in his room. He and Alexis did not want to remember them, all the nameless and the faceless. They did not and could not dare to do so. In silence they would down a shot, then another, they would empty the ritual bottle

---

[1*] Artel is a general term for various co-operative associations that existed in the Russian Empire and the Soviet Union between the 1860s and through the 1950s. Historically, artels were semi-formal associations for various enterprises including fishing, mining, logging, commerce and manual labour; the term is also used to refer to associations of thieves and beggars.

neatly and a sighing Alexis would say, 'I'm off to feed Elena'. (His wife hadn't left her bed for several years now. Little Elena, one more forbidden memory: the womb frozen by the black snow, the hands that had made fabulous sausages. Elena, the ant with her legs pulled off.)

Alexis and his Elena disappeared and Ona did not reply or give any kind of sign. Vytautas's daughters fought daily with their husbands before making up again. Sometimes they asked if their father needed anything and if he could use some help. What did he have need of? He was sturdy and not especially old, he could even help others including his daughters if the need should arise. Summer was at its peak, but Vytautas Handless liked Vilnius: the old, hot streets were dearer to him than the quiet solace of the lakes back home.

Desire ambushed him, stung him like a snake biting a naked, unprotected leg. The poison dispersed throughout his body immediately, fogged up his brain and even disturbed his dreams. The poisonous desire pulsed in his heart together with his blood; maybe the blood itself became the desire, his heart, kidneys, liver and his entire body became it. The strange temptation to conquer himself burned like an icy fire. Vytautas Handless suddenly felt that he had not dared to admit to himself throughout his life who he really was – he had pretended to others and tried to fool himself. He had devastated an important part of his soul, without which he was not the real Vytautas Handless; he went on existing like some other person – someone with a different face, name and soul. The cock having crowed scarcely three times, he had denied himself, he himself was Jesus and the apostle Peter. He had to recover himself, return to himself at least before he died.

The thought struck him that perhaps Ona didn't answer because he had kept his essence from her. He hadn't told her about his hand, wandering the world, or perhaps the heavens. Now the hand was calling him.

His grandfather Raphael had once advised him: if you're ever confused, cast a spell or better yet wait for a sign, but not from this crucified God. Wait instead for one from the oaks, from the altar place, from the current of the sacred river, from the cry of the sacred wolf; simply go on living, he'd say, don't be afraid that you'll miss seeing it or hearing it. No, when it appears – and it will appear – you'll recognise it right away, it will speak to you in a loud voice and you'll know everything. You won't be able to deny understanding it – choose a holy place and wait. Vytautas Handless did just that, wandering the Vilnius streets (after all, Vilnius is also a dreary kind of temple), looking at the mouldings on the cornices of the old roofs, inhaling the odour of the city, which perspired gasoline, all the while secretly listening to the conversations of passers-by. He wasn't in any hurry for he knew the fateful sign was looking for him and was searching with equal tenacity, and that inevitably they would run into each other.

He found the hardcover booklet in a passageway. He flipped through it before his quivering hand stuck it in his pocket. Suddenly he felt the urge to run away from himself, to hide in a gloomy forest, dig himself into the ground and burn the book because he already knew that this booklet was the sign. He knew this with certainty, just as that other time when he had picked up a ring of sausage from the damp ground between the barbed wire. It was a genuinely delicious Lithuanian sausage. Without any hesitation he had recognised the smell of home wrenching his soul. Then, as now, he cursed his abominable fate, feeling that any freedom of decision or choice had disappeared and that just as he had once been guided by fate in the form of a sweet-smelling sausage, now he was being led by a slightly damp booklet. It was leading him into the unknown, into perdition, or maybe even into non-existence. His fate was always decided by the strangest or most shockingly trivial things.

Winter in that land lasted eight months, but the river never froze completely even in the depths of winter. As if alive, its current had to breathe air and be able to see the world. It surrendered to no frost; it was invincible, like the common current of the lives of all the people who had been relocated to its banks. Tens, hundreds, thousands could perish, but there was no power that could destroy every single

125

one of them.

They brought the twenty-six of them to an abandoned logging camp. There were supposed to have been twenty-five, but at the last minute the supervisor of the zone had shoved Vytautas Handless over by the others.

('Your odour gave you away, boy,' he said in an almost matey manner. 'You smelly thief, you.'

Handless was still aware of the bitter taste of garlic and rosemary, the scent of juniper smoke, the smell and taste of home, when the zone superintendent crept along the row like a dog sniffing each one of them. He had nothing doglike about him; rather, his appearance was that of a tired geography teacher. But he was approaching Handless like death, like Giltinė, the mythological goddess of death. Instead of the scythe, he grasped a polished riding crop.)

The guards swore out loud, wading those few kilometres from the rusted-out tracks of the branch line. No one had cut timber here for several years. The file of men dragged along silently; only Alexis, when he first got off, muttered: 'The sausage was mine. Elena is only in exile, she sent it to me. And as usual they filched it. Did it taste good?'

Here the snow didn't crunch at all; people's voices momentarily froze into ice and fell into the snow banks without a sound. Around them stood trees that one could only dream of; many of them were probably two centuries old. They were painfully beautiful but at the same time sombre, as though they existed in a frightening fairy tale with no happy ending. Looking at them you were overcome by the fear that nothing else existed in the universe, that these stern and soulless trees had overtaken the entire earth. (They have no soul, Bruno was to shout later. Oak has a soul, ash can have one, even aspen – but not these ghastly giants.) The men clambered over the snow banks, each with his own sign, his own angel overhead. Bruno was being followed by his gaunt Dzukish muse, Alexis by the image of his Elena, while above Vytautas Handless's head floated only the spirit of fragrant Lithuanian sausage, shining like a halo.

Finally, the abandoned logging camp lay before them. Satisfied, the guards stamped their feet, shaking the snow from their boots as if they had arrived home. The camp was impossible to take in with one glance; in this country everything was inhuman, you would think that once upon a time giants had lived here. But the giants had long ago disappeared. Only the guards remained, and they kept stamping their feet, almost like they were testing the ground's durability. But the ground here was harder than steel, a steel earth.

'Tomorrow we'll bring the rations,' one said in a hoarse voice.

'By tomorrow we'll escape!' snapped Zenka from Kaunas. He was the only one who felt good.

The guards didn't bother replying or even to shrug their shoulders. In winter no man could move more than twenty or so kilometres in this country – not even on skis or being armed with a gun. Even seasoned hunters didn't stray too far from their cabins. No one and nothing could escape from here including the animals and birds. The clouds that kept drifting and drifting in the same direction were the only possible exceptions.

'Are they going to leave us alone?' said Bruno in amazement. 'It can't be.'

'In the Land of Miracles anything can happen. Anything!' shot back Zenka.

For some reason everyone called that part of the country, the valley of that river, the Land of Miracles.

'We'll bring food tomorrow, food for the whole two weeks,' boomed the guard, walking away.

He played with the hardcover booklet like a cat with a mouse, even though he understood perfectly well that it was the book which was playing with him, making him suffer, entrancing him like a boa constrictor hypnotises a rabbit petrified with fear. It burned his fingers, but as soon as he would fling it down, he'd pick it up again, open it, look over the face in the small photograph for the hundredth time. It reminded Vytautas Handless of Ona's face: the wide lips, protruding cheekbones and the large, dark eyes. The woman in the photograph looked kind and tired; she was probably a champion milker, or perhaps a weaver. For some days he debated with incredible seriousness which would be more likely, as if this had any meaning at all. Only the document itself was important, the miserable little book whose owner gazed at Vytautas Handless with kind, sad eyes – Ona's eyes – understanding and justifying him, allowing him to act as he saw fit. She offered her help without his asking. She didn't begrudge him the booklet with hard covers, that respectful testimony, which gave its owner rights and privileges – after all, she was an ordinary woman, a milker or weaver. Maybe she wasn't even aware of the privileges that he needed so much – needed briefly, not forever, just for the trip there and back for an ineluctable journey into the forbidden, dangerous past. He had to find his past and look it in the face. A man who has forgotten his past and renounced it is nothing but a wind-up doll.

He didn't ask himself anymore why the desire existed – he only wanted to comprehend why it arose now of all times, earnestly believing that neither his retirement nor all the spare time it created had anything to do with it; after all, painful thoughts had always tortured him, taken away his breath and suffocated him, had howled in the deepest closed-off subterranean passages, knocking at the iron door. But he had never broken down the door, had never even attempted to break it down. Why now in particular? His life had finally settled down quite nicely: a job in an enormous artel with responsibilities of a sort; certificates of merit and a medal of seniority; and two beloved daughters as well as other relatives and friends. Nothing reminded him of that which he himself didn't want to remember, if anything it helped to keep shut the subterranean door. Why now in particular? Why not right after Ona's death? Why not some other day or week or minute of those thirty-five years?

Having thought it all over calmly, he decided that there was no reason for it, but he felt that the pressing desire would still win and had already won over him. It seemed like some other Vytautas Handless had occupied his soul, but a different one from the one who through all those years had lived, worked and strived harmoniously and correctly. The first version always knew how to force the world to be the way it was supposed to be. He could put his things and thoughts in their proper places, while this one, the new one, sowed confusion and ruin not only in himself but in the whole world. In his mind, the sun didn't rise in the east and set in the west, odours changed to tastes, ideas to clouds, always drifting and drifting over the frozen earth. Suddenly the world lost its harmony, each item existed in isolation and it could mean whatever one wanted – now this, and in the blink of an eye, that. But what was worst was that this new Vytautas Handless could remember that which had been forgotten for eternity, that which perhaps had never even existed. The world fell apart and would not go together again. Vytautas Handless had felt this way only once in his lifetime – during the great council of the nineteen men who were all that was left of the original twenty-six. Once he caught himself talking to the hook-nosed neighbour's cat, asking for his childhood friend Martin's advice. He realised that the unquenchable desire had overcome him for good. He had to stop stalling on his commitment or go out of his mind.

'It's like a desert in my head. Camels are grazing, nibbling the sand.'

'The raft won't hold two. It won't even hold one. It won't hold anything.'

'Did Elena's sausage taste good? Did it?'

'Men, the famine and cold have shocked our spirits. Our thoughts don't belong to us anymore. Men, pull yourselves together, think of something very ordinary. Don't do it, don't do what you've decided to do. Come to your senses! How are you going to live afterwards, if you survive?'

'It's the voice of God! Whatever comes into everyone's head at the same time is the voice of God!'

'I have many heads. And they're all so empty, so light. Men, listen, I have many heads. And each one of them talks in its own way.'

'An idea of greatest lucidity. Of the greatest clarity. A mighty idea. Great lucidity. Great clarity. A great raft. The great message.'

'Do you agree, Handless?'

'Did Elena's sausage taste good? Tell me, was it good?'

'I'm a doctor. Everything is going to be okay, no pain. I have a

medical degree.'

Carefully, Vytautas Handless tore the picture of the kind and tired woman off the document, having previously apologised to her out loud for his grandfather Raphael had always taught him that at least a tiny part of man's soul was hidden in his image – it could hear, understand and sympathise. He kept repeating to himself that he was making the document for himself, wishing only to find himself. He wasn't aiming to become another person or to steal anything from the woman he didn't know. The honourable certificate was only a key, a magic phrase like 'open, sesame' – only in the cave that was perhaps about to open neither gold nor emeralds were waiting for him, but rather himself: gaunt and malnourished, thirty years younger, he himself in the shape of a dragon, his jaws open wide, greedy for victims, the last of twenty-six men. Vytautas Handless, the last of twenty-six men, holding in his hands the document with a woman's last name, while in the pocket next to his chest was the picture of the real owner of the document, so similar to pictures of Ona.

Suddenly it struck him as incredibly funny that he was setting off on the most important feat of his life under the cover of a woman's name. He choked with laughter until the tears came, tears that turned into the most real bitter tears, although Vytautas Handless didn't understand for whom he was crying – whether it was for himself, the woman, Ona or for the future journey. He only knew that no one would notice the woman's name; from previous times he knew that there, far beyond the Urals, in the former Land of Miracles, no one recognises or remembers Lithuanian first names or even last names.

The snowstorm stopped raging just as suddenly as it had started roaring. And all at once an eerie frost set in. Not one of the twenty-six men could remember such a frost. The storm released its fury for two or three days. No one could say how many nights of terror there had been in the shaking shed. Several of the men became totally confused.

The frost pressed down relentlessly for several days. It seemed that even the air would soon turn to ice and start to crack. The entire world froze: only the river and the twenty-six shabby men did not surrender. They kept the fire going day and night, as only a few matches remained. In that land fire and life often had the same meaning. The men mostly kept silent. Only Bruno constantly muttered, repeating that they were little male vestal virgins and would survive if they threw just the tiniest piece of oak into the fire. But oak had not grown here since time immemorial. Bruno kept getting up to search for the holy wood, and the men would hold him down sullenly but without anger.

The last leftovers of the January rations were running out. Some of them went out into the forest and returned with bark and pine cones, and tried to bite into them. Others shovelled snow, kept the fire going outside and attempted to dig out some miraculous roots. But the frozen ground here was stronger than human patience. At least twice a day volunteer scouts would wade out to look for the train tracks without any luck. There were no tracks; they had disappeared forever together with the guards and their dogs. All that was left were waist-high banks of snow and the ethereal frost, which caused the trunks of live trees to crack. Then there was the river; as if alive its current had to breathe air and view the world. It refused to surrender even to this eerie frost; it was invincible, like the common current of the lives of all the people who had been relocated on its banks. Ten could die, all twenty-six, thousands of others could. But there was no power that could make every single one of them disappear.

They came up with idea of building rafts, but the ghostly tree giants did not wish them well. The axes and saws fractured and crumbled like glass. Though the men constantly returned to the fire of the shelter and patiently heated the helpless iron, the steel of the trees was more durable. Even the most patient ones, sacrificing almost all the axes, produced only a small raft; it wouldn't have carried even the lightest of them.

Toward the middle of the second week the men started to rave. One of them, screaming at the top of his lungs, would constantly rush out of the shed into the unknown. Some of them never returned. Those who retained at least a little common sense were still able to comprehend that one should not leave the fire. No one knew in

131

which direction to go or where to seek help. They had only one good axe. Only a few matches remained, and the men were secretly afraid that even those might not light. They chewed on pieces of their clothing, bark and woodchips. A few had collapsed into a heap in the far corner of the shed and were raving deliriously, as if they were communicating in a secret language or were singing ghostly chorales. Francis knocked out Vaclov's remaining teeth when all he had done was mention that someone was bound to come looking for them – after all, they were human beings. Valius held up the most steadfastly. If it hadn't been for him, the men would long ago have waded out into the unknown in the direction of an indifferent death. Valius wouldn't say anything, he'd only glance at those who'd gotten up with his fathomless eyes, which were sculpted into the shabby face of a saint, and the men would suddenly become hesitant. But there were some that even he could not restrain, and they were increasing in number. The men's conversation had long since lost its meaning. One of them claimed to be flying, another told the same story about a fox hunt over and over again, and a third was possessed by naked women. This couldn't go on. Something had to be done.

Somehow they had to send a message to the world of men, they all realised this. The only route was the river. The only messenger was the meagre raft, which would probably get caught in the first bend of the river. The men argued and raved. They couldn't write anything; uselessly they tried to engrave something on the wood of the raft. They had to think of a sign that anyone would comprehend at a glance. The men decided to call a Great Council. This idea, which had struck Bruno, united them all for a moment. Even the delirious bunch fell quite and crept closer to the fire. Chewing on chips, bark and the ends of their felt boots, they all tried to think of something with their frozen brains.

Only the two foreigners remained immune from the encroaching madness. They didn't go searching for the spur tracks, they didn't run over the snow banks screaming, and they did not succumb to delirium. They scrupulously washed their hands and faces, and even their feet, five times a day. They always faced the same corner of *the shed and intently began to murmur a prayer. They were the very happiest. They didn't care about the great message, the raft, food, probably not even about life. They were the happiest.*

Only after he had gone there, after he had descended into hell and climbed out of it again, only after he had written and sent out the first letter did he understand what it was he had hoped for all along and secretly awaited. He did not expect to find anything there that had been there before, then he could turn around and go back with an unburdened heart, paste the photograph of the tired weaver or milker back into place and settle accounts properly with himself. He tried to do everything he could and even more, but fate itself erased the evil nightmare from the surface of the earth.

Fate had no desire to help him; it was probably sitting comfortably in a soft, easy chair with its knees crossed, carelessly watching to see what Handless would do and how he would behave. Now, when everything was over and done with, he could remember it, even though it was with shyness, always convincing himself that nothing terrible had happened, everything was simple; it hadn't shocked him and wasn't driving him crazy. The hangover also helped – it had been a long time since Vytautas Handless had had occasion to drink pure alcohol.

He wrote the first letter just after he arrived in the familiar town, which had turned into a noisy city over the years. Bulldozers buzzed around and construction crews in lorries sang songs at the top of their lungs. The weather was beautiful; he was constantly taking off his coat and carrying it over his arm, always fearful that he'd lose his money and papers. It seemed to him that everyone he met was looking at him suspiciously, but soon he realised that no one was paying him any attention, that he wasn't in anyone's way, he was simply unnecessary. All the stares said: what did you come all the way here for, what are you looking for, wake up before it's too late.

But it was already too late. He said as much in the first letter, still naively rejoicing that the city was so big, noisy and completely different from the muddy town with wooden sidewalks that had remained in his memory. Everything had changed here. Vytautas

Handless carefully copied out his address on the envelope; at that time he didn't think then that there would be many such letters, letters to Ona. Being so far from home, from the chain enclosure of her grave, he suddenly felt that she was still alive. It was thanks to her that he had survived thirty years ago and he'd survive now too, for his Penelope had repulsed the young men and was waiting for his return from the wide and sombre banks of the river.

A solitary raft of rough logs was floating down the river; it was making its way forward slowly, as if dead tired. Driven by the cold, animals stopped on the riverbank and followed it with fearful glances. But the raft did not care about them. It was searching for people who could receive the message. But still there were no people.

He climbed into the bus while whistling fitfully and looked out of the window at the skeletons of factories and power stations, having no doubts that he was performing only a formality. A bad premonition stirred under his heart only after he saw the swamp where they used to dump piles of sawdust back in those days. Even now the stench it gave off was exactly the same. It was even harder to see the barbed wire fence.

It was hard to go inside and step into the living past, to open the zone superintendent's office door before putting on the mask and making a proper face – one which was both solid and ingratiating, conspiratorial but insistent. Hardest of all was to speak out – up to that second it was still possible to retreat, to flee, to pretend to be lost. The zone superintendent looked at him with his piercing gaze for an infinitely long time, took him apart bone by bone and investigated each one separately, squeezed them, smelled them even; he spent even more time squeezing and looking over the document. To Vytautas Handless it seemed that he would never get out of there; that any moment now he'd be put behind the barbed wire fence for falsification of documents. But finally the superintendent slowly and unwillingly got up from his chair, came around the table and gave him his hand. From that second on everything would succeed. He understood that he was victorious, that he'd calculated everything correctly and that the current of destiny had caught him and would carry him forward like the frozen river had carried the mute raft of rough logs.

Vytautas Handless's insolence knew no bounds, but he had calculated correctly: everyone here was seeing the certificate of a Supreme Soviet deputy for the first time. It acted like a magic password and right away the secret door opened slightly. The zone superintendent immediately fell to pieces. He was afraid of only one thing: did this not, perhaps, reek of some dangerous inspection. But Vytautas Handless didn't allow him to collect himself. He had learned his part well and had rehearsed it in front of the mirror a hundred times, even though now he was doing everything differently. He had intended to speak matter-of-factly, but he poured out an entire monologue about old age, the desire to retrace the paths of his youth and said that he had worked here once (it was, after all, true). He related an enormous level of detail, bombarded the chairman with questions, made idle jokes, asked that his visit not be made public, pulled out the grain alcohol and cognac as well as the snack he had brought – the host's eyes lit up – and kept calling the superintendent 'my good colleague'. Afterwards everything that took place felt like a dream in which nightmarish landscapes are more real than real ones, monsters are more alive than the most alive of men, and meaningless words have much more meaning than all the wisdom of humanity. But it was far from being a dream. It finally dawned on him that he was caught in a horrible trap. Everything here looked different than it had in the old days, but this had absolutely no meaning. Vytautas Handless visualised the old barracks and paths. He saw the hill that had now been levelled, the holes had been filled, he recognised every tree that had been felled long ago, he smelled the old odour that had dispersed heaven knows when – the odour of injustice and despair that could not be covered up, which had enmeshed the zone more tightly than barbed wire. And the people now looked quite different: gloomy, staring creatures and insolent kids wandered around, but he didn't see them at all. While he was watching the kids, their faces kept changing and they became completely different. They became the faces of others, familiar and unfamiliar.

'What're you in for?'

'For the cause,' said Valius. 'It's okay, good times will come for me, too.'

'And you?'

'I don't know,' replied Handless. 'For nothing. It was a mistake.'

'They accused me of aiding the guerrillas,' said Francis. 'How are you not going to help them? Did they ask my permission when they showed up at night?'

'Me, I'm in to make up the quota,' said Zenka from Kaunas, grinning as usual. 'This good-for-nothing guy, a mate of mine from school days, shows up. He says go, take off to the countryside and hide – your turn's up according to the quota. You can hide out in the countryside; they'll take someone else in your place. But by the time I got my stuff together, they nabbed me there and then.'

Vytautas Handless finally figured out why there had to be two of him, who needed the second Vytautas Handless who was doing everything differently. Now that the other one was cracking jokes and looking around with an eager eye, he was acting the way he himself, the real Vytautas Handless, never could have managed to act. He certainly could never have pretended to be his own warder here once, to have sent himself out through the snow banks to work, to have left himself and twenty-five other men to slowly go out of their minds in that terrible and frightening winter. He made the zone superintendent laugh and made fun of the prisoners, and then courageously drank the undiluted alcohol and invented even more details. He allowed the real Vytautas Handless time to recollect everything leisurely, let him cry quietly and honour the men with a minute of silence, an endless minute of silence, while the other one carried on and drank and almost fell down the steps before being brought back to the hotel in the zone superintendent's car. But at one point he couldn't take it, he suddenly grabbed his host by the shoulders and roared: 'give me back my hand, return my hand!' But no one caught the gist of his words, thank God, no one understood. And later he spoke to the bare hotel room walls, to the stars, hidden by the clouds, to the ghosts who had gathered in his room. He wrote the second letter, then the third and the fourth, perhaps even the thousandth, or perhaps none at all. He tried to write on behalf of all twenty-five men, tried to carry within himself twenty-six souls. He heard the men's voices, saw their faces, felt himself to be all of them at once, but this feeling could not be described in any letter.

The Great Council lasted until evening, without reaching any decision. They had the puny raft and the single axe. They could stick the axe into the middle log and send it off downstream. Would this be a sign?

With their brains frozen, the men's thoughts turned to ice and had to be thawed out. The men bent their heads closer to the fire, scarcely able to bear the heat, but the ideas didn't want to come.

The men continually glanced at Valius, but all they saw in his eyes was helplessness and torment. They looked at Bruno, begging, but he only raved on, first more quietly, then more loudly, murmuring his own and others' confused utterances. Vaclov was incessantly counting his broken teeth; he raked them in the palm of his hand like bits of gravel. Francis for some reason got the urge to take off his clothes and run around naked. Alexis was patiently chewing on Elena's sausage, one long lost in someone else's stomach. It was the Council of the Great Silence. The silence of each of them joined with the general silence, and the latter flowed into the silence of the indifferent century-old trees, the blinding snow and the clouds floating across the heavens. It was a council without debates or suggestions. No one could find a sign that all people would understand at once. Perhaps such a sign announcing that they were here, slowly dying in body and soul, did not exist. Before he began to rave, Bruno had suggested that one of them turn into a dwarf so that the raft could support him. Finally Valius spoke and said that in such cold even a dwarf would turn into a piece of ice within the hour.

No one was aware of when and how the great idea dawned. No one knew who was the first to utter the words out loud. Suddenly it seemed to the men that each of them had long harboured this thought. They burst into words, each one talking louder that the other; they didn't even need to vote. Only Valius tried in vain to make his voice heard over the din of the others. No one was listening to him, they all kept glancing at Handless. He had to be the one to agree. They all waited for him to speak, although there could be only one reply.

'I agree,' Handless finally said, 'I agreed long ago. It's my destiny. My grandfather warned me a long time ago.'

'Come to your senses, you madman!' Valius was the only one to exclaim.

The two foreigners, having understood not a word of the entire Council, sadly nodded their heads and started to wash their hands with snow. It was already midnight, the hour of the final prayer.

The stump had been hurting for a long time; it had already started hurting in Vilnius as soon as the miserable, insane desire had overtaken him. An oppressive, sick feeling troubled his heart too, and periodically everything would get confused. It seemed to Vytautas Handless that his tortured heart was beating somewhere beyond the confines of his body in place of his lost hand. It seemed that he wanted to recover not so much his hand as the heart he had lost. He didn't blame the men then or later – he never thought about the horrible council at all, and most amazing though it was to him, he didn't even dream about it. His nightmares were quite different.

But now the awful council appeared, welling up from the depths. He was sitting once more in the shaky shed and by the fire, and he couldn't run away anywhere because beyond the thin board walls there was the eerie frost and there was no road that would lead him to people. Vytautas Handless wandered around the buzzing, reeking city. He saw the dirty streets, the holes in the foundations, people's pale faces, but at the same time he was there, at the council. He heard every word, saw everyone's eyes. Periodically he would stop, lean helplessly against a tree or a wall, concerned passers-by would inquire if he felt all right, and he'd just nod his head. How could he explain to them that just now, right by this tree, he heard Francis's voice and saw the distorted face of Zenka from Kaunas, that he already knew what his decision would be and was trying to concentrate, summon at least one clear idea? But there was only one idea: if the enemy takes away your hand, this at least is understandable; if your own people tear it off – it means the end of the world has come. He was just waiting for the angel of perdition to trumpet and for the book with the seven seals to be brought.

Vytautas Handless could long since have gone home. It wasn't easy to get out of there, but with the miserable falsified document he could have brought a ticket at any time, without even waiting in line. It had been a week since he had gone anywhere, but every day he would write a letter and post it. Only the dead could read letters like those without feeling fear.

He felt that he had to explain that which could not be explained. He convinced himself that he wasn't going home because he was waiting for Ona's answer. But in reality he was detained only by the pain in his heart, the heart beating beyond the confines of his body, in place of the lost hand. He couldn't return without having found the hand – which meant his heart. On the evenings of his letter writing his grandfather visited him, smoked his curved Prussian pipe, and nodded his head sadly.

'My child,' he would say in a mournful voice, 'that's our family emblem. You can't change it, it's been that way for centuries. Even our family name is that way. My hand was torn off by a shell, your father's chopped off by the Bermondtists. I've said many times: prepare yourself ahead of time, child, say good-bye to it. It belongs to you only temporarily.'

'If we send his hand off, anyone will recognise this kind of sign. You understand, if Handless really becomes handless, the secret will of the gods will be fulfilled. You understand? The gods themselves call for it.'

By the middle of the second week he had made up his mind. Now he gave up hope of finding anyone there in the deserted logging camp from those times. If he tried with all his might, he could visualise a vast area of stumps, piles of trunks and the rotten shed. He could make out the gigantic stump that looked like a bull's head and could feel the hand hopelessly pressing the handle of the last axe. Grandfather sat beside him in the shaking four-wheel drive and for the last time tried to talk him out of it. However, Vytautas Handless knew that he would go there in spite of everything – indeed, he had already gone. It was an accomplished fact, even though it was hidden in the future. The future, the current of time didn't mean anything anymore. He knew well what was to follow. He could relate everything in the greatest detail to anyone ahead of time and then take them to the logging camp so that they would see that in reality everything would be just as he said.

It is only when he gets out of the vehicle that he will suddenly have the urge to turn back, but his muscles will not obey him. Finally, he'll comprehend that he can't leave his hand, his heart, to the will of destiny because at the same time he will be leaving the twenty-six souls imprisoned here. He'll be taken aback because the spot will be exactly the same as it had once been, even the remains of their fire will be untouched. Without anger he'll kick at the rotten skeleton of the shelter, with a firm step he'll walk over to the stump that looked like the gigantic head of a bull – now it is looming quite close to the shed, but then they spent a good half hour crawling to it – and he'll fix his eyes on it. The stump will glance at him, and he will glare back. They will battle it out in the clash of stares; they will contend for a long time, oblivious of time, or perhaps, turning the clock back some thirty years. They'll try to crush one other because this will be the most important thing in life. He wasn't afraid at all. He knew he would win just as he had won back then. He knew that he was invincible and had always been so, especially now, when he has twenty-six souls. He was invincible like the river's current, like the sunlight, like Ona's eternal patience waiting for him. He knew that in the end the stump would surrender and shake its death rattle when he put his right hand, the good hand, on it, resolutely and firmly.

Four of them went out into the freezing weather. The doctor was carrying some bandages, torn up from filthy underwear soaked with sweat. Formerly he was called Andreas, but for several days now he had ordered them to call him by some other name. Sometimes he would secretly admit to having several heads. Zenka from Kaunas and Alexis went with them. Zenka said he'd seen everything there was to see in life and therefore he had to see this too. Besides, once upon a time he had worked as an orderly. Alexis came along just in case. If Handless should happen to faint, he promised to carry him back in his arms like a baby. Alexis knew well that now he was the strongest of them all – while the others had been starving, he had kept eating Elena's nonexistent sausage. They hurried along so that the axe, which they had heated in the fire, wouldn't get cold and crumble. They thought that they were going along at a good pace in an orderly fashion, though in reality they were only crawling waywardly and staggering at their own pace and direction, like gigantic snails, groaning every now and then. The doctor wouldn't stop repeating out loud that this kind of frost kills off all germs. Zenka from Kaunas kept telling the same anecdote, to which no one was listening.

They went behind a small hill so that they couldn't see the dilapidated shed, which was enveloped in puffs of steam. Handless wanted it this way. He was silent even when he had approached the large stump, which resembled a bull's head. He only pointed to it with his hand. He flourished the axe three times, but each time he didn't chop. Zenka from Kaunas muttered that the axe would freeze and offered to hold down the hand stretched out on the stump so that Handless wouldn't pull it back involuntarily.

'I'm not going to wait for others to take it away from me, Grandpa,' said Handless to the empty space. 'I'm going to do it myself.'

The axe bounced back from the stump without a sound. Alexis caught Handless, who was falling, while Zenka from Kaunas grabbed the axe and slipped it inside his coat. The doctor finally shut up, quickly holding the bleeding limb tight and bandaging it. Separated from the body, the hand moved its fingers as if in surprise, then fell on its side and froze. There was almost no blood dripping from it.

The linden trees in Vilnius had finished blooming. The pavement gave off an almost imperceptible unhealthy steam. He fetched the letters, which a woman in the neighbourhood had collected, and counted them diligently, even though he could not remember how many he had sent. His home seemed totally alien to him. He didn't go to visit his daughters and he only went to the store and back for some fresh potatoes and to fill his refrigerator full of canned meat and eggs. He locked himself in, opening the door to no one and ignoring telephone calls.

Vytautas Handless had to think. He had to get used to himself, a quite different Vytautas Handless, a man who had dared to open the forbidden door, to descend into hell and return, a man who had gotten the urge to experience for a second time that which it is possible to endure only once, a man who was carrying twenty-six souls. He found it strange that he wanted to eat and drink, and later urinated and defecated. He found it strange that he fell asleep and dreamed of himself without a hand. Throughout his life, he had dreamed of himself having both hands. Hopelessly, he tried to get a sense of whether his victory really was such, and if so, over whom it came. His mind was of no use now, it had long ago forbidden him to leave Vilnius. It could explain neither the incomprehensible desire, nor the journey, nor the return. Vytautas Handless couldn't understand what forced him on the ill-fated journey and what he expected to find or experience. Yes, twenty-five men mournfully invited him, the last of their group, but he didn't have to go – it wouldn't have been a betrayal. He could feel nothing with his heart; all the feelings he had experienced during those two weeks didn't belong to him, they were someone else's. Yes, he had won the battle, he could calmly recall any moment of those days, the memories long imprisoned had broken free, but they had no power over him. The stretch of life that had been torn from him once upon a time had been put in its place. Everything was in place, but Vytautas Handless himself had disappeared somewhere, he didn't exist and had to be found, or perhaps created anew.

For four days he read his letters – the letters of that other Vytautas Handless – and forced his way through the tangle of words, wanting to understand, at least a little, the other Vytautas Handless, the one who had never broken away from that freezing land, who had remained there for all time, who sat on the banks of the river that didn't freeze solid as he waited for the log raft to appear with the sign, who kept hoping that his hand would come slowly floating back on the black waters. He read and kept asking the paper out loud why all that he had experienced and forgotten had to be experienced one more time. Was it because a man can't live without a memory? But how can he go on living now that he has become the living memory of twenty-six men?

On the fifth morning he placed the letters in a neat pile and tied them with a ribbon. The day dawned bright and clear, the near-deserted city hummed quietly, several times the phone rang irritably. Vytautas Handless put some water on to make tea and carefully ate his breakfast. He wasn't terribly hungry, but the tea seemed excellent. Shutting himself in the bathroom, he rinsed his mouth and returned to the kitchen because he had forgotten the matches. The phone rang endlessly and obstinately – this was the last sound that Vytautas Handless was to hear.

If his soul had been able to see into his home and his dead body from the outside, a few days later it would have seen how the neighbour with the fat lips sidled in, together with the men who had broken down the door, and curiously, showing no disgust, looked over the blue, bloated face, the black tongue hanging out, the greasy, shiny rope, scarcely to be made out on the swollen neck, the bathroom full of ashes from burnt paper. With sincere sorrow she said: 'Well look at that! And I would have bet anything that Vaciukas from number forty-six would go first.'

The men who had broken down the door prudently flipped through the document with the woman's name and the picture of Vytautas Handless pasted in and asked the neighbour if recently he had started acting a little strange. For instance, had he shown any desire to turn into someone else, or had he commented that life was better in the world of the dead? The woman proudly shook her head and said that Vytautas Handless had been the calmest and most sober of all her neighbours and had never talked any nonsense. He had cared for nothing, she added, except for his daughters and the cat of the man next door.

Winter in that land lasted eight months. Four were left for the other seasons.

The frost overcame everything – that which was alive and that which was inanimate. Only the river never froze completely. Its current was invincible, like the common current of the lives of all the people who had been relocated on its banks. Tens, hundreds, thousands could perish. But there was no power that could destroy every single one of them.

A solitary little raft of rough logs floated down the river. It was empty. Only by looking extremely carefully could you make out something pale and crooked on its middle log. A man's hand had been attached to the icy bark with a rusty nail. It was white all the way through, not even the contours of the veins could be seen through the dull skin. This hand was the sign that every man had to understand.

The raft made its way forward slowly, yet obstinately. And still there were no people.

1987

First published in *Come into my time: Lithuania in prose fiction, 1970-90*, Urbana; Chicago: University of Illinois Press (1992).

Translated by Violeta Kelertas from Ričardas Gavelis, *Nubaustieji*, Vilnius: Vaga (1987).

Ričardas Gavelis (1950–2002) studied theoretical physics at Vilnius University and worked for several years as a researcher before becoming a full time writer. In his trilogy of Vilnius novels, *Vilnius Poker* (*Vilniaus pokeris*, 1989), *Vilnius Jazz* (*Vilniaus džiazas*, 1993), and *The Last Generation of People on Earth* (*Paskutinė žemės žmonių karta*, 1995), he delved into the core of totalitarian coercion and the perversions engendered by social change. He is the founder of Lithuanian post-modernism, having created complicated and multi-layered narratives that did not shy away from themes such as illness, exile, murder and sexual coercion. In his work he uses images of sexual coercion to help lay bare the elements of power and the desire to manage and control impulses. He uses irony to recreate the ideas that were fashionable in the first decade after the fall of Communism as part of his focus on the 'birth of the elite' and the suffering experienced during that time.

Year of the Lily of the Valley

Jurga Ivanauskaitė

The lilies of the valley withered
From the yellow northern wind.
A glowing red hull
Passed through the sky three times.
An old, blind seagull
Whispered his prayer to me –

Saulius recited while mincing down the road in graceful pantomime-trained steps. A whole host of the most unbelievable expressions wafted across the cold features of his handsome face. Saulius removed his glasses and his glance became extraordinarily sharp such that it seemed odd that when it fixed upon something, the object of his gaze was not rendered in two. Saulius was the ideological leader of our group. We worshipped him unconditionally and didn't bother to question why we were so attracted to him. Fifteen-year-old Danas tramped along beside Saulius. He was the youngest among us and therefore had certain privileges. He was allowed to admire Jack Kerouac, while the rest of us delved into the apologetics of Zen Buddhism and Dostoevsky. Danas even gained the privilege of talking about what he would do if he became a millionaire or a rock star.

The only 'Miss' in our group, Vilija, walked with her eyes fixed on Saulius – no explanation is necessary – and for this reason she often tripped. Now, I kept my eyes fixed on Vilija. If you saw her you'd behave this way too. Of course, if you prefer Hollywood starlets or the women of Renoir or Kustodiev, you might think I'm crazy. Though it must be said that Vilija was great bait for drivers. When she stood in the middle of the road, her red garment, black hair and tiny glittering beads flapping, she looked like a plant cut out of a Max Ernst painting, and not one car would drive by without stopping. The rising and receding of the tide of her soul was visible in her face, her movements and her speech – they changed in a heartbeat and one could stare at them almost unblinkingly. By contrast, I was a terror to motorists. For some reason, my shaven head had acquired a sickly, grey hue and my old green riding breeches – I found them in my uncle's attic – were always getting torn. Vilija had to mend them constantly.

No doubt you've already gathered that we were hitchhiking. The journey was a great success. We left Vilnius early in the previous morning, spent the night in the bus station in Daugavpils, and now, around noon, we were only ten or twenty kilometres from Pskov. Yes, we were headed for Pskov and Novgorod, the kingdom of the pealing bells and a million white Russian orthodox churches.

Saulius continued his recitation:

When that bird sang
The lily petals fluttered –
I concluded and bit my tongue:
And a horrifying ghost
Suddenly appeared –

'Romas, you ridicule everything,' muttered Vilija.

We, or rather Saulius, decided to walk the final ten kilometres. It was a wonderful time of year – the beginning of June, when the first thunder explodes from the clouds and pours mad greenery upon the ground. That greenery filled the space around us and entered the tips of our being.

> *The lilies of the valley withered*
> *And the church bells tolled!*

I didn't interrupt the poetic mood of our group any more because there really were a great number of lilies of the valley around us. They grew along both sides of the road: the marble white blossoms gleamed, while the sturdy green leaves were almost invisible.

Vilija was the first to dive into the lilies of the valley, and she began to pull them out of the ground, willy-nilly. Danas followed, ever faithful to the traditions of the 'flower children'. Saulius hesitated a bit (he was probably wondering how it all related to Zen aesthetics), but then he took off his shoes and waded in as though it were a well of milk. The lilies of the valley were perfect and the coolness wafting from them was so seductive that even I swam into the fragrant flora. We frolicked like ponies let out into the pasture.

Vilija let out a scream and dived into the very thick of the white flowers. It looked like bathing in champagne, I thought disdainfully. Nevertheless, when Saulius and Danas sat down among the lilies of the valley, I, of course, followed suit. The fragrance floated around us like a lost angel.

Saulius lay down and Vilija picked the flowers, placing them on his face. I watched as the blossoms moved on top of his quivering eyelids and expanding smile.

'Why didn't your wife come with us? She would have liked it here,' said Vilija as she brushed the flowers from Saulius's face and placed the palm of her hand on his forehead.

'I think I've explained it many times. She's working, writing her dissertation. And besides, just because she's physically not here doesn't mean that she is not here with us.'

No doubt I've forgotten to mention the most important thing! Saulius's wife! When he was in the eleventh form Saulius read in some brochure that there were Buddhists in the Buryat ASSR (Autonomous Soviet Socialist Republic). He borrowed money from all of us just before exams began and travelled to see the holy mountain of Alhanai and the miraculous spring of Arshan. And then he returned – with a wife who was ten years older than him. But her parents, grandparents and great-grandparents were real Buddhists! Her name was Cagansara, which meant 'white moon'. She was beautiful, exotic, spirited, eccentric and temperamental but she wasn't interested in Buddhism. We all thought Saulius had made a grave mistake. Her intellect was boundless: she was interested in semantics, politics, parapsychology and exobiology; she painted placards and wrote poems, songs and plays campaigning for peace. Saulius, who was completely apolitical, a child 'angry with the world', before our very eyes became a man within a few months. He championed love for humanity, pacifism and decried the events in South Africa and Ulster. He began playing political songs in our school band. He was thoroughly familiar with the situation in El Salvador and Kuwait. He chose journalism as a course of study, even though he had always dreamed of being a painter.

Everyone was stunned, but it's not all that easy to remove the glorified Saulius from the altar! Instead, we concentrated our anger on Cagansara (she would sometimes pick up Saulius after class on her motorcycle). Nevertheless, the anger turned to fascination and Cagansara soon became an object of our veneration, just like Saulius. Now she's writing her dissertation, shockingly titled 'The Cultural Crisis and the Philosopher's Total Responsibility'.

Saulius and Cagansara have lived together for four years and their love for each other is boundless. Two years ago they had a son whom they named Marcel, in honour of Proust.

'You love each other so much, how can you stand to be apart?' Vilija asked in a strangely artificial voice.

'We're together all the time... she, myself and Marcel,' said Saulius, biting a lily of the valley. 'It is not important that our exterior shells are not always next to one another. I feel that her love floats over, like gusts of warm air from some yellow distance and caresses me with long strokes frozen in time…'

'But, judging from your wife's accounts, the physical is not totally meaningless. I've heard her say that an absolute communion between two people is possible only in the physical realm,' said Vilija. (Cagansara really did recount some very intimate details about herself and Saulius – and not always in a very dignified manner.)

'Spiritual forces and soul games have very little meaning in your fantastic love story,' Vilija continued. 'Talk to Freud and he'll tell you it's nothing more than frustrated libido. Everything is much simpler than you'd like to believe.'

I looked at Vilija and saw a flash of fear cross her face. I knew that she realized that rather than getting closer to Saulius, she was drifting further away – burning her bridges and constructing barriers. I knew that she did not believe a word she was saying. I saw that she was beginning to tremble with terror when she saw Saulius's eyes fill with shining sadness instead of anger, irony, or indifference, which were our usual defensive reactions. I understood her perfectly. I remember once when Saulius talked for a long time about the war in Vietnam. I sat and tried to seem disinterested in political matters – even the world at large – but my leg swinging nervously betrayed the fact that I would much rather hear of his and Cagansara's nightly games. And then Saulius suddenly took out a photograph. It showed an American soldier holding an infant only a few months old by the feet and smashing him into the head of a huge, stone Buddha. Several bloodied little bodies lay close by and the mother was standing there stripped naked. I remember that I grabbed the photo with a disgusting greed and uttered a few revoltingly ironic words. I looked at Saulius and it was as though I was scalded with hot water. His handsome face held so much sadness and wonder, like a small boy who has suddenly realised that he will never find a magic wand and will never be able to fly.

And now, again, I felt something pulling at my tongue: 'Vilija belongs to the Society of Lonely Maidens who Love Saulius. Those who have been lucky enough to spend a night with you tell of wondrous things…'

To avoid seeing the expression on Saulius's face, I looked at Danas's orange hair burning among the lilies of the valley.

'I know very well that you are not what you pretend to be. Your ideas are the same as mine. Otherwise, you wouldn't be able to survive,' Saulius said suddenly. 'Remember Kant's categorical imperative? A person does good deeds because he is essentially good and noble-minded, independent of motive or circumstance. You waste so much energy on fits of anger and sarcasm when you could live in goodness and love. I see how your faces twitch nervously with indifference when I say that all men are equal socially and spiritually – talent, intellect, thought patterns notwithstanding. The world's greatest art is to love people. The need for precedence and the desire to demonstrate your superiority are signs of spiritual poverty.'

'But, listen,' interrupted Danas, 'remember Kerouac? Or punks? They were mistreated in life and protested against urbanism with their anger,' and then he blushed having uttered such a 'daring' notion.

'Anger and disappointment – this is not a form of protest but rather reverse conformism. Life gives us rain and sunshine equally. There are things that are eternally sacred, which fill even the most miserable souls with goodness and harmony. Japanese art, the music of Bach, the paintings of Chagall, even these lilies of the valley,' Saulius said and stood up. Then he quietly added: 'Of course, there are other things – war, oppression, inequality, but enough of this, you're already sick of my sermonising.'

'Easy for you to say,' remarked Vilija, also rising to her feet, 'when everything is going so well for you. You have a woman who loves you, whom you love too, you have a wonderful child. Everyone loves you, so it's easy for you to love everyone. And me? I love you and that is all I exist for. If you disappeared suddenly I would suffocate. I would explode as though in a vacuum. Everything that I do, I do for you: walk, sleep, eat, read, draw, think, interest myself in world events, try to be good to others. But I know that you only love her, and I can't ask that you show some interest in me. If I fell to my knees before you as before God, bathed your dusty bare feet with my tears, if I dried them with my hair, if I immolated myself in your presence, if I carved your name upon my face, you would still love her and not me and you would be absolutely right!' Vilija suddenly knelt down and embraced his legs. Saulius straightened up like a bow-string, then bent down, lifted her up and kissed her. Danas and I stood crushing the lilies of the valley in our fists and stared like idiots. Finally I said:

'Oh, Vilija, Vilija what would the great Shakyamuni Buddha say to you! In your speech you repeated the personal pronouns 'I', 'mine', 'me' many times!'

'You still love only her,' said Vilija.

'I love everyone,' replied Saulius, putting on his glasses.

'Yes, of course. You love all humanity. Perhaps you're the incarnation of Buddha? I have placed all of my love at your altar, there is nothing left for anyone else. You say that the idea of goodness is eternal; I say that the forces of destruction are eternal. Forces, not ideas. And war. Everyone wants peace, but war prevails. It's an elemental force. You and your wife dedicate your lives to the fight for peace, but that is like the shaman's effort to forestall a hurricane or an earthquake. Some rock star donates the proceeds of a concert to the starving children in Bangladesh, but that's like trying to ladle out the sea with a spoon. You say you love all of humanity, yet you are unable to help a single person, even me.'

'According to Santayana, an entire ocean of goodness cannot wash away the suffering of one individual,' I said, lighting a cigarette. (You've probably noticed that I am completely crazy?)

Saulius continued: 'When the desire to destroy is overcome, suffering ceases. And you have needlessly constrained yourself with such a love. I think that if you love a person, you love the whole world within him, all people. I don't know if true love can elicit anger and despair, even if it is unrequited. If love renders you a stranger to the world, if it dissociates you from your fellow man, then you do not love me, even if your love is attached to me. You love something within yourself, not me. It's not the object of love that is important, but love's special qualities. If I love someone, I love all of humanity

152

within him, living things, and myself as well. You must join yourself with the outside world so that you can feel it as your twin. Rather than indulging your torments, you must close your eyes and learn to hear the eloquent peals of silence. Dissolve within the moment, absorb the gravity of the universe without reflection just as the moon does not decide whether to reflect itself in the lake or not...'

Saulius stopped and listened. A strange, bewildering music wafted over from a nearby dwelling.

We went back to the road carrying bunches of lilies of the valley. The music played on. My blue-hued bald head thought that this might be a funeral march. And indeed, soon after this thought a funeral procession turned onto the street from a side road. We mingled with a group of people dressed in black. They blocked the entire road, holding up cars that rudely and impatiently blew their horns. The deceased was lying in an open casket. I was taken by a strange curiosity. It was hard to believe that the dead man could not see the springtime fields and the sky arraying themselves for the last time before his closed eyes. Vilija boldly stepped up to the coffin and placed a bouquet of lilies of the valley on the dead man's chest. I saw how her hand trembled and her glance froze upon the face of the deceased. A woman near the coffin grabbed the lilies of the valley and threw them to the ground.

'No, no, darling, only not lilies[1],' she said in Russian.

Vilija jumped back and grabbed Saulius's arm. I clearly saw that she was very scared.

And then strange things began to happen. I was loitering some distance from the group, not mingling with the black-clad crowd when a girl, maybe sixteen years old, approached me and took my bouquet of lilies of the valley.

'No need for lilies[2],' she said in Russian, dragging her clenched hand up the stalks of the flowers. Only bare stems were left in one hand and the other held the tiny white blossoms.

---

1 Original text in Russian: *Нет, нет, голубушка, только не ландыш.*
2 Original text in Russian: *Не надо ландышей.*

'No need, just listen to the bells ringing[3],' she said in Russian and walked away, dropping the small white bells on the ground.

I looked at Saulius and Danas. Their flowers had also been taken and tossed on the ground, crushed.

We held back from the procession as it turned into a cemetery by the forest.

Again, we sat down near the road among the lilies of the valley.

'Strange customs – just like in the times of Rublyov,' said Saulius. 'Why were they so troubled by the lilies of the valley?'

'I don't suppose you would be really happy,' I said, 'if brutes like us threw bunches of wild flowers gathered from the roadside on the remains of your kin?'

'Clearly. This is a rural area. What do they know? They haven't even heard of beatniks, hippies, Kerouac, and the avant-garde,' you've probably gathered that this was Danas speaking.

'They weren't angry, and they didn't yell at us. They just politely took the flowers from our hands,' Saulius muttered and lit a cigarette.

Vilija was quiet, then lit her cigarette off Saulius's cherry.

'Saulius,' she said very quietly, 'I got very close to the dead man. His entire face, his neck and his hands, were covered with tiny, tiny wounds, as if he were pricked all over with a needle.'

We didn't find this at all strange. There are many types of diseases.

We reached the city in the evening. I remembered Saulius once saying, 'If you ever travel to Pskov you should time your arrival so that you first enter the city in the evening, when a viscous dusk begins to conceal the sunlight. Innumerable white orthodox churches, enveloped in the pealing of bells and the calls of black birds, swaying gently, twinkling with copper-topped cupolas, suddenly rise toward the heavens. And just as unexpectedly as they rise, they fall down upon the low hills without disturbing the grass. It happens within a blink of the eye. You may not even notice it, but just feel a gust of damp wind rising, as if from a giant cellar.'

We wandered the city for several hours, from one Russian orthodox church to another. We bought copper bells and thin scented

---

3 Original text in Russian: *Не надо слушать, как звенят эти колокола.*

candles. Vilija and Saulius stopped to kiss every five minutes. Later it became as though Saulius was enclosed in a case made of mirrored glass. We saw him, but he didn't see us.

We headed toward the suburbs looking for a place to stay. We didn't want to sleep in a station again. Besides, we missed normal people (there were after all none to be found among us). The people were wonderful in this country!

We had barely left the centre of town when the lilies of the valley appeared again. They glowed white in the twilight, as though someone had splashed kefir in the fields. The air was full of a refreshing fragrance. We were tired and silent. Danas said that we were all very dear, as though we had stepped out of the pages of *Dharma Bums* or *Satori in Paris*. I was trying to imagine what my little sister Rasa was doing at the moment (she was the same age as Marcel). Vilija walked while staring at Saulius, her lips moving.

On the outskirts of town, we came upon some small wooden houses. We opened a gate and walked into one of the yards. There, as in all the other yards, a campfire was burning. The yard was smothered with harvested lilies of the valley. A man holding a scythe stood by the fire. A small boy with a red woollen hat was throwing the lilies of the valley into it. There was a cat lying by the fire, and I moved closer to stroke its back. As I bent down, I saw that he was covered with tiny wounds, as though someone had pricked him with a needle or a nail.

A woman came out of the house carrying an armful of lilies of the valley. We asked if she had any rooms available. She welcomed us, served us tea and potatoes, and showed us to an empty room. It was completely empty save a few lily of the valley leaves on the floor. We heard the voice of a football commentator – someone was watching television in the other room. The mistress of the house gave us several blankets, although we had some of our own. We were pleased, especially Danas, and we lay down on the floor.

'If you sense anything strange, call us. Good night, everybody[4].'

---

4 Original Russian: *Если что-нибудь почувствуете, зовите нас. Спокойной ночи, ребята.*

the woman said in Russian as she smiled at us and left the room.

'Such mysticism, my dear friends,' I said. 'If anyone sees a vampire looming over him tonight, shout and scream. The mistress of this house is Prince Dracula incarnate. He's watching television right now, but at night, my dear friends, at night...'

'At night an orange abyss will open up beneath us and we'll fall, birds will scream and before our eyes we'll see the span of our lives from the present to the day life began,' said Saulius.

Vilija opened the window and hung our copper bells on the latch.

'Maybe you shouldn't open it,' said Danas, looking around anxiously. He had spread his blanket out in the farthest corner of the room.

I spread out a huge plastic sheet, as though I were planning to sleep in the middle of a swamp. We lay down and this time for some reason we did not play our usual game: to say whatever comes to mind. You know, fantastic chains of verbal reactions arise out of the subconscious. You should try it yourselves sometime before falling asleep. I have long imagined recording such a session. But this time, everyone was quiet because Saulius was quiet. He once said that he didn't want us to communicate with words alone. He never spoke about his spiritual victories.

I awoke during the night with a strange sensation: as though someone was pricking my hand, which was lying on the floor, with needles. The air was full of the fragrance of lilies of the valley and a barely audible tinkling. I thought that the scent was wafting in from outside and that our copper bells were ringing. However, the tinkling was not a copper one and the scent was both around and within me.

Suddenly a sharp pain pierced my right hand. I opened my eyes and lifted my head. I was surrounded by nothing but lilies of the valley. Again, I felt a pain in my right palm. I looked and was horrified to see two seedlings rising from my hand. Shocked, I jumped to my feet – my friends were bursting with lilies of the valley. It was as though they were nailed to the floor by delicate, tinkling stems; they couldn't move.

A mild pain stabbed at my bare feet like mosquito bites. I began screaming wildly.

The mistress of the house ran into the room.

'Oh, this is the year, the year of the lilies[5],' she wailed in Russian before rushing to my friends and pulling up the lilies of the valley from their dead bodies.

I could barely tear my feet off the floor – they were already in bloom with lilies – as I ran toward the window. Something like a strong whirlwind struck me, or maybe it was a whirlwind of emptiness. I drew back suddenly and knocked the glass out with my elbow. As I turned around, I could see that the lilies of the valley on Saulius's body were swaying gently. Cagansara?

I jumped out of the window and ran.

I've already mentioned that we were bound by words alone. And the year of the Lilies of the Valley separated us entirely.

Do you want me to defend myself?

Here!

Wait a minute, someone is knocking at the door.

It's Cagansara and Marcel, both with bunches of lilies of the valley in hand...

Translated by Ada Valaitis From Jurga Ivanauskaitė, *Pakalnučių Metai*, Vilnius: Vaga (1985).

Jurga Ivanauskaitė (1961–2006) was a prose writer, essayist and dramatist. While she was still a student of drawing at the Vilnius Academy of Arts she published the cult short-story collection *The Year of the Lily of the Valley's* (*Pakalnučių metai*, 1985). It was thanks to this impressive debut that she became one of the most popular authors among younger readers. Her later novels, *The Witch and the Rain* (*Ragana ir lietus*, 1993), *The Magic of Agnes* (*Agnijos magija*, 1995) and *Gone With the Dreams* (*Sapnų nublokšti*, 2000), established a new narrative in Lithuanian literature, one full of song, independent women characters and a feminist worldview. Eastern themes also permeate her work.

5 Original in Russian: Ах, этот год, год ландышей.

Tūla

(an excerpt)

Jurgis Kunčinas

Chapter VIII

But then, *Domine*, I was already in the Second Section – I've already mentioned it rather vaguely. Vasaros, Rudens and Olandų streets, right up to the rise of the Polocko line on the southeast, were its natural boundaries, where I felt at home for almost two months. The hospital's territory was, obviously, much more restricted. On the east side rose a steep, pine-covered slope, which, when climbed, opened the valley to the Butterflies Cemetery. It was above it, *domine*, that I would fly on sleepless nights to the corner of Filaretų, and there, making a turn to the west, I'd be fluttering into Malūnų Street...

There's no reason to hide it: the Second Section was a poorly disguised alcoholic sanatorium – most of the time they'd write into the hospital admission records that such and such a person suffered from a disturbance of the central nervous system. That's certainly truthful, but there wouldn't be a single word about hallucinations or phobias, or about hangover syndromes or cirrhosis. It was an open secret, a finger on the lips when someone from outside asked: Second Section, what is that really?

It was the dullest section. Those slaves to the bottle, whose remains of reason still whispered: 'go on, take a break, then you can booze it up like a man again!' – accompanied by tearful wives or girlfriends, or else alone like me – came to this shady park, lived in blocks that were built in a style reminiscent of a whimsical summer house and would loll about there for a good month, guzzling vitamins and tranquillizers. In their free time they would corrupt the unhinged young girls who filled both the beautiful park and the woods around the lunatic asylum. The beige blocks held only an assemblage of recovering alcoholic males. In the other sections enclosed by brick buildings with barred windows and a tall, wire-entangled enclosure for walking there were would-be suicides, handsome young men beset by depression, curly-haired schizophrenics with eagle noses and fiery glances, unfortunate students who had decided it was better to sit in a nuthouse than go into the army, hysterical teenagers in conflict with their parents and lonely old people who no longer wanted to go anywhere except the kingdom of heaven. The latter were the ones who fluttered off to that vale, to the Butterflies Cemetery; there they would be quietly buried in a still quieter slope, mostly at night for some reason. I saw it – the soft sand, the restless butterfly graves, the pockets of the dead filled with wind-blown sand.

The alcoholics got better right in front of your eyes – they would lift a rusting two-pood[1*] weight by the door, hang around the kitchen, play cards, and nearly all of them had a handle that would open almost every door.

As not just a drunk but also a homeless drunk, I felt particularly good there. Clearly the Second Section was also, in a certain sense, a concentration camp whose administration and personnel attempted to turn the 'drinking animal' into a human again, even though the detox specialists and psychotherapists had long since given up believing in miracles and therefore in the meaning of their work. But they did what they could, or at least pretended to do so. A thin, nervous doctor with a sternly twitching cheek signed me up for the experimental group right away – I agreed to all the conditions. Every other afternoon he would take six or seven of us wretches to the attic and lie us down on roughly chest-high platforms, brown oil cloth-covered couches. He would slowly repeat pleasant words before

1* A pood is a unit of measure used in the Russian Empire equal to about 36 pounds.

urging us or even forcing us to relax. After a filling lunch the body would grow lazy and the eyes would shut of their own accord.

During these séances Glebas, a freight-handler from the 'Krasnūcha' industrial zone, who lay to my right, would frequently start snoring to our collective horror and to his own misfortune. I'd want to laugh but the psychotherapist, giving an angry shout, would poke Glebas in his bare stomach and start the next part of the experiment. In a high voice, full of drama, he'd start passionately cursing vodka, wine, and beer, comparing the bottle's neck with a nipple; his eyes probably sparkled. We couldn't see that – we'd been ordered to lie with our eyes tightly closed and not to stir, otherwise everything would go to hell. But it's questionable whether he himself believed in the strength of his influence when he reached the culmination and suddenly spouted: 'There it is, that damned vodka! There! That's the reason,' he cried, jabbing the nearest prone chest with a finger, 'that you lost your job! It's because of the vodka that your wife left you!' (He could have correctly jabbed almost anyone at that moment.) 'Vodka destroyed your brains! Vodka! Vodka did it!'

By now, nearly hissing in fury, the doctor would order us to open our mouths as wide as we could. Pulling a full bottle of the newly-damned vodka – which had been diluted by half – out of somewhere, he'd start slopping it into our open mouths. He sloshed it about and it would splash onto your face and eyes – so that's why he told us to close them! Having emptied the entire bottle of spirits he would collapse limply into an armchair, cover his eyes with his palms and, brushing away the black hair that had fallen onto his forehead, ask us in a more normal voice to get up slowly. There were red and blue plastic buckets set on the ground between the couches, but it was only a rare patient, influenced by the doctor's words or by the vodka splashed on his lips, who would throw up. But that was the purpose of this cruel treatment – to force vomiting, to cause as much disgust as possible. The pukers were encouraged and held up as an example to the non-pukers.

After a séance like this the doctor would ask every lab rat: 'Well now, how do you feel? Do you still want to drink?'

'Oh *doktor*!' my neighbour Glebas, the freight loader from Krasnūcha, would moan, '*Nikogda bol'she, ei bogu!* – Never again, oh God! *Chto by ja etu gadost' bol'she buchal!* – I'd rather drink lye than drink this filth! *Basta, zaviazyvaju*! – That's it, it's over!' The doctor's bad eye twitched, and he marked something down in his observation notebook.

'Well, and how are you doing, sir?' he asked me one beautiful autumn afternoon. Grey, green and red maple leaves bigger than your hand fell just beyond the narrow, white window and rays of warm sunlight glittered. How badly I wanted to answer this good person with words like Glebas uttered! Alas! The saddest part was probably that I, like the majority of the inhabitants of this colony of alcoholics, did not, by any stretch, imagine I was some kind of invalid – well, maybe a tired boozer who didn't have anywhere to live and didn't, in general, have a life.

I was ashamed to look at this thin, nervous person's troubled eyes. After all, he addressed me politely, and it was actually his brother, an actor who had yet to find his destined role, who helped set me up in the sanatorium. He even requested that they did not go overboard with me there and force me to take medicines. It was this doctor I had to thank for a bed in the corner by the window and for the fact that they had already, on the fifth day of my voluntary captivity, allowed me to go into town. I walked down the street knowing I had somewhere to go home to and a blanket to crawl under. 'I don't know,' I'd say to the doctor, the actor's brother, when I was asked.

'It's disgusting, of course... believe me, I try, but I don't get nauseous... I don't puke! You know, a person gets used to all kinds of smells.'

'No matter, no matter,' he'd cry almost elated. 'You just need to hold yourself together and not fall apart, and everything will be okay!'

I'd nod and together with my other grey-faced colleagues march out to rake armfuls of falling leaves and pile them into the little tractor's rusty trailer.

In the evenings, when the guards would wipe the puddles of milk soup and bacon rinds off the long tables – family members would bring the smoked products over; recovering alcoholics were overcome by monstrous hunger! – I would often settle down under this refectory's dim lamp. I could read there until the middle of the night, or, when woken by my neighbour's mighty snoring and finding myself unable to manage to fall asleep again. I'd go there with a notebook. I would write down my impressions and try to compile a slang dictionary; but most often I'd write letters to you, Tūla. At that time I didn't send them anymore – and not just because I didn't have any address for you. Frequently, one of the other guys also tortured by insomnia would pester me – most of the time they were overflowing with a passionate need to let it all out. I would unwittingly fall into empty conversation or listen to interminable monologues about riotous all-night parties, quarrels and fights with drinking buddies, endless escapades in bed and constant battles with authorities, wives, neighbours, with the entire world! Sitting around in the night-time cafeteria, I wrote and wrote letters to you – I wouldn't cross out anything anymore. I'd tell you about everything in turn, or sometimes just the opposite: I'd confuse everything so badly that I could myself no longer distinguish what was true and what was an invention smacking of quiet insanity.

> *It's as if a deadly spider's thread*
> *spreads through darkened streets*
> *where buggies of blue will convey*
> *The sleepwalkers out of Tūla.*

Something like that. A rhyme like that came into my head and later, I believe, you liked it? Yes, you liked it, you even asked me to write it down. I scribbled it down on the grey wrapping paper that the Rytas café used for napkins. I didn't write to you much back then. Excerpts from the life of a beetle or a wasp. Reflections on *aminazine* and amnesia. A short essay: 'How do Ethics, Aesthetics and Epithets differ?' The answer: ethics and aesthetics are frequently only epithets, for which... Bah. Not a glimmer of hope.

In a hospital you're supposed to sleep at night – that's the way the majority of our grim contingent behaved. Only Glebas, getting up after midnight, would start lifting the two-pood and pester me with his absurd questions: 'What do you think, if you poured kefir from one bottle to another for six months, would it really turn into pure alcohol?' And once, on the same day in which he swore to the doctor that he would never '*buchinti*' – drink – again to the day he died, he pulled a bottle of vodka out from under his arm right in front of me, rummaged in the cabinet and retrieved an onion and a dry crust of bread, and threw back his head and emptied more than half the bottle. He would have drunk it all, but it was more than one gulp and I coughed at the wrong moment. He gave me what little remained and said: 'Go on, drink it!'

I shook my head. Then Glebas clenched his labourer's fists – they looked like real three-pounders to me! – and grabbed me by the flimsy lapels of my pyjamas: 'Well!?'

His eyes were already crazy by now. I drank it. I didn't have the slightest intention of turning him in to the 'caliphate', what difference did it make to me? I hadn't drunk in a long time – my head spun, my chest got hot, and opening the air vent wide, I flew out into the star-studded autumn night... And Glebas was left sitting there staring with his red eyes – he couldn't believe what he had seen! Then he snorted and fell headfirst onto the table. They found him dead in the morning.

That was the first time I flew to you as a bat, Tūla, without even knowing whether I'd find you at home or whether you still lived next to the Vilna River. I flapped my webbed wings, obeying entirely new instincts; I felt the never-before-experienced giddiness of flight and rose higher. I flew above the Butterflies Cemetery – from above the frost on the grass looked like a white shroud... Off in the distance the Belmontas forest glowed in the throes of the damp, but I turned to the west, to you, Tūla. There was nothing I wanted to say to you anymore, nor to remind you of, nor to explain. I just wanted to see you and be near you for a while. Even if I were invisible, what of it?

But I only saw you on the following day when, after it had gotten quite dark, I once again went out into the city. It was a city preparing to entomb itself – I don't ever remember streets so dimly, so dismally lit; the lanterns and arched lamps merely emphasised the grimness. To me the people passing by looked like they had only just now been pulled from the water. Half-dead, they staggered lifelessly towards home or some other place. It seemed that the city had forgotten how to talk – only the car engines coughed, sounding like they'd come down with a cold. Yellow trolleybuses would slide past, silent as real ghosts, like coffins with glass windows loaded with someone's dead loved ones seated side by side. Maybe I didn't deserve a better life, I thought, creeping down the cement embankment towards the city centre – the 'heart' of the city also barely moved – I'm of no use to anyone.

Many think otherwise and that I'm harmful, a destroyer bound to provoke a citizen's intolerance; didn't the episode in the Second City confirm this? Well, then! Yesterday, when I was flying back to the Second Section, my colleagues – several real bats, *chiroptera*, the common noctule – attacked me. They didn't want to admit a stranger into their domain; maybe they were from the pan-Slavic *Severozapad* organization? Now my hand and shoulder hurt, but I got ready to go into town anyway. The evenings had started to feel longer because of the real madmen, who had been sent out for an evening walk in the exercise yard enclosed by the wired fence and were howling and laughing, their voices not drowned out by either '*Ja uedu v Komarovo!*' playing at full blast in our block, or the heart-rending cries of Glebas's wife. For the third day in a row she hadn't left the door of our block, unable to believe that her little Glebas was no longer there. I think they were getting ready to admit her to the women's section – apparently she wasn't just wailing but guzzling the wine she'd brought along. And they say no one loves a drunk! They're loved by the same kind of drunks, and how they mourn when they lose their loved ones!

I headed down the boulevard. Even the drunk people, who one happened upon with practically every step, rollicked, yelled and shoved as if driven unwillingly by a greater force. Gloomy shadows passed – women carrying huge bouquets of white chrysanthemums – All Saint's Day was coming. Nothing buzzed in my sober head as I walked and walked; I had no purpose and no one I wanted to see. But at the end of the boulevard, past the square, I bumped into Tūla. She was walking by herself, just like everyone else and looking the same way, as if she'd just been pulled from the water. We really did bump into one another. She mumbled 'tsorry!' and was going on her way. I held her by her shabby sleeve and then she turned around and recognised me. Hello, hello, she stirred her swollen lips, hello… should we stop somewhere? But she didn't take hold of my arm.

***

Even this tiny, narrow, normally always jam-packed café, where petty passions eternally boiled over at the bar and where those waiting their turn to down a glass breathed impatiently on the backs of the necks of the drinkers, where almost everyone not only knew one another but saw clear through one another, even this place was half-empty. We sat down at the bar on the high stools – Tūla next to the rough-textured square pillar, me next to her.

'Oh,' she whispered, 'it's pretty dark in here.'

I asked for coffee and vermouth. It seems we didn't talk about anything, or if we did then it was just trivialities. I took her hand and together with my own put it on her cherry-coloured wool dress. She drank greedily, in small sips. I just watched her in silence. Then she ordered another round of tasty, slightly bitter vermouth from the still brotherly land of Hungary. I felt her inspecting me with her eyes from her comfortable twilight; I was afraid to as much as stir. I just found out today where you are, she said, and here we meet each other, not bad, huh? We drank again. Her eyes glistened but I saw nothing in them, not the slightest desire to talk. Maybe I should have explained everything? Hardly.

When I remember that evening in the dim café, now when Tūla is no more, a shameful sorrow flows over me. Shameful? Who knows?

Hey, I don't display that sorrow, I don't wear it on my sleeve and what of it, if I did? So why am I ashamed? Maybe it's my lack of determination, my sheepish, submissive thankfulness for the fact that she was sitting next to me? Perhaps. That gloomy, half-empty café keeps coming to mind as never before. Now that evening seems to me like a clip from a sad Italian film, one of those black-and-white ones they used to call neo-realist. At the time, of course, it didn't seem that way; it didn't even occur to me. A gloomy evening with a beloved person and vermouth that triggers sadness. During the dusk, when you look at the chrysanthemums outside the window, all that's breathing on your neck is the approaching All Saints' Day and the draft when someone opens the door. Maybe you'd remember everything exactly the same way, Tūla. The café is still quiet with a distinctive, but barely detectable smell from the unseen kitchen. Two stools away from me sits, as I remember, a grey-looking conductor with a pointy goatee; he feeds his cat tender, boiled beef and slowly sips brandy. He's already quite drunk – would he actually take his cat to a café otherwise? The conductor doesn't pay any attention to me either, even though we're acquainted. Not far from the big window is a young film and theatre actor, practically a genius. He's so modest that even in an empty café he shrinks from the glances of chance admirers.

'See,' I showed Tūla.

'I see,' she says. 'What of it?'

'Take my hand again, take my hand.'

I take her hand but look at the actor. An artist: a black, thick moustache, a wide, low forehead and the neck of a master wrestler. Stocky, strong and angry. I know he's a mean gymnast, fencer, marksman and horseman. His only shortcoming: he can't pronounce short vowels and so stretches them out like blades of grass. But is that really important? If necessary, he's Romeo or a Red Commissar or an *SS Bannführer*, or else Hamlet, Gasparone, Oedipus. He can produce at will a fiery glance, the kind that makes the ladies' groins wet.

'Hey,' Tūla tugs at me. 'Where are you?'

I turn to face her again. She's in the shadow. She orders us both another glass of vermouth and a piece of cake.

'You'll get in trouble there, won't you? They let you rot there in solitary, don't they?'

'Yes,' I said, 'we get in trouble for everything, they let us rot in solitary, stick us with needles. How do you know all that?'

'Oh,' Tūla says seriously, 'I don't know. I just make an effort, just try to guess.'

Her cherry dress is nearly black too. We drink vermouth and get depressed, like that grey rough-textured pillar with nothing beyond it. Like beyond Polocko Street? She draws the symbol for gold on the napkin – you could still find them sometimes in cafés – with lipstick.

'You started using make-up?'

'No, I just carry lipstick so that when I meet you I can draw the symbol for gold.'

Depressing talk. My stiffened fingers on the constantly darkening dress. The meowing of the conductor's satiated cat.

Now when I look at that single photograph of you I have left I always remember that café – and it hasn't been there for some time now! – the same shadows and twilight, and somewhere beyond the edge of the photograph a glass of vermouth giving off the scent of ashes. And not just ashes – maybe gall. Beyond the window white and pink chrysanthemum blooms keep floating by. The superstar actor's hair shines like a crow's feathers above a battlefield – he's drinking vodka while his girlfriend guzzles champagne, of course.

I see the fleshy barmaid press the 'old-fashioned' tape-recorder button. The tape screeches, the machine blares and at last a passionate woman's voice whacks right in the ear – my ear, your ear, the bat's wide ear. The barmaid staggers offstage somewhere – what else does she have to do here? Cold wafts from the door and only Gerasimas Mucha, a former pioneer captain and now a doorman, can stand it next to the platform and that is only because from time to time he downs a glass of spirits proffered by a visitor. Inside it's dim and outside it's dark. I see the tape in the recorder become tangled. I see the theatre and film actor go behind the bar, first judiciously and respectfully consulting with his lady – a remarkably thin, big-mouthed girl with fishnet stockings – and press one button, another and then a third. The tape slowly straightens out, stretches, crackles and blares again. This evening I want for nothing.

Adriano Celentano is then heard singing 'Yuppi Du'. It was still the era of 'Yuppi Du'! For some it's yupidoo, but not for others, of course. I'm still yupidoo. Yupidoo, yupidoo, yupidooo... yupidododoooo... To others it was an era of hopelessness, of *Sturm und Drang*, a time of souls and gloomy indifference. But there, in that narrow, cramped café, this dramatic 'Yuppi Du' completely overwhelmed me. I didn't even say anything to Tūla about it. That's the way I remember that 'neo-realist' Italian evening; you couldn't imagine a gloomier one, but still! I held her plaid coat – it was the first time I'd seen this one – while she aimed her arms into the slippery sleeves and giggled.

It was horribly biting cold in the street with those same corpse-people with corpse markings on their foreheads. We got on an empty trolleybus – now that really was a glass coffin. I let you in first. Go on, Tūla, they'll nail the lid on right away. I went along as far as the Antakalnio traffic circle. I didn't even ask where you were going, or who's waiting for you, since it didn't really matter. I went knowing that when I returned I'd find the door to the Second Section locked. No clever handle would help me, it's already late and if the sister on guard writes in the book that I returned with a smell of alcohol on me, they'll throw me out of the alcoholics' sanatorium tomorrow and onto the street again. At night I'll wander around as a bat, but during the day?

'Maybe I'll come visit you,' says Tūla, her eyes lowered at the cracked sidewalk. She strokes my old jacket with her glove and leaves so quickly I don't even have time to ask: when will that be?

I return plagued by the sweet torture I'd already forgotten – that's the kind of guy I am! I was with her for a few hours, and I'm happy! Only an honourable person, only a person who loves selflessly can do that! I headed for the sanatorium's white gates without in the least blaming myself for flagrantly breaking the rules. I sobered up quickly in the biting cold, but I chewed on some green cedar from the hedge just in case. Maybe its bitterness will overwhelm the bitterness of vermouth and chrysanthemums?

I was in luck, for the sister who smelled the reek of alcohol from the door and was already leaning forward to write my surname into the journal of miscreants, unexpectedly raised her eyes and briskly asked if I wasn't... Domicėlė's... Domicėlė's cousin? I stared and asked: whose? But I immediately confirmed: aha! She really is my relative, my cousin, yes! The middle-aged sister shone with little golden wrinkles which didn't age this woman in the least. She and Domicėlė had danced in the same ethnic folk dance group in exile! Oh, those were the days! Exile, of course, was an injustice but when you're young... Domicėlė played there, and sang, and what a comic!... Domicėlė a comic? I thought. And why not? It's just in the long run that everything atrophied – humour turned to sarcasm, irony to malice, and so forth. The sister forgot both her infamous journal and my bad smell. She reminded me of how pretty, intelligent and friendly Domicėlė was... But how badly things turned out for her there! Of course, no one did well, but for her? She was madly in love with an Estonian, you see, this mechanic who played the accordion. But it turned out he was already married and ridiculously stubborn. He wouldn't agree to divorce the wife he had left somewhere on the islands – you know how it is with those Estonians. I didn't know this dramatic detail from my relative's life, how could I? So that's what happened! The sister nearly cried because she was so sorry for Domicėlė. Even now, after so many years! She made me swear not to let anyone see me, but when I started moaning that I badly needed a little drop, she sighed and trickled a drop of pure alcohol into a beaker, diluted it with water out of a fly-splattered carafe and gave it to me: 'Go ahead, choke!' she said, but not angrily, not angrily...

**

Incidentally, our senior doctor, the actor's brother with the twitching cheek, would cure the most hopeless drunks with spirits. Not everyone, of course not – just those who were brought in already flying with the pink elephants. The sisters and veterans said they were *delyrikai*, the dis-lyricists instead of the usual diagnosis of delirium tremens. At first I just shrugged – those guys didn't resemble degenerate lyricists, or artists of any kind for that matter. Defined by their dazed eyes, crazed movements and endless struggles to get free, they would be tied up in the tiny sixth ward not far from the bathroom. They would tie the drunks up tightly with sheets, soaking them first so the knots wouldn't come loose. We, the comparatively recovering ones, would take turns watching at their deathbed, moistening their dried lips with a rag and wiping the cold sweat from their brows. Furnished with an intravenous drip, continually poked and otherwise prodded, the dis-lyricists either recovered or rather quickly gave up the ghost. They'd have time to rave all kinds of nonsense, some of which really would have been worth writing down. Actually, they did manage to haul some of them off to the intensive care ward where they would bid farewell in peace to the seas of vodka and their drunken non-life.

But to my great surprise, after a few days those who returned to this terribly imperfect and disorderly world began looking longingly again at the woods beyond the wire fence and towards the noisy street where the dreary Rytas loomed – a store that sold liquor. The orderlies, and even the sisters would say, as if in their defence, that they didn't remember anything. So you see, it was those raving under a death sentence that the doctors would water with pure medical spirits. With a sudden, well-practised movement they would open their firmly-clenched teeth and slosh in a good dollop of burning liquid, all the while holding the jawbone pressed in a way so that not a drop splashed out to the sides... I've held one by the feet during this operation: the poor guy thought they wanted to kill him – maybe strangle him? Lo and behold, most of the time this medicine would raise them from the dead. The revived patient would start demanding a second dose and the doctor almost always poured him some.

One day the senior doctor called me in. A week had already gone by since the meeting on the Boulevard and the visit in the café – don't tell me they'd sniffed out something? I waited all that week for Tūla to show up but she didn't come. On my way to drink tea I'd glance at the intersection, loiter in the gateway, sit around on the bench next to the registry office – but no, she's not coming.

The senior doctor took my blood pressure and listened to my heart. I saw how he loathed these procedures. Then he punched me and his eye twitched, maybe even more than usual.

'You see,' he began, 'my brother told me everything... well, you know, that you're... this vagrant.' He tried to giggle. 'Forty-five days have passed already, it's actually even more now...'

I looked at him silently. That's how long the course of treatment takes, as determined by the specialists – forty-five days.

'I'm releasing you,' the good man decided. 'Tomorrow. Stay somewhere for a week, okay? Well, drink or not, whatever works out for you. It'd be better not to, of course! Then come again on Monday, I'll take you in. You can stay today.'

He only wished me well, this neurasthenic who, as I later discovered, was an unhappy man in his own right, but he wasn't omnipotent, either. I used to see that type, men and women with folders and briefcases, dashing into his office, some of them waving their hands in the doorway or even wagging a finger. No, not omnipotent. Apparently even he fails to carry out some responsibility or another, or treatment plans, or maybe even the percentage of cures is too small. So there you have it, he has worries up to his ears! Maybe even serious vexations. But to me he only complained that his brother hadn't gotten the lead role again. Instead, he'll be standing there again with a halberd, like a stuffed dummy! He tried to smile. This time he almost succeeded.

I went out into the yard, smoked a cigarette under a brown chestnut, and from a distance saw Tūla hurrying along the gravel pathway. She ran straight for the horribly green office door. So she wasn't here to see me. My heart beat calmly again, my blood pressure returned to normal. Not to see me. Just to the office. I gave a shout. She turned, squinted and recognised me. She waited for me to come up to her. She looked thoroughly irritated, maybe even angry, even though she spoke in a half-whisper like she always did. She needed some paperwork from the hospital office.

'Wait a bit, if you want,' she said. 'If you want,' she emphasised again, or maybe it just seems that way to me now, suspiciously assigning significance to everything? Possibly.

What paperwork could she need there? To travel out of the country? Hardly likely! Or maybe she is leaving, what do I know. After all, anyone travelling beyond the cordon has to show that they're not insane – the insane asylum bureau searches through its extensive card catalogue and if you aren't in their archive, they give out a certificate that maybe you won't pull any tricks and you can go... I waited for you for a good half-hour. Coming out you looked even more grim and angry. Not a word about paperwork. No polite questions about how I, the patient, was feeling. We quietly headed off to that same Rytas for a coffee. I climbed the stairs and stood in line while she ran into the store and said something to a woman standing in another line. It was only as I finished slurping the coffee that I suddenly realised it was Tūla's mother. I was itching to ask her what the two of them were doing here, what they needed here. I barely restrained myself. Tūla was no longer in a hurry. The muscles in her face composed themselves, her lips seemed more seductively swollen than ever. The wrinkles next to her lips relaxed and straightened out. Apparently her mother had agreed to wait somewhere for her. There was surely a great deal I didn't know. We went out into a cool sunny day. When I suggested a smoke, she nodded vigorously: let's go!

Manoeuvring between the cars, we ran across the inhumanly wide Olandų Street. On its opposite side the comfortable two-storey townhouses that had earlier belonged to Polish military officers had been completely renovated some time ago. Their entire grey and brown neighbourhood nestled in what was once a quiet and remote area next to Vilnius. The main road seethed, roared and wheezed now; the cars, it seemed, climbed atop one another as if marked with the sign of death. To me, at least, they resembled those pedestrians I had seen – barely animated drunks, bodies just pulled from the water.

There were no doors left anywhere and the two of us entered a narrow corridor and then went into the former kitchen. A smashed gas stove still stood there. I picked up the air-vent frame – the glass had been smashed out – that had fallen from the air vent and raised it to the hole that was once the window.

'The frame,' you muttered, 'what a beautiful little frame!'

I immediately noticed the writing in black paint on the wall, which for some reason was in German: *Wir sind ein okkupiertes Land!* Oh well, at least it was there, in those Polish ruins. It should be photographed and sent to *Der Spiegel,* I said, and I translated it: 'We are an occupied country!' But it seemed occupation didn't much concern you, Tūla; you sniffed your little nose and that was all. I even remember what we smoked then as we sat on a fragrant stack of boards – it was Salem, long cigarettes smelling of menthol and packaged in Finland according to some kind of licence. It was you, Tūla, who had them. You even gave me a couple of those cigarettes; I smoked them later, thinking about this strange meeting of ours. It was completely different from the other one, the meeting in the café.

It was as clear as day that she hadn't gone there with her mum to visit me. But it wasn't because of that fictional paperwork, either. And what of it, if after so many years I know the truth: you, Tūla, were supposed to be committed to the First Ward with the milder cases and the losers tortured by romantic depression. But your mum, when she found out that my sullen shadow dragged itself around even here – you never did, after all, hide anything from her? – she immediately dropped the idea. Yes, Tūla, it was only because of me that you evaded milk soup for supper, MGB in the vein, the silly interns with their psychological test folders – all of that merry madhouse. And after you left I was there hardly a half a day! Maybe something else really would have happened? You know, patients are like family. Maybe something would have changed? Changed where? Well, in our relationship, maybe even to our fates, what do I know? Maybe we would have been together after all, smoking fragrant Salems, spicy Ronhills or ordinary Primas, turning endless circles in the madmen's lanes, climbing the wooded slopes, snuggling in the cold shade or even wandering as far as Butterflies Cemetery? You always did want to see it, at least once. I had filled your ears talking about it. Maybe we would have laid down there ourselves?

I put an arm around your shoulders and you didn't so much as stir. I quickly pecked your cold, bloodless cheek and for some reason jumped back, but you sat there like a stone. Only the hand with the smoking Salem cigarette slowly swung down as you blew out a column of white smoke before swinging up again. You greedily inhaled, the cigarette shortening by nearly a centimetre.

'Nothing would have turned out well for us anyway, nothing at all!' you suddenly shouted so angrily that I cringed and slid off onto the ground. It was the first time I had heard your low voice so angry, Tūla. It was so different from all the tones, nuances and modulations I had heard up until then! I wanted to ask: what wouldn't have turned out well? Or maybe I was already asking, what *should* have happened? How badly I wanted to be disappointed in you then! Certainly all it would have taken was a single glance full of scorn or disgust, or even a carelessly thrown 'drunkard!' No, no, nothing of the sort! You sat there as before and from the little tip of your nose a clear drop trickled.

You sniffed, wiped it off with your plaid sleeve and laughed: 'You see, I'm crying! You should be pleased!'

You announced this so solemnly, so seriously, that I was astonished – you weren't putting on an act, you weren't mocking me? I didn't even suspect what it was that threatened you, but you already knew: from the Second City our militant, organised family had already raised its wings to move to somewhere near the border with Belarus... But even if I had known! Everything was already decided, as if it had been precisely drafted on a white piece of paper. This was the plan and I know this now: the daughter would rest in the hospital, and when she had recovered she would go straight to the refuge of the peaceful, natural surroundings of the small town of Pagudė. There were too many ghosts of all sorts in the Second City. That's the story!

I was powerless, but you, Tūla, were even more so. Anyone

observing us from outside would probably have said: run as far as you can from one another, you're doomed! I'm already doomed as it is, I would have said to any such prognosticator, but what would you have answered, Tūla? After all, you still suffered and how! But no one asked anyone anything. We stubbed out our cigarette butts and went out the opening into the suddenly gloomy street. Goodbye!

You went off without turning around even once, a grey knitted hat pulled over your head. Back then half of Lithuania wore hats like that. Some peevish guy who came out behind us started yelling – all the scum that come around here! – but I continued to watch you, silently. You walked faster and faster. All I saw was a woman come out from behind a dogwood bush – your mum, that time I recognised her. You linked arms and immediately disappeared from view. I didn't even see where the two of you turned off. And how could I foresee that the next week I'd finally fall into the hands of the bluecoats, that after rotting in a temporary holding cell they wouldn't release me into the sodden autumn but instead take me straight to the Drunkard's Prison? Actually it was called by a much more innocent name. I didn't foresee either that I wouldn't see you, Tūla, for three whole years or that when we did see each other again it really would be the last time. No premonition. Only an emptiness in my heart and completely normal blood pressure. All I knew then was that I wouldn't be returning here on any Monday. Or any Tuesday, either.

Having made up my mind about this, I slowly crossed the roaring racecourse of Olandų Street and it was there that I was stopped by a writer I knew who was wearing dark glasses, a white coat that reached to his ankles and the elaborate walrus moustache. He was the one who was actually preparing to travel past the cordon; to West Germany no less, or the 'moneyland' as he himself called it. So it was he who had gotten that piece of paper, Tūla. Even I was certain this guy wasn't going to raise a stink while he was away; he'd know how to use both a bathroom and a fork. That type doesn't disappoint. '*Wir sind ein okkupiertes Land!*' – the writing on the wall in the Polish townhouse's kitchen came to mind...

Translated by Elizabeth Novickas from Jurgis Kunčinas, *Tūla*, Vilnius: Lithuanian Writers' Union Publishers (1993).

Jurgis Kunčinas (1947–2002) began his literary career as a poet, but later became one of the most prominent prose writers of his generation, as well as a respected translator from German. His novels *Glison's Noose* (*Glisono kilpa*, 1992), *Tūla* (1993) and *Movable Röntgen Stations* (*Kilnojamos Rontgeno stotys*, 1998), and his short story collections, including *Good Morning, Mr. Enrike* (*Laba diena, pone Enrike*, 1996), are notable not only for their plots, but also for the copious histories that flow from his narrators' memories. His prose works, which are full of humour and irony, most often depicted Soviet era Vilnius through restless, bohemian characters who cannot adapt to the rhythms of official life.

When the Weapons are Silent

Herkus Kunčius

Stubborn battles persisted in the mountains. Yet here, in the division, the storms of war were distant. About to ascend into his fifth decade, the chief of the division's political branch, Lieutenant Colonel Afanasy Kazimyrovich Pak, returned from work every day at six in the evening, changed into a comfortable tracksuit and lay down on the couch.

'You're tired today, Afanasy,' his beautiful wife Nadezhda Pak would say. He had brought her back from the Kuril Islands.

'Hardly,' said Lieutenant Colonel Afanasy and he'd wave his hand. 'People get really tired over there,' he'd say and his wife Nadezhda Pak understood that her husband was referring to the battles in the mountains.

Lieutenant Colonel Afanasy Kazimyrovich Pak, chief of the division's political branch, longed for a transfer to the mountains. He wanted action. This was an understandable desire, because for the warrior Afanasy a life lived in peace behind a desk passes by without purpose. Afanasy tried everything: he wrote reports to the leaders of the division and the military district; he even flew to meet personally with Army General Nursultan Genrikhovich Mitrofanov – they were well acquainted from their days at the military academy.

But it was all in vain.

The laconic response was always the same: 'Request denied'.

Afanasy Kazimyrovich Pak was vexed; he even began doubting his military prowess. He was a descendant of a renowned military dynasty – his great-grandfather served under Denikin, his grandfather wore the *budenovka*, his father, First Lieutenant Kazimierz Lionginovich Pak, fell fighting the counter-revolutionaries during the Budapest revolt. The men of the Pak family were all heroes, having shed more than their share of blood in the fields of battle. And here was Afanasy – a failure, a disgrace to the family.

At first, the Lieutenant Colonel searched for flaws within himself, but alas, he could not find a reason why the leadership mistrusted him.

'I'm politically mature, I march well, I have a powerful commander's voice. What else do they want?' Lieutenant Colonel Afanasy mused, lying on his sofa.

His wife Nadezhda Pak saw Afanasy's anguish but she was unable to help him, though she tried her best. She swept the floor earnestly, sang Korean folk songs animatedly in the mornings, washed the laundry until she was blue, played tunes from variety shows on the piano, brushed his uniform assiduously, polished his high boots, thought up tasty meals to cook and even managed to acquire a rather racy negligee from a junior officer's wife. Wearing it she hoped to distract Afanasy and remind him of erotic delights, long forgotten.

'You look like a whore,' said the Lieutenant Colonel, lying on the sofa, when one evening, Nadezhda came into the room wearing her new negligee. 'Disgusting,' he added.

'You don't like it...' Nadezhda said glumly, and Afanasy turned toward the wall not even glancing at her.

'Afanasy, make love to me,' moaned Nadezhda Pak, clinging to him. But the chief of the political branch was unresponsive, cold as ice. Women, including his wife, did not interest him; he only longed for the mountains.

His relationships with the officers under his command were no better. Major General Konstantin Abramovich Stanislavski, the chief of the division, even called Afanasy into his office one day and said: 'Comrade Lieutenant Colonel, I'm beginning to doubt whether I should recommend you for promotion.'

After such a 'hint' the chief of the political division Afanasy Pak fell into a profound despair. He left all functions to his subordinates, abandoned his political education duties, and once was even late for morning drill, for which he was reprimanded by Major General Stanislavski.

'See that this does not happen again,' Major General Stanislavski said. 'Do I have your word?'

'You have my word,' muttered the chief of the political division Afanasy.

However, Afanasy soon forgot the warning.

He thought about the mountains and oftentimes, gazing at the political map of the world in his office, he would daydream. Here he would see himself in the mountains with an AK in his hands, lobbing a grenade into a cave, returning fire, interrogating a captured enemy, carrying a wounded comrade over a mountain pass, giving commands to attack here and retreat there before, at last, the Minister of Defence awards him a medal for bravery...

During those moments, Lieutenant Colonel Afanasy Kazimyrovich Pak was reinvigorated: cheeks flushed, he would feel a stirring manliness and resume writing his reports.

Alas, a negative reply would arrive and Afanasy again roamed the division dejectedly. Officers and soldiers began to avoid Afanasy and had nothing to say when he addressed them.

It pained Afanasy to hear new arrivals to the division, who had already served in the mountains, talk about their experiences. They spoke of clandestine ambushes, raids, intelligence operations, and battles waged not only by the artillery units but also fighter pilots, tank crews and saboteurs. The chief of the division's political branch, Lieutenant Colonel Afanasy, despised the newly minted heroes – many among whom sported the order of the Red Star on their chests. The yellow ribbon worn by light casualties and the red ribbon given to those who had been seriously wounded in the course of duty so enraged him that he could not look; he would turn his head away. Lieutenant Colonel Afanasy was incandescent with rage.

After a while, Afanasy, unable to get a posting to the mountains, became utterly despondent. He showed no tenderness toward his wife, he retreated into himself and became even more careless in the execution of his duties as chief of the division's political branch. He was no longer interested in the party plenaries, decisions or programmes; he became apolitical. There were rumours in the division that the army political leadership was even considering whether or not Afanasy Pak was competent to carry out his duties. Afanasy viewed all this with indifference. He had, it seems, arrived at a critical point, and his wife Nadezhda began to worry about, God forbid, suicide. She no longer thought about love or emotions.

It would not have taken much for him to announce that he was transferring to the reserves without waiting for retirement and to cross the border into the mountains as a volunteer. Lying on the sofa, Afanasy imagined himself as a free agent – a sniper. Well hidden in the mountains he would wait for the enemy convoy. When it appeared, he would shoot every single one – he would finish off the wounded with a shot to the head. Once the task was completed he would shoulder his weapon and move forward to wait for another enemy convoy. He was invincible. His bravery and accuracy was legendary, yet no one knew what he looked like. Afanasy Kazimyrovich Pak had no need for glory, medals or rank – he was a warrior. Afanasy Pak loved to imagine himself wounded in the belly. He would rip open his shirt, pour some alcohol from his canteen onto the wound, sterilise his bayonet in the flame of his lighter and, suffering the most excruciating pain, extract the bullet from his stomach. He would lose consciousness after the operation but not for long. Upon regaining his senses, he would bind his wound, rise and continue fighting more bravely than ever.

'Afanasy, Afanasy, let's make love,' Nadezhda Pak would beg, but Lieutenant Colonel Afanasy would pretend that he was asleep. Such was the marital bliss of the couple who knew that critical battles were being fought somewhere in the distant mountains.

And then, one day, the chief of the division Major General Konstantin Abramovich Stanislavski summoned Lieutenant Colonel Afanasy.

'You have a patron, Afanasy,' the major general said gruffly. 'I never would have authorised it myself, but Comrade Army General Nursultan Genrikhovich Mitrofanov has ordered it. Get ready, you fly out tomorrow.'

Lieutenant Colonel Afanasy needed no explanations.

'Yes, sir,' said Afanasy. 'May I go?'

'Forward march!' commanded Major General Stanislavski, while his eyes followed him out suspiciously.

Afanasy got down to work as soon as he entered his office. There was much to do: he had to prepare graphics for the political lectures, write reports, minutes of the party meeting, personnel evaluations, data on party fees, and so on, for the officer who was to take over his duties. So much to do – enough to make you lose your mind.

Lieutenant Colonel Afanasy looked at the stacks of paper and realised that he would not be able to complete the work by tomorrow without exhausting himself. The work was boring, but the notion that soon he will face the enemy eye to eye gave him strength.

'I've been negligent, yes, negligent,' he repeated to himself and then he called for the ever-willing *praporshchik*[1] Ekaterina Leblan. She had served in the housekeeping section of the division for many years. The obliging woman never declined a task assigned by the chief of the political branch.

'Comrade *praporshchik*, I command you to come to my office at six o'clock,' Afanasy said to Ekaterina Leblan in a peremptory tone.

'Yes, sir. May I go?' asked the surprised *praporshchik*, for it had been quite a while since she'd heard his imperious voice.

'Dismissed. And don't be late,' Lieutenant Colonel Afanasy said in a loud, commanding voice. And suddenly, for some reason, he thought of his wife Nadezhda Pak dressed in her seductive underwear, slinking like a cat toward his sofa with a peacock feather behind her ear.

It lasted but a moment. There was work to be done, and Lieutenant

---

[1] *Praporshik* was originally a rank, equivalent to ensign, attained by junior commissioned officers in the military of the Russian Empire. The rank was restored in the 1970s in the USSR and was used for non-commissioned officers equivalent to the rank of warrant officer.

Colonel Pak dismissed the indecent memory without much effort.

Praporshchik Ekaterina Leblan, who was plump and not known for her seductiveness, came into his office at exactly six o'clock in the evening. Lieutenant Colonel Afanasy was exhausted and he had not progressed toward his goal of organising the political division's paperwork.

He was inefficient; his mind kept wandering to the mountains. As he picked up a paper marked 'Secret', he imagined himself again a member of an elite paratrooper unit, parachuting from a helicopter and raking an enemy encampment with gunfire before hitting the ground. The enemy soldiers run in all directions, the wounded fall. Afanasy lands and disentangles himself from his parachute. He fires again. He pursues. He tosses the AK aside and engages in hand-to-hand combat. He throws his opponent down and pulls out his entrenching tool. He strikes, he strikes again. Or else: Afanasy is crossing a minefield and only Lieutenant Colonel Afanasy knows the route. A step in the wrong direction means instant death. Or yet again: in the aftermath of a battle, Afanasy and his troops sit around a campfire. He talks about Khrushchev, Lenin and Brezhnev and describes the proceedings of the latest Party Congress.

'Excuse me, comrade Lieutenant Colonel, allow me,' *praporsh-chik* Ekaterina Leblan suddenly interrupted his thoughts and accidentally touched his hand.

Afanasy feels a tingle that, while gentle at first, suddenly resembles a bolt of lightning through his body.

Afanasy glanced at the clock – there was only half an hour left until his departure for the mountains. He felt a stirring manliness.

We've worked too long, I won't have a chance to say goodbye to Nadezhda, he thought and was surprised to see how quickly daybreak had come. And then there's that mischievous...

The chief of the political branch Afanasy Kazimyrovich Pak raised his eyes, smiled wryly and sighed. *Praporshchik* Ekaterina Leblan, although she had been a member of Communist party for twenty years, flinched. She stepped back as if anticipating trouble, but she didn't dare scream.

It's impossible to say why – the paperwork, the desire to get out to the mountains as quickly as possible, the nearness of the *praporshchik* and the sudden erection – but Lieutenant Colonel Afanasy's eyes grew dim.

He swayed and then straightened, growing tight as a bowstring before giving a military click to his heels.

And then suddenly the chief of the political branch Pak howled like a coyote and pulled the retreating *praporshchik* Ekaterina Leblan into his embrace.

The woman, although she had experienced worse in the course of her life, tried to free herself. She bit him, but their strengths were unequal and Afanasy was as quick as a rabbit.

The chief of the political branch Lieutenant Colonel Afanasy, overwhelmed by spontaneous passion, pressed Ekaterina, mother of two children, to him, gnawed at her double chin, tore at her eyelashes with his teeth, ransacked her mouth with his cockade, licked her armpits with his boot tops, scattered the stars from his epaulets upon her neck, pinned his breastpin to her bottom; he became a pervert such as the army had never seen.

The political branch chief's powerful hands tore *praporshchik* Ekaterina Leblan's tunic, ripped off her epaulets and medals, groped at her breasts and kneaded her thighs.

A true beast, and not the chief of the political branch, decided the manhandled *praporshchik* Ekaterina Leblan, when Afanasy overstepped the bounds by cutting into her nipple with the visor of his cap.

'Comrade Lieutenant Colonel, stop! We are at work – you'll be leaving in ten minutes for the front line!' pleaded the *praporshchik* but Afanasy, blinded by lust, did not hear her.

'Katya! Katya!' he shouted, pushing Ekaterina Leblan onto the table where no less turbulent meetings of the infantry division party had taken place. 'Nadya! Katya! Nadyusha, I've come to say goodbye! Katenka! Nadenka! Nadya, I'm leaving for the mountains! Nadya, so long!'

'Comrade Lieutenant Colonel,' wailed the *praporshchik*, who was being hacked at by the visor of the cap and scratched by the Frunze Military Academy pins. She had served as inspector at the penitentiary for many years. 'Afonya, it hurts! Comrade Lieutenant Colonel, have mercy, my children, my grandchildren are waiting for me at home…'

'Nadyusha! Nadyusha! So long!' shouted the chief of the political branch as he, still wearing his uniform, forced himself into the *praporshchik*.

No one knows how this would have played out if there had not been several staff officers on duty.

Later, when the military procurator delivered Lieutenant Colonel Afanasy Kazimyrovich Pak's sentence at the court martial the chief of the division, Major General Konstantin Abramovich Stanislavski, wiped away a tear and testified: 'Comrades, it is hard to accept the fact that in a few days you will be shot. So does it matter how, where, when and under what circumstances it will be?'

The tribunal judge asked the general not to stray from the matter at hand, and although he understood the subtlety of 'where, when, and under what circumstances', he, too, longed for more vivid effects – he had waited for a chance to preside at court martials in the battlefields of Afghanistan for more than a year.

'Continue, general,' said the tribunal judge after a while.

'I have nothing to add,' admitted General Stanislavski.

Afanasy sat behind bars in the dock, stared at *praporshchik* Leblan, and bowed his head as if to apologise. Later, he turned toward his weeping wife Nadezhda and thought: I will never go to the mountains… To hell with them. And then Pak finally decided as he stood to listen to the sentence given out by the court martial: I'll serve my time, and when I get out, I will only hunt for *praporshchiks*.

Translated by Ada Valaitis from Herkus Kunčius, *Išduoti, išsižadėti, apšmeižti*, Vilnius: Lithuanian Writers' Union Publishers (2007).

Herkus Kunčius (born 1964) is a prose writer, dramatist and essayist.

Having studied art history at the Vilnius Academy of Art, he worked for some time as an art critic and conceptual artist before becoming one of the most prolific authors in post-Soviet Lithuania. He is known for his post-modern style and his prose is distinguished for its erudition, intellectual brilliance, subtle humour and irony. His grotesque charades reveal the absurdity of existence. In his novel *Don't Pity Dushansky* (*Nepasigailėti Dušanskio*, 2006), his short story collection *To Betray, To Denounce, To Defame* (*Išduoti, išsižadėti, apšmeižti*, 2007) and his play *Matthew* (*Matas*, 2005), the absurd logic of the Soviet system is highlighted through explicit sexual scenes, a technique that has annoyed some conservative critics.

The Murmuring Wall
(an excerpt)

Sigitas Parulskis

Martynas stood leaning against the wooden wall and looked forward. He looked, but didn't see anything. And if he did see something it wasn't what was in front of his eyes. It was like he was looking at his inner being, at his past. There are those moments when you feel like you're not here. At the same time you are here and somewhere else, in your past and your memory. You come across a moment that is unbearable, that you need to get rid of, that you should pull out like a painful sliver. That moment can last for eternity. It can last and torture you. And you can't do anything with it because it is your life.

He had sat on the edge of the stool for a whole hour already. His back ached; his arms and legs hurt. He tried a few times to move his rear end from the edge of the stool without being detected, however he got a smack to the head each time he made an attempt.

The partisan was questioned by two interrogators. They changed every five hours or so, perhaps every six. Martynas didn't know whether it was day or night anymore. Just sometimes, when they took him back to his cell, he would see wavy light or gloomy nightfall through the little window decorated with two sets of bars. One day the warden came into the cell and closed the little window. However, even through the closed window you could hear the cheering of Soviet citizens on Lenin Square – a revolutionary parade was taking place, processions marched with flags, and you could hear Soviet marches played by a brass band. The Lithuanian people were greeting their great leader. The Lithuanian people rejoiced in the achievements of October – a splendid showpiece for Martynas' torture.

He was captured in October, which meant that it was now already November for he had been in Lukiškės Prison for more than two weeks. At first the interrogations were very intense but now they had lessened. The main rule that he found out from a cell mate, who also introduced himself as a figure in the underground, was not to talk with anyone in the cell. He was quickly taken away and never returned, but Martynas made a note of this lesson. Regardless of how hard people of all sorts tried to talk with him later on, he didn't get into a discussion with any of them.

A farmer, at whose place he wanted to stay for the winter, had informed on him. Martynas remembered very well that on the evening before his arrest he was reading notes from Student, a fellow partisan. He felt very ill – he had a cold, and his throat and head hurt. The farmer, knocking on the hiding place, invited him to come and have dinner with him. They ate mashed potatoes, and then the farmer poured some moonshine. Just one glass, the host said, it will get rid of the headache right away. Another was proffered before he descended down into the hiding place and started to read. He woke up in a lorry, wet; it appeared that they had poured water on him so that he would sober up before wrapping him up in a tarpaulin so he wouldn't try to jump out of the back of the lorry.

Feeling like he was soon going to lose consciousness, Martynas warned the interrogator watching him through the little window.

'I'm going to fall,' and he fell from the stool. He woke up from a blow to his back. His interrogator, standing near him, never let down his guard.

'That's enough, take him away,' the interrogator said without turning around, and they took the partisan to his cell.

After another week of intense interrogation, they stopped. He refused to collaborate and while he was being interrogated, he mentioned only the names of dead partisans and the addresses of those who he knew to be collaborators.

'You will put me up against the wall sooner or later anyway, so the earlier the better,' he said. The interrogators were enraged and beat and cursed him, however the partisan felt that a shadow of respect for him was hidden under this hate. The local Soviet militia and NKVD officers in the town of Olandija were worse – just as soon as they caught him they beat him brutally with sticks and ropes. Afterwards, refusing to say anything, they took him near the lake, near the wall of the manor estate storehouse, referred to as the Murmuring Wall by the people of the estate, and ordered him to dig a hole. Having finished digging, Martynas leaned against the wall, closed his eyes and heard the wall making sounds. It didn't speak, it murmured and it emitted a vague but pleasant vibration that was reassuring and compassionate, which reached his tired, pain-inflicted consciousness, and Martynas smiled for the first time since his captivity began. They placed him next to the hole he himself had dug and pointed their rifles at his chest. But Martynas did not feel afraid, just an unbounded longing, an all-absorbing, all-embracing emptiness near his heart, an emptiness that, it seemed, should swallow him for all eternity. But suddenly that flow of all-encompassing emptiness crashed into something, perhaps the wall, the Murmuring Wall. The NKVD officers threatened him but did not shoot, and they took Martynas to Vilnius.

Once a day he was taken out for ten minutes to walk around. He was taken through three iron gates; at each of them he would have to stop, wait until they unlocked it and then wait until they locked it again. Since all the buttons of his clothing were cut off, Martynas walked through the yard holding his trousers up with both hands. A few other prisoners from neighbouring cells were taken out to walk, and the sight was rather comical: grown men walking like children with their trousers falling down. Martynas would have perhaps smiled, entertained by such a sight, but his split lip was very painful and abscesses had formed on his right cheek from lying on the cold cell floor. He had spent a few years underground in various bunkers and in damp hiding places, sleeping right on the ground, covering himself with pine branches or digging himself into the snow. But he had never complained about his health and there had never been anything like this. Freedom worked like medicine; in captivity the organism lost its immunity. Martynas decided that he needed to pay little attention to bodily things because now he did not need his body anymore. Everything had fallen to pieces and now it was death or Siberia that awaited him. He became so indifferent toward his body that the weekly mocking by the guards didn't even concern him anymore. A thorough search took place every week: the prisoners were told to undress and ordered to open their mouths wide, crouch and then pull their buttocks apart to show that haven't hidden anything. Afterwards they would go through your meagre belongings and if they found something suspicious they would take apart even your last stitch of clothing right down to the seam.

One day everything ended very quickly. A guard took him to a small room with two windows with no bars. A table covered with red material stood in the middle of the room with three people sitting at it. Martynas, almost unable to hear with one ear, most likely due to an eardrum rupture while being beaten, calmly listened to the sentence: twenty-five years in a camp and ten years of exile. He stood, almost not hearing the list of charges. He was sure that this disgustingly red cloth was dipped in the blood of his murdered brothers-in-arms and all those Lithuanian citizens who were tortured, beaten to death or exiled to Siberia. He had seen a lot of blood, enough to paint all the Communist flags and all the tablecloths. There would still be enough left over for the Pioneer's ties.

It was all just smoke and mirrors – now they would take him to a storeroom, put a bullet to the back of the head and it would all be finished. Funny, but he didn't feel fear – just a barely tolerable heaviness in his legs and stomach. It would be embarrassing if he couldn't walk and the NKVD officers would have to carry him like a calf to the slaughter.

'Do you want to say anything?' asked a short man with round glasses and a narrow moustache under his nose, who was sitting to the side.

'I fought for my homeland, and now you are sentencing me for betraying my homeland. Doesn't that seem ridiculous to you?'

Martynas asked.

'Take him away,' came the terse order.

Siberia greeted him coldly. On one stop along the way over the Vologda, Martynas, standing near the cattle car's window criss-crossed with barbed wire, saw a strange spectacle: a sleigh on a road blanketed with snow full of unhewn logs that was being pulled by a short-legged one-horned cow. It was the first time in his life that he had seen a harnessed cow. The beast stamped on the snow, turning his head to the side, and it seemed that the cow was suffering unspeakable pain while the driver, a stocky, broad-faced Russian woman, occasionally slapped the animal on its sunken sides and hollered, 'Hey, hey!' Finally the tired cow stopped and slowly kneeled down on its front legs before its behind collapsed into the snow bank. Its eyes bulged, and thick, white steam gushed out of its nostrils. The cow was similar to a locomotive that had stopped and did not plan on moving anymore. It was as if something had gone awry in the mechanism and had been irrevocably damaged. The water or coal reserves were used up, like the will to live. The train moved forward but Martynas remained standing near the little window, still looking at the fallen cow that didn't want to suffer anymore in the endless Siberian expanses that were quickly becoming dark.

The train would stop constantly as living and breathing cargo would be unloaded. Lined up in ragged ranks and marched to a transit point, from which later, a day or even many days later, they would travel to a camp where lice, hunger, unbearably hard work and an emotionless, lonely death awaited them. As the train made its frequent stops, to those sitting in the sealed cattle cars who had not been called from the list, it seemed that all of Siberia was one enormous concentration camp, full of stops all bearing the same name – Death. The backbone of the railway line, travelling through the eternal frozen ground and the roads stretching from it, the legs of the journey where one had to walk to other camps – it was the skeleton of the merciless Lord of Death.

***

The Lord of the Dead will cut off my head, tear out my heart, rip out my guts, lick my brain, drink my blood, devour my flesh, gnaw on my bones, but I won't die. I can't die, because it's not right, it can't be like this, it can't all end like this. I have to return so I can look them in the eye. Who are they? My wife and sons are already in the ground; all my friends are in the ground. The communists, collaborators, betrayers – it wasn't worth looking into their despicable eyes.

***

The deportees were bathed in a shabby barracks with the wind blowing in, their heads were smeared with a smelly liquid soap using the end of a narrow strip of wood. Some men were given wooden buckets filled with barely lukewarm water and ordered to wash themselves quickly because others were waiting. Martynas shivered from the cold, but the image of a hot day arose in his memory: there were six naked partisan bodies lying behind the headquarters of the local Soviet militia in the town of Olandija. Among them were two women, their stomachs bloated from the heat, bulging out like repulsive stones at the edge of a field. A militia officer came out of the headquarters and stood and urinated on the corpse closest to him. Afterwards he said something to his associates inside and started to jump on the bloated intestines of the corpses.

The column herded from the sauna was met by a sledge in which lay barely covered bodies. The sledge turned through the gate and stopped, having driven just a few metres. The bodies were buried right there, behind the fence. A guard who had accompanied the sledge stabbed each body with a bayonet, and once again searched their shabby clothing – some corpses were almost naked – before two sickly looking men threw them into a shallow pit and buried them with a mixture of earth and snow. The new arrivals, arranged in rows opposite one of the three barracks, waiting to be called, watched this burial ritual.

When the sledge with the guard and two gravediggers crept past them, one of the exiles whispered: 'There won't be hide nor hair left of us.' Suddenly a sound could be heard amid the silence: at first something resembling chuckling, later turning into laughter. The man was laughing so heartily that he was quickly joined by several others standing next to him. And the angrier the guards became as they tried to calm them down, the louder they laughed. They laughed even though they didn't want to laugh anymore, as if laughing for the last time.

Martynas wasn't afraid to go down the mineshaft – he had after all lived underground on and off for a few years: in bunkers in the forest, in hiding places under gardens, in the houses of farmers.

Martynas spoke to his neighbour on his plank bed after hard work in the mines: 'It's all the same everywhere underground – darkness, dampness, a lack of air. But there, in Lithuania, the smell is different underground. Familiar, rich, full of life... But here, there's methane, a spark and you will explode like in the eighteenth mineshaft... They say that two of ours were burned horribly, a Pole and a Tatar... I wanted to live, I believed that we would win, that an American would come to help us. Maybe he will still come, though nobody believes it anymore... I don't know, I don't believe it anymore... And Student didn't believe it. Nobody believed it...'

His neighbour, an elderly airman named Peter Žemaitis, didn't say anything to him at that moment, maybe just because he didn't have the strength. Žemaitis didn't mine coal underground. He pulled the ropes used to erect the columns that supported the mineshaft ceilings. The work was easier, but wet clothes, hunger and fatigue turned any work into hellish suffering.

When they would finally come up from the 400-metre depths to the surface, a cold that was just as unpleasant was there to meet them. Wet clothes hardened, froze to the bone in an instant, becoming sharp and rattling like tin, so that it was hard to take a step.

'Good lord,' Žemaitis would say. 'It's the 20th century, technological progress, planes and radios, and it's like we're in the Stone Age with clothes made out of stone.'

A month later Žemaitis was run over by a coal wagon. Martynas guessed that it wasn't an unlucky accident: Žemaitis was praying and crying hard the night before it happened.

After his death, laying next to the empty bed of his friend, Martynas tried to pray for his unlucky soul, however he was unable to do so. He tried to remember something nice about Peter Žemaitis, but his head was empty. Neither sympathy, nor compassion. The wagon was almost the same as a grenade, Martynas thought. He died honourably, but what remained of Žemaitis, from a person who had once been a soldier, the head of the family, a father of three? Nothing, just a little mound of snow. The only thing that Martynas' fading conscious was able to recall was how Žemaitis would remove the outer bark from the trunk and eat the white and relatively soft layer underneath. Cheesecake, he would say. A wooden cheesecake, that's all that remains of a person.

Martynas was also quickly moved to the surface to work. One day a layer of coal toppled onto him, and if it weren't for the German POW Ott Bartel, Martynas would never have seen the light of day again. He broke a few ribs and a shinbone, and suffered concussion.

After recovering a little in a local hospital, where the only medicine was ointment for scabs, he was given a job in the carpentry workshop. The work was easier, but it was accompanied by unceasing and excruciating hunger and cold. It wasn't the lack of medicine that killed people off in the hospital, but the starvation. A thick broth with a big piece of bread would have made a number of people rise from their deathbed.

There were forty-three mineshafts in the coal mines of Vorkuta, and there was also a chalk and cement factory, a cattle farm with a hide-processing workshop and a soap workshop.

Summer lasted one month in Vorkuta. Nature managed to do in one month what it takes at least half a year to do in Lithuania: the buds built up, blossomed and then the fruit ripened. The summer was short, like the life of a deportee, as farmer Zibolis liked to joke. He was very ingenious: seeing that the Germans, who were even more ingenious, would buy sweaters, he himself started to buy torn clothes from his co-workers that didn't suit anyone anymore. He would mend, wash and sell them to the Germans from the Privolzhsky district.

Later Zibolis discovered a clever scheme for providing rabbit meat to the deportees. At one point he didn't go to work anymore. He was barely alive and would stay in the barracks, washing the floor and feeding coal into the stove made from two metal containers. One day after returning from work, a few of Zibolis' closest neighbours – you couldn't call them friends, because there were no friends there, just neighbours – had an unexpected surprise waiting for them. The meat that he gave them to try was not salted or sweet, but very soft. 'Siberian rabbit,' Zibolis said proudly and laughed. 'Siberian rabbit,' the deportees repeated. They ate, laughed and chewed with mouths that were not used to such delicacies anymore. Later a few of them threw up, but not because their stomachs weren't used to food all of a sudden. It's possible for people to forget how to walk, but not to eat. Zibolis told us how he had hunted those rabbits.

Left alone to wash the barrack floor, he noticed that a number of rats would come up through the holes in the floor when it was quiet in the barracks. They ran around in groups from one bed to another, smelling the shabby rags thrown on the plank beds, and constantly chewing on something. Zibolis collected gum from the prisoners, made a sling, and the rabbit hunt began. Those that threw up were recent arrivals, and though they already knew what hunger was, their imagination still worked according to old habits. There were no habits that were important anymore for experienced prisoners, except for one – to eat something.

The carpentry workshop was situated near the soap workshop. Martynas would go there because women worked there. He wanted to look at them. Women reminded him of home and what he had lost: something very human, fragile and miraculous. He longed for the experiences of two people while they are silent or doing some sort of simple, everyday work. Perhaps he also longed for love or was moved by a memory of sexual attraction. It was just a memory, because the attraction itself wasn't there. When you walk, constantly hungry and starved, when you lose half your weight – Martynas, who earlier had weighed more than 170 pounds now weighed about

100 pounds at the best of times – sex becomes merely an exotic, rare memory that means little.

He would come and look at the women like they were moving pictures. Life would become more comfortable and warmer, as though some sort of meaning appeared for life that had been extinguished by being in the camp.

He met Casper on precisely such a day, having come to the soap workshop, the only venue where he could feed his aesthetic hunger for humanity – to watch how the women walked around the big metal vats, using long pokers to mix the bubbling, horribly smelling mass, which was used afterwards in making cheap soap that didn't lather.

'Well, you want one of them?' asked the one-eyed man, who looked like an old pirate with an eye-patch as he approached Martynas.

'If you'd spread her on bread,' Martynas replied.

Casper was one of the first deportees taken in 1941.

'I haven't spoken Lithuanian for a long time,' said Casper when they met once again in a dilapidated shed near the carpentry workshop that was used for storing firewood and other kinds of junk. It was possible to stop briefly there and take a break from the work and despicable supervisors.

'No one is left from our group, no one,' Casper said, shaking his head sadly. 'They took us from Kaunas. I was a simple teacher, I didn't wish any harm to anyone, I didn't speak badly about the Soviet government, but it seems that somebody denounced me, and in the middle of June 1941 they knocked on our door in the night, perhaps in the early morning, I don't remember anymore... Sometimes it seems like I don't remember Lithuanian anymore. I think about some object, for example, a tool of some sort, that got left behind in the house. I had a lot of tools – I liked to work with wood and I would make furniture myself. I want to remember what things are called, but I can't. Tears well up, my hands shake, I can't and that's it... They took us to the Šančiai neighbourhood, and there were a lot of people there, very long lines of wagons stood there, two trains right next to each other. I was carrying the children in my arms, I couldn't hold onto our baggage any longer, they only let us take one hundred kilograms. I don't know what we took there, I don't remember – warm clothes and pictures. The NKVD officer shouted that it was too much, that it was all going to go missing anyway. Then he started to divide up our things with the soldiers right there and then. When I went to the wagon, a soldier ordered me to take my suitcase, leave the children and go with him. I said, 'Shoot me here, I'm not leaving my family.' They shoved us into a wagon in the middle of the train. It was raining outside, we were all wet, the children were crying, it was hot in the wagon and it was damp from the wet clothes. We laid down on the bunk planks. You couldn't see anything in the darkness – no window, no ventilation, while the biggest problem was with the toilet. No one let you get off, you had to do everything in the wagon. A hole, a small one, the size of a child's fist, had been made in a wall of the wagon to pee. A little trough was fixed there. That tray was more than half a metre high from the wagon floor. For us men, obviously it was still all right, but the women and children couldn't reach it. The piss ran on the floor and seeped through badly joined planks. When the time came for bigger business, people covered the ground with a rag or paper so they could throw the shit out, but the hole was small – only a kitten's head could get through such a hole. We had to push the excrement through with our fingers. before wiping off our shit-covered fingers on the sides of the bed, the walls, whatever. Nobody gave us water to wash or drink. As we were travelling the sun started beating down and the tin-wagon roof got hot. People fainted from the heat and thirst. They pounded on the walls of the wagon when the train stopped. The NKVD officers would answer that they would shoot us right there, because there could be no mercy for counter-revolutionaries and enemies of the people. Women died, two while giving birth, and a sick child died. But they were just the first victims, those who reached the end point of the journey. I remember that we were on a large Siberian river, I don't remember which one, I don't remember anymore. We were happy that we got fresh air, but most started to get diarrhoea from the fresh air and a number of those who arrived went on to the grave, children and the elderly were the first to succumb; the others were put to work. There weren't any mines where we were taken so we were made to cut down trees for our own firewood. We were constantly on the point of starving. You right now, you're living like royalty. But we were told, bullets were needed for the front, which was why we weren't shot and that we had been sent here to perish. Then they transferred me to railroad construction. I don't know why I stayed alive. Only about seventy of us of the few thousand men survived, and why I should be living when my wife and two children are all in the ground... They put them into the Siberian soil, and they'll put me there too. Maybe that's how God mocks man. I begged like Job for the One on High to send me to death, but still he took my children and wife and he left me to live on purpose so I would understand my pain even more, so that suffering would sting me even more, and as if that wasn't enough, I ended up in a camp where there were more criminal prisoners than political prisoners. And God, he thought up yet one more humiliation: the criminals, the biggest thieves, pederasts and murderers of Russia played cards with me as the thing they used to bet, and the one who lost dug out my eye and gave it to his buddy as a debt. If God were looking, if he had eyes, he should have let me die, but I stayed alive. People ask me what I'm here for. I don't know, that's what God wanted, I say. They made up a case for me, that I had supposedly betrayed my homeland. How could I have betrayed it sitting in a camp? How, when I am living with Siberian bears, wolves and the dead who they stuck in the ground like potatoes in spring – how could I betray my homeland? I was lying in hospitals for a long time and still I lived. Now I think, well all right, I will intentionally not die, I'll return alive to Lithuania. I'll go through the villages and towns and tell everyone, let them put me in prison, or send me back to Komi, Yakutia, the Altai Territory. But I will return again, like an eternal Jew. I will once again go through the towns and villages and tell everyone the truth: that the Russians are worse than the Germans, that the Germans thought up concentration camps only during the war years, but that the Russians had established them ages ago after their god-awful Communist Revolution in 1917, and no one destroyed people so horribly as the Russians – and it wasn't just the Lithuanians or the Latvians. They destroyed their own: millions, millions…'

Casper fell silent, looked at Martynas, smacking his dried-out lips, swallowed, with difficulty, the saliva that had collected in his mouth. 'What can you say,' he asked with a heavy voice ringing like a cracked dish.

'Maybe you have something to eat?' asked Martynas, who had not said a word.

One day Casper pulled out a carefully folded scrap of newspaper. The ends of the folded squares were worn away from the endless rubbing in his pocket. He quietly unfolded the scrap in front of Martynas. It was a fuzzy photo – Martynas barely recognised Casper, waving a pickaxe. Next to him were a few prisoners with shovels, and below a caption in Russian said: 'Our wonderful Komsomol youth are laying the Siberian railroad.' All newspapers that ended up in the camp were read down to the last detail, and then smoked just as eagerly down to the last scrap. Casper was very proud of this preserved shred of newspaper. He would only show it to trustworthy people and only on some special occasion. It was like his family album, a thin thread tying him with that other world of freedom and people, left for a long time on the other side of the barbed wire fence. That scrap of newspaper, though it was absurdly false, was for him a proof of his existence.

'We're not the ones that have been deported,' Casper would say. 'It's the world that's been taken from us. It's closed, fenced, hidden, though it's right here. We don't see it.'

It was then that Casper invited Martynas to come to the soap factory after work. It was spring and nature, though not very noticeably, was already stretching itself under the snow. The earth was flexing its frozen ice muscles and was getting ready for a short life cycle in summer. It was dark on the premises when Martynas met Casper and a young Ukrainian named Mykola Netrebych, with whom Martynas helped Casper make furniture. The manager would say with a vulgar smile that the furniture was travelling straight to Moscow, but that such counter-revolutionaries as Casper and Martynas were not good enough to make furniture for the capital of this grand state.

Casper's voice could be heard in the dark: 'No, here.' Turning in the direction of the voice, the men saw Casper sitting near a barely glowing stove. He stood up, waved to Martynas and Mykola, brought them near the low tables used for skinning cattle, and pulled out a metal tub from under one, with large pieces of meat swimming inside.

'Our steaks!' Casper said with a voice suppressing his euphoria. Earlier, Protasov had worked here; he was once an accountant for some company and had got ten years for fraud. He had recently fallen ill and died. Now his spot had been taken by Casper, the one-eyed devil, as the exiles called him.

The premises quickly filled with the smell of roasting meat. All three men sat with their eyes glued to the stove, their jaws moved slowly, as if they were already chewing on their steaks.

'What do you think, is it beef or horse meat?' Martynas asked, wiping his greasy lips and reaching for another piece of meat.

'Elephant,' Casper said. All of them laughed.

Having finished eating, the men decided that they should quietly roast another piece for later. Casper went to the table, the sound of the metal tub being pulled on the floor could be heard, the dripping of liquid, a loud curse word, and then silence.

'Casper?' whispered Mykola, a man with golden hands and a beautiful voice from the western part of Ukraine. 'Casper, did you fall asleep?'

Martynas together with Mykola chuckled in unison, but the next moment they were speechless; a naked, white arm of a person popped out of the darkness, held by a dark and calloused hand.

The men sat in the dark in silence. Afterwards, Casper got up and, saying nothing, started walking toward the door. He turned back when he reached it and with a strange, hoarse voice yelled, 'Not a word to anyone!' and left.

Martynas couldn't eat for almost three days. Each time, right when he put something in his mouth, it seemed to him as if the piece came alive and was struggling to get out of his mouth. A few years earlier he had worked at the local morgue. The corpses were frozen with their limbs akimbo; the faces of some of them had been chewed on by rats along with the lips, noses and sometimes the genitals. I never thought that I would become a rat, Martynas thought, and this idea was almost worse than the constant hunger and lack of sleep. He was already unafraid of death – as a partisan he saw the deaths of many close friends and relatives. He saw corpses dumped in the town square and the bodies of friends dying from their wounds. But that was a different kind of death. Watching through the barbed wire fence how a worn-out horse pulled a wagon with dead souls, like a wagon filled with logs, he didn't feel the fear of death. It was something else – the desecration of life. Before burying the corpses, a guard would stab their chest with a bayonet one more time so they wouldn't bury them alive – so a person wouldn't escape to that other world alive. That was the essence of death camps. That's how it was when they just got here, that's how it continued, endlessly. Nothing had changed. But a thought struck Martynas: it had changed; I'm not a person anymore, I'm a rat.

Living standards did get better, though only slightly. More food appeared as well as tolerable sanitary conditions, more time and more desires and dreams.

As summer ended, Martynas ended up in a punishment cell.

Aldona didn't say anything when Martynas came inside. She suddenly stood and began to undress. She threw off her prison clothes and was soon totally naked: her breasts, which earlier had been full, were now sagging, and only by straining your imagination could one recreate their former beauty and see more than the skin and bones.

'Do you want me like this?' the woman smiled.

They had gotten to know each other a few months earlier. Martynas would come and watch her work in the glue factory. He would bring her a tasty morsel. Last week he secretly gave her a flower. Afterwards he wrote her a letter: 'You are a devilishly beautiful woman. Like bread.' He received a reply the next day: 'And you are devilishly brazen – like salt.'

Saying nothing, Martynas also quickly threw off his clothes. His body appeared even uglier – his arms and legs were even thinner, his muscles like rags wrapped around his bones.

'And you want me – like this?'

They both received three days in the punishment cell.

She smelled of sweat, unwashed clothes, bad soap and something else – of what exactly it's hard to say – that special womanly smell that each one has but is different with every woman, putting off some men and casting spells on others. Martynas licked her neck, shoulder, nipple… He didn't remember anymore when he had last been with a woman; perhaps it was ten or fifteen years ago.

'I was still a child fifteen years ago,' she said.

'It was so long ago,' he said, 'that I've forgotten things.'

'You can't forget it,' she smiled. 'It's the same as eating. Let me help you.'

She touched him, just barely, softly, but at the same time demandingly, and Martynas was surprised that he was still a man. Goodness, he thought, her hands are miraculous, and Martynas put his heavy hand on her stomach, spread his fingers apart and pointed his middle finger down. At first it seemed that he and his fingers were not the same at all, as if his hand did not belong to him. The white hand of a person flickered in his conscious for a second. It was the one that Casper had held onto like a torch. He grunted: 'I am a cannibal, I will eat you.' He bit the woman's nipple and he sensed that very gradually, but more and more surely, blood was pouring into the valley of her pelvis. He read it like a blind person with his fingers, felt that Aldona understood this as well. While he carefully looked her in the eyes, they narrowed and looked at him from up close and from far away, from the depths. He had not seen anything more beautiful than those narrowed eyes for ten years, nothing more beautiful and more attractive. They made love slowly, so slowly that Martynas even cried. His tears ran down Aldona's face. It seemed that she was crying.

'I said that you were brazen as salt...'

The supervisor found them asleep, half-naked. It might have been that someone had snitched on them.

When Martynas got out of the punishment cell he found out that Casper had died. A prisoner, a thief and murderer from Leningrad with the nickname Krasavchik, pulled out the scrap of newspaper with the picture from Casper's pocket without him noticing, ripped it up and rolled a cigarette in full view of a horrified Casper. Casper didn't talk for a couple of days, then said to Mykola the Ukrainian that his life wasn't even worth a scrap of newspaper. He calmly ate lunch and, when everyone lined up in a row for work, he ran and jumped on the barbed wire surrounding the barracks. The guard who shot him received a ten-day vacation for good service, while Casper's body hung for the whole day on the wire because, for pedagogical purposes, the camp's superior didn't let the prisoners take him down.

Aldona was quickly moved up a level to another camp. All that remained for him were a few of her letters on birch bark. 'The evil sorcerer turned us into rats, but the light of freedom will turn us into people again,' she wrote in her last letter. 'It's easy to die, but to survive in such conditions is true heroism. We have to bear witness. Don't in any way give up, just survive.' Martynas would sometimes take out her letter and feel that her words had miraculous powers. Perhaps because they were written by the hand of a beautiful woman, a woman whose taste he would remember for his whole life.

After the Arctic blizzard ended, he stood leaning up against a wooden wall of the barrack, while opposite him, like on a huge film screen, tongues of light that were greenish, yellowish, bluish and a host of other colours and hues all mixed together. There had been so many events during the last years, so much news. Stalin, who was supposed to live forever, had died, Beria had been shot, a riot that arose in the camp was suppressed, conditions improved, hope had even appeared that he just might someday return to his homeland. However it all seemed distant, as if it was just next to him, as if it wasn't attached to him.

Martynas stood near the wooden wall and felt like he was one of the logs from the wall – unfeeling, heartless, unable to be happy, or cry. He looked at the sky, which was unbelievably beautiful, grand like some medieval painting or immortal poem by Dante. Who was this beauty for, that divine light above such a horrible place, above factories of death, above camps where everything dies, even hope? It seemed that God himself, confused, was rummaging through the nooks and crannies of the sky with a huge projector looking for the reason why he created his world if he himself allowed it to become a place for horrible suffering and jeering, the triumph of death. What was God looking for, what could it be, Martynas thought – perhaps a wooden cheesecake? Casper's picture? Aldona, from whom he never got even one letter? An angel with a bag full of presents or the promise of eternal life for those who went through such suffering, the kind even Dante hadn't thought up? Light was all that was left, the northern lights that shone painfully above the everyday hell of people not wanting to say anything, just to shine and that's it.

Translated by Jayde Will from Sigitas Parulskis, *Murmanti siena*, Vilnius: *Baltų lankų leidyba* (2008).

Sigitas Parulskis (born 1965) is one of his generation's most important poets as well as a dramatist, prose writer, essayist and literary translator. His poetry was awarded the highest prize in Lithuanian culture – the National Prize. He developed a cult following with his novel *Three Seconds of Heaven* (*Trys sekundės dangaus*, 2002), which was based on the author's own experience as a paratrooper in the Soviet army. His monumental novel *The Murmuring Wall* (*Murmanti siena*, 2008) is an original, dramatic metaphor for 20th century Lithuania. He is one of the most translated Lithuanian authors.

You Could Forgive Me

Jaroslavas Melnikas

He crawled through the window while we were sleeping and he wanted to rob us, or maybe even kill us all. It's why I didn't really understand very well what I was doing, shooting at him with a revolver and aiming for his head. He, of course, was a scumbag, a criminal. But to see the death throes of the person you killed in your bedroom, well, it isn't very nice either. And it was like he deliberately lay there dying for a whole half hour, gurgling and crying, all bloody and foaming at the mouth. My wife's eyes were as big as saucers, her face turning green, sweating and shrieking (she couldn't shout anymore). The children, standing in the doorway, were red from their ear-piercing screaming, which usually accompanies an endless fright.

I ran out into the yard in just my underwear because otherwise I would have lost it. My body hit the eighth degree of irritation of my nervous system, or something along those lines. Of all the windows, why the hell did he have to crawl into mine?

So, the ambulance, together with the police, took him away. Now I was supposed to go back to my good life, wife and kids. We threw out the carpet with the huge bloodstain – to hell with it. But something's not quite right. At night I lie down in bed next to my wife, but she moves away from me. 'I don't understand,' I say. And I move closer. And again she unconsciously pushes me away. 'Luba, what's with you?' And again I move closer. And at this point she's almost in hysterics, whispering unintelligibly, as though to herself: 'Murderer...' Honest to God, I'm dumbfounded. 'Get up,' I say. 'I don't understand.' And she's afraid of me. 'I don't understand,' I say. 'What, would you have preferred it if he had robbed us, killed us?'

'Maybe he wouldn't have killed us,' she says. 'Just robbed us.' What a fool. 'Maybe,' she says, 'he would have taken something and left. But now...'

'Now what?' I ask, barely able to control myself. 'But now he's gone,' and then comes the shouting and screaming.

Good God. These are the facts. So, I killed a man. I am a scumbag killer. 'Vitek, I understand,' she says, shuddering from the crying, 'you defended us. But why in the head?'

'I don't understand!' I shout.

And she says: 'When I remember how he lay there dying, poor thing... right here. Dying and crying. Oh, I can't...!' And she starts wailing. I see the kids in the doorway, looking and once again shaking from terror.

'Out! Go to sleep!' No, I... What, am I suppose to go and kill myself? It's not possible to live like this anymore.

So I went to his home. I went there on purpose to see just how much of a scoundrel I really am. As if on purpose, his elderly mother looked like my mother: she sat there and did not cry. She just held his dead hands. It was horrible. And then there were his children: a boy and a girl, who were now orphans. The girl, the younger one, was crying, while the boy stood with a look on his face that I will remember to the day I die. Suddenly the girl spoke through her tears: 'Daddy, my dearest.' And two teardrops fell on daddy's forehead. 'Dad-dy, get up. Daddy.' She clearly loved him. The little girl with the puffy little red nose, still just a baby.

I left, holding myself up against a nearby wall. What was this? I didn't understand. Who am I? What was I supposed to do in that moment? Now that he's lying there, he's so innocent, an angel, a son, a dad. God's creation. But then, when he crawled through the window wearing his mask, he was simply a criminal, a scumbag thief who I put a bullet in – a worm who had the gall to interfere in a stranger's peaceful life. And I suddenly had the desire to eliminate a few more of those vermin in my bedroom, so that the children of those sons of bitches would cry their eyes out, asking their dad to get up out of the coffin.

I sat down on a bench at a playground near their home. Good God, what had I done wrong? What? I was living my life, not harming even a fly, when he crawled into my home and my life. And now he's not here anymore. What did I do wrong? Why was I suffering so much?

When I talked to myself like this it seemed to me that I was thoroughly in the right. But then I remembered the little girl, that little voice of hers: 'Dad, daddy, get up, please.' Oh, I can't do this anymore. I am a scumbag. Luba's right. Yes, a scumbag. Sure, maybe I had saved Luba and my children from being killed, but I was still a scumbag. And Luba was afraid to touch me. And yes, now I can walk with my head held up high. There aren't many who have killed a man, who have ended a life. But I have.

And now, overcome with horror, I understood that I could never wash away this stain. I'm a killer. I will die like that, like a killer, with sin weighing down on my soul. A sin? I stopped right there. What the hell – a sin? What did I do wrong? So I sat on that little bench near their home until they carried him out – that son, father and criminal. Just now I heard real shrieking: the mother started wailing and I almost went crazy from her pain. 'Son, son!' It was just impossible to listen. That poor woman, she could hardly move her legs. She had given birth to him, raised him. I sit and cry a river of tears. I didn't understand, I don't understand anything. And then a young man comes up to me. He seems intelligent. He says in a low tone: 'Leave. You had just better leave.' And then he looks me straight in the eyes. But, good God, what is this? Well he's a brother or a relative and recognises my right to defend myself and all that. But he personally blames me, only me. You hear me, guy, you were in the right in your own bedroom but now go, get out of my sight and out of their sight. Don't stand there, you killer.

So what of all this, ultimately? I leave. Like a beaten dog. There's shouting, crying, his kids are screaming – that son of his as well – out of grief. The mother is wailing. God, what had I done? I, I alone.

With this hand right here.

So I calmed down in a café. Now they are putting him in the ground. So, what is there left to do? Did I really understand what I was doing when I grabbed the revolver from the nightstand? He approached with a knife, for God's sake. All right, maybe he wasn't planning to kill me. He most likely just wanted to scare me so I'd lie in bed without resisting while he emptied out our drawers. Then… Now I understood Luba. Goddammit, so in other words, let's just say he would have robbed us and disappeared, it would have been better than what's happening now. So what, we would have taken a hit financially, but everything in our hearts and minds would have remained just like before. And what now?

I went home, but Luba didn't even say a word.

'So, what's wrong now? How can we live like this? Luba, do you hear me? Don't be silent.' And instead of answering she's silent. 'Don't be silent, or I'm going to smack you!' And then she looks at me. 'So, why are you staring at me? Huh? I'm a murderer, right? You see a murderer?'

And then she, incomprehensibly, says with a shaking voice: 'Yes.'

And she runs out of the kitchen and cries alone in the bedroom. So I start breaking the dishes and the furniture. I broke a stool and the table then fell right down onto the floor. And here I cut my hand, the blood's running. What am I supposed to do? Luba began to wail even louder. It was good that the kids were at kindergarten. I was going to go crazy.

'I'm going to kill you!' I say. Suddenly I leap up and Luba, seeing me in the doorway, retreats to the corner, her eyes glazed with terror.

'Don't kill me,' she screams.

So, I think to myself, those are the facts. It's not far to the mad house for me. My nerves are totally frayed. I turned around without saying a word, took out a half-litre bottle from the cupboard and drank from the bottle, right there.

And that was what saved me. I knew that I was acting like the biggest lush in the world, but I put it to my lips and emptied it right to the bottom. And ten minutes later I collapsed to the floor. Of course, it would have been better to take some strong sleeping pills – a triple dose of Tazepam. But we didn't keep anything like that in the house. Ultimately, I needed to relax for a long time because otherwise my nerves would have gone haywire and it wasn't clear how it all would have ended. So I acted correctly in getting drunk.

Luba was still somewhat hysterical all alone in the bedroom (she told me that she had pushed the chest of drawers in front of the door so I couldn't get in, though she knew she was acting the fool – she scared herself deliberately). Afterwards, when everything quietened, she calmed down a little. The foolishness evaporated from her head. She put the chest of drawers back in its place and went into the kitchen to take a look. I was lying all twisted up on a pile of broken furniture. Of course she started to scream, thinking I had killed myself. Afterwards she found the empty bottle and she understood everything. While I was lying there I felt sick a few times. But having lost consciousness, I don't remember anything.

I slept something like thirty hours. I sobered up in the bedroom and even smiled. Somehow my soul felt good.

The sun was in the window. Luba came in. 'So, how are you feeling?' And she came to hug me. Good God. Everything's fine again. I remembered that something horrible had happened, but it was like I saw everything through some sort of filter. In other words, I gained a little perspective. My nerves calmed and my heightened senses subsided as did Luba's. She would have a cuddle with me; it was entirely different now. It seems that she also got some sleep.

A year later and I had forgotten everything. An unpleasant feeling remained, but there were no more recollections of how that man died, crying in our bedroom, and the other family came to terms with it and got used to living without their son and father. That lonely old mother and that girl with the swollen little nose continued to stand there before my eyes, but in time they disappeared as well – especially after the one time when I was walking by and saw that very same mother angrily arguing with a neighbour. I didn't feel anything good and noble towards her then.

Lately for some reason Luba and I have been fighting over petty things. We came into a little money, but it seems we aren't happy. Our eldest, Vova, goes out partying and doesn't come home to sleep. I've noticed that Luba looks at me like I'm not even here. 'Take out the trash,' she says while she is scraping at something in the kitchen. 'The Yelizarov's are flying to Paris this week.' Now she apparently wants to go to Paris. 'Luba,' I say. 'What?' she says annoyed. 'Nothing.' And I take out the trash.

Good God, what a life. What is going on with us? Are we bored with each other or what? The trash. Vova. Paris. Money, and what's more, it seems that I killed a man. Yes, I did. I've got work tomorrow morning. Yawn, I'm getting sleepy. Neither feeling nor meaning. Still, back then, in those horrible days, I lived to the fullest. I cried out of grief with that old woman and I suffered.

In the evening I said 'Luba, do you still remember that incident?'

'What incident?'

'When I killed that person?'

'And what were you supposed to do? Wait until he killed us?'

And she taps her spoon so nervously against her plate, thinking to herself.

'I'm a killer, after all.'

'Stop it, you acted like a proper man.'

It was nice to hear, of course, but then came the comment: 'Fix the sink in the bathroom. How long can you put it off?'

I went to his grave. A horrible longing overcame me. I thought it would get me feeling. I'd remember how he died right before my eyes. Maybe something would tremble in my soul. But I didn't besides the crooked cross and the headstone with 'Pavlov Gennady Konstantinovičius', I didn't see anything. I didn't feel anything. The grass and the remains were under the ground.

I ended your journey, friend. You could forgive me.

Translated by Jayde Will from Jaroslavas Melnikas, *Rojalio kambarys*, Vilnius: Lithuanian Writers' Union Publishers (2004).

Jaroslavas Melnikas (born 1959) was born in Ukraine, studied literature in Lviv and Moscow, and later settled in Lithuania. He has written books of prose, philosophy and criticism. His work is distinguished by his paradoxical way of thinking, his philosophical narrative tone and his humorous renderings of existential situations.

Obituary

Giedra Radvilavičiūtė

I'll begin with some information intended for pretty much everyone. Please turn off your mobile phones for about twenty minutes. It's a mournful evening in the Interpol Kebab Restaurant in the Old Town. If any foreigners are looking for it, they'll find it by the smell.

My dear Ladies and Gentlemen, on this busy Saturday we could certainly pay our last respects to the dearly departed in the usual way with a few well-rehearsed phrases that conform to the sad rules of the obituary and our tired traditions. We would face less gossip and insinuation if we simply said: 'She will always remain in the hearts of those who knew her. From now on we will be united by the gentle sadness of remembering. May her journey be an easy one for her...' Or something like that. But clichés and concrete truths have always irritated me, and her as well. And the saying, 'It is better to speak well about the deceased than to say nothing at all', we find absolutely infuriating. I feel I have the right to remember my best friend more or less as she was. Why? Because of all of us present here, and perhaps in all of Lithuania, I knew her best: all her biographical details, buried in that small village, all her unfulfilled plans for the future. Although I am painfully shy, and my friend was a live wire, we had some things in common. Some people even confused our faces, tastes and opinions when we would appear in public together at book signings, book fairs or literary events.

True, she aged, got fat, went grey and became melancholic quite a bit sooner than I did. She once said that it wasn't the years, but her experience and understanding that were making her grow old. I, too,

211

have noticed that it is always the most infantile, temperamental and optimistic people who remain charming and attractive the longest. If my friend ever lost her earrings, she never bothered to replace them. I, on the other hand, would go out and buy new and fancier ones the very next day, usually from Swarovski. If she ever found that her lipstick was down to the end, she'd be sad that it was almost all used up. Whenever I see the same end, I always think it is just the beginning. My friend would contemplate death – and obituaries – much more often than I would. To this day I have kept in shape and kept my shape. She had dentures for her top teeth put in five years ago whereas I only did this year. The last man she had was a very long time ago (I'm talking about a lover). My boyfriend is here tonight among those gathered to pay their last respects… Thank you, Artūras.

As I've already said, neither of us ever liked the way in which in final farewells, or in election campaigns for that matter, people are suddenly transformed into moral, beautiful (especially in the photographs enlarged hurriedly by undertakers), hospitable beings, almost without sin, who were neither licentious nor alcoholic, but if they did drink irresponsibly it was for a good reason. A year ago, in a small town cemetery, as I was standing by a graveside and listening to the eulogies, I became frightened by the thought that we were probably burying a still-breathing former elementary school teacher, who was 'eternally young, eighty-four-year-old, energetic and hardworking, forever forging ahead with his creative plans'. Perhaps the saying 'he lives forever in our hearts' means precisely that (especially in its most horrifying sense). Perhaps we sugar-coat a medically unsanctioned act intentionally with this euphemism? I am certain that in the accursed rush that generally forms our lives, we do end up burying the occasional body without adequate inquiry into whether the person is really dead. Usually, it's those elderly folk taking an afternoon nap, who seem to have intentionally showered and combed their hair and covered themselves up with a newspaper as people used to with a prayer book in the old days. Do you remember? I think it was Tsvetaeva who requested not to be rushed to burial, asked for someone to put a mirror to her lips and check a few times whether the silver surface wasn't dampened by the fog of life too subtle to be seen with the naked eye. And Gogol turned in his grave – or was it Gogol who was checked and Tsvetaeva who turned? I don't remember now. They're all the same to me.

Our dearly departed, if she really is departed (please allow me, as her closest friend, to think of her as 'missing in action') was neither energetic, nor beautiful, nor good, nor especially hardworking. Besides that, she drank enthusiastically. Every day. Worst of all, it was without any justifiable reason. So don't ask why. I look you all in the eye now and I see, nonetheless, that most of you would be happy to hear the answer to this none-too-difficult question. If she were to appear here in the flesh, she would respond as any alcoholic would in the sincere voice of Jerzy Pilch: 'I drink because I have a weak character. I drink because something in my head is turned upside down. I drink because I am too anaemic and I want to be rejuvenated. I drink because I am nervous and I want to calm my nerves. I drink because I am sad and I want to clear my soul. I drink because I am happily in love. I drink because I am hopelessly looking for love. I drink because I am almost too normal and a little bit of insanity wouldn't hurt.'

It's true that during her last few weeks, the departed drank only swimming-pool water and nettle tea – the latter by the litre. Her cousin, the cybernetic, suggested she use that harsh but nutritious weed to clean out her joints. Diuretics… Dear God, what for? Her job was exclusively intellectual. She did not exercise and she walked like a duck. She rode her bicycle like Molloy… She went to her mother's house again and again. It's true that sometimes, seated in front of the computer screen, she would stiffen up and her daughter would have to massage her for about half an hour to loosen her muscles enough so that she was able to stand. Once every two months that same cousin would come to her house dressed in his black mourning suit to repair her computer's interface with her modem. He wore this suit because he was ready, every time, to bury the computer. Yet when he arrived he would be warm and gentle. He had genetically inherited his gentle demeanour from the May winds. May was the month he was born. It's odd that he is not here with us today. On his way out he would leave, pasted on the monitor, a photograph of a nettle field along the Vilna River, and in the thoughts of the dearly departed he would leave a longing for a healthy consciousness. While having a smoke in the kitchen he would ask her to make some nettle tea, and once, having worked seven hours and perhaps becoming a bit frustrated, he said that my friend's relationship with technology was the same as Goethe's wife's relationship with spiritual values: 'She was respectfully conscious of the huge importance of art to humankind.'

It was probably because of the nettle tea that my friend started having trouble getting to the bathroom in time. This handicap was another thing that she and I had in common. Handicaps, not love, are what tie people most intimately. A friend once told me the story of when she figured out that she really loved her husband. Coming home after a difficult operation, she was being led up the stairs to the third floor by her neighbour; she was bundled up in a winter coat because they had brought her to the hospital in January but released her in February, and she felt confused, didn't know who or where she was. On the second-floor landing she felt sick. She leaned against the wall, and instinctively put her sleeve to her mouth. That was when she saw that her husband was holding out his large construction worker's palms with white plaster crusted into his wrinkles out under her lips – just in case she had to throw up on the stairs... One time last year when I was crossing Žirmūnai Bridge I, too, did not make it to the bathroom in time. You know what I did? I stopped in the café by St. Peter and St. Paul's Church and splashed my jeans until they were soaked so that they would be dark blue throughout, because I still had to stop by the Ministry of Culture. Fortunately, it was raining.

We really were identical, like two halves of a coffee bean. That's why once, a long time ago, she entrusted me and no one else to burn the twenty-five letters that her husband had sent to her in addition to the seventeen that she had never sent out to various men. 'Dust falls to the ground, smoke rises to the heavens.' Of course I never destroyed them because I thought that it might be worth publishing one or two of the letters, because the most popular literature these days is the kind that falls between fact and fiction. The other reason I made this decision was that her husband, a man who had stood patiently by her for a long time, became famous. It's telling that the other seventeen, to whom the letters were never mailed, met unremarkable fates. I took some interest in them: most of them were her contemporaries, pernicious leaders now midway through their fifties who, having achieved their *prostatus quo*, had married women ten or twenty years younger. My friend reacted to this phenomenon positively – she supported adoption, no matter at what age. The divorces in her life were also telling. She got on with (and did not get on with) her children's father like a suddenly awakened nervousness in an ever-vigilant mind, like quicksilver and a thermometer, like *vers libre* and a quatrain poem.

Although we were born in the same town, we met and became friends only during our first year at university. I compare my student days to an intoxicating journey on a cruise ship – few passengers on that ship are still alive today. During my first years in Vilnius, images and events from my hometown would enter my consciousness, usually at night: the cracking wooden banister of my stairway, the overwhelming smell of malt along the riverside, the infestation of green worms. I would recall that disgustingly memorable summer when those worms hung from the stairwells and balconies, crawled on the sidewalks, benches, windowsills and along the spines of books, and crept among carpets of Asian dahlias as if in an odalisque by Ingres. I remember a lonely little goat nibbling grass in the field. From a distance she looked like a rock. Within five years the field had been developed with identical houses. Each of those houses became a home to people who dressed the same, ate the same food and who unlocked their French locks into the same rooms. A scratch on the underside of the hand from tuberculosis turned into a dangerous mark the colour of a sunset, but our lungs remained healthy. I remembered the theatre, to which it was impossible to get tickets. My friend liked to repeat the saying of the cruel but beloved director: the most valuable treasure is the one that's impossible to lose. This would bring to mind the statues in the bank in the city centre: titans who held up the vaulted ceiling so that it would not crash down onto the roubles being counted and recounted below. Those roubles financed the rockets that the Russians launched into the cosmos. The cosmos was like the dome of the glass ceiling of the bank. I would recall the track at the school playing field – shiny, as if it were paved not with cement but with the sweat of teenagers running a hundred metres in ten seconds. Sometimes I will remember a particular event like when a silent, barely noticeable woman who worked in the sugar factory gave birth to a child during her lunch break and shoved it into the toilet. I can't remember if they put her in jail or if she had herself committed by virtue of insanity. But for the next few weeks every time I went to the bathroom I would carefully examine the water in the toilet bowl below, imagining that a slippery baby, like a *kulak*, could swim anywhere through the labyrinths of plumbing, even up to our house.

On our block lived a lady who dressed all in black. She kept a bowl of milk for the cats who came begging on her doorstep. However, the entire neighbourhood knew that every night when she climbed into bed she would step onto a rug made of kitten fur. We would imagine that she had skinned them in the bath in the same way most normal people peeled huge quantities of wild mushrooms in the autumn. On dark evenings, when November turns unnoticeably into December and fallen leaves turn into roughly frozen earth, we would take off at full speed with our sledges right past the black hag. We'd shove her shoulder, gasping out of fear: 'Murderer! Murderer!' and she wouldn't even turn around. Half-blind, she'd focus her milky eyes on the emptiness and wade through the soft snow as if it were short-haired fur. Recounting this now, I feel guilty. What if that rug at the foot of her bed was nothing but an unproven legend? And she herself – what if she were an unhappy, lonely woman, incapable of making friends with her neighbours, whose parents and relatives had all died, for example, in Siberia?

There was one Veronica[1*] – the name is associated with unhappy love stories, not only in literature, but also in real life – who was abandoned by her lover and jumped off a three-storey rooftop, breaking her back and legs. Later she married another man and gave birth to identical twins who resembled her former lover, even though seven years had passed since they'd broken up. Back then I didn't know that with men, the ones with whom you feel a deep – one should say clinical, because it is almost poisonous – attraction of both the body and soul, the relationship can develop in one of two ways: either an all-encompassing but short-lived love with a dependence that is almost identical to hatred, or a long-lived flight from one another that only results in getting increasingly mired in thoughts of each other, like trying to move through sweet syrup, and ultimately all of this turns into nothing.

There was the town cinema with the films like *Mackenna's Gold*, *Phantom,* and *The Spinster*. Those days seem so long ago, like an Annie Girardot heroine's shyness on a rocky shore. In the morning at the beach, the girl would change out of her underwear into a swimsuit under a special long skirt, the gathered waist of which would pull up to her neck. A reporter once asked the actress how she imagined misfortune. Annie answered: 'As a beautiful, young woman dressed in black, crying on a park bench on a sunny day.' I wonder now, how my friend imagined happiness. We can no longer ask her... But she probably would have answered very simply: 'recounting your own life experiences and those of others'; 'swimming in a lake until it freezes over'; 'listening to my daughter's impressions about school'; or 'watching how the cat sticks out his backside as he stretches in the morning'.

Some people thought her recently-acquired affection for that household pet was funny; there are those who would argue that this behaviour testified to a slight indication of dementia. First of all, that cat was not a household, but a greenhouse, creature. It had gooseberry-green eyes, while its tail squeezed between its hind legs

[1*] Veronica was the protagonist of the famous work *Paskenduolė* (*The Drowned Woman*) by Antanas Vienuolis.

like a dog's and its fur electrified into sparks during thunderstorms. My friend became quite offended when, one day in a café, a woman sitting at another table saw the animal in her bag and asked: 'Excuse me, is that a dog or a cat?' My friend responded to the question with a question: 'Excuse me, are you a man or a woman?' Nonetheless, to call that creature an animal is hard for me as well. My friend would visit her mother's grave together with the cat. (This seemed pointless to me – the cat did not know her mother.) Together they'd go shopping at the second-hand clothing stores. The cat would grab onto some drapes or warm children's clothing with its claws, and my friend would buy these for him immediately. At the outdoor market he would effortlessly help my friend choose the best minced meat. My friend believed that he didn't disappear in order to join the all-too-promiscuous alley cats, but that he walked through the mirror. Like Alice.

My friend had brought the mirror from her deceased mother's newly-sold house in her hometown, and wanted to hang it in the bathroom. That was the only place in the apartment where you could have seen yourself at full height. I saw it leaning against the kitchen wall; I fitted into it with my head chopped off. My friend said that she could see history in the mirror. The simple past fitted in that one-dimensional space like a ship built out of matchsticks by an inmate residing inside a narrow-necked bottle, even though from the outside this might appear impossible. During certain hours at dusk, the mirror would decide to reflect not an image of the hall, with its untidy shoes, sack of potatoes, the half-open bathroom door, and jackets and coats hung on hooks, but rather a slice of memory: also a hall, but in another city, fifteen, twenty, or even thirty years ago. In the old apartment, the mirror was hung facing the entrance, reflecting a variety of people entering and departing – now into my friend's kitchen. Usually her mother would appear. She would step through the door into the mirror. She was young, dishevelled, indecently licking an ice cream that she had purchased on the street, or dressed in a flannel robe, and on crutches. It was a month ago that I sensed in that kitchen the strange aroma of turpentine and eucalyptus. My friend thought that it must have been the smell of her mother's arthritis ointment.

Other relatives were also reflected in the mirror. Sometimes her uncle would appear with a stool and a bowl; setting the bowl on top of the stool, he would use a rusty grater to grate farmers' soap into the bowl. He used the soap to wash her newborn daughter's nappies. He would play the saxophone or a game of chess on a special table; sometimes, with tears in his eyes, he would declare checkmate on himself. Although a lost game would not mean the end of her uncle's life, he would immediately remind us that he wanted to be cremated: 'Don't pour my ashes into an urn. I can't stand them. Sprinkle me into a paper bag, blow up the bag, and burst it on Sunday at the outdoor market, as children do.'

My friend's two-year-old daughter would also appear in the mirror. Smiling at the kitchen furniture, the barefoot girl would come so close that it looked as if she were about to step out into the other side; but having come close in her imagination, if she wasn't sick, she would pick her nose and wipe the snot on the mirror. Then, swearing, my friend would clean the mirror from this side with a little rag. Grandmother would re-wind two balls of wool into one, a fatter thread would be made out of two. She'd wind it on paper spools made of the wrinkled-up letters of her dead husband to another woman. The neighbour, who had once had a large two-acre allotment, would appear. She would bring us carrots, cabbage, beetroot and dill. I began to doubt my friend's sanity when she would take those vegetables (from the mirror).

On her kitchen floor there was always parsley, mint, dill and scraps of thread, but I think that these were brought home from the Halė marketplace stuck to her shoes. The neighbour who brought vegetables had a dog. She would take him to the garden as well. The retriever didn't bite, but he barked at every cyclist passing by, every piece of newspaper floating on the wind and every starling pecking the ripe cherries. Some breeds of dog are big, but timid and unthreatening. My friend's cat attacked the neighbour's dog in the mirror and chased him away, thus violating the permissible boundary of healthy fantasy. The mirror broke into five pieces, which slowly, almost as if they were weightless, dispersed and settled in the kitchen's darkness, like metal garden puddles reflecting the herring-coloured sky.

My friend said that after this event, her memory suddenly became weak. I noticed this without her needing to mention anything. Before, she could remember perfectly the Arabic surnames of all the terrorists who so meritoriously contributed to the history of their countries, but now she confused them. She said that the Ministry of Education had finally chosen an adviser who was well acquainted with the literature of the period between the world wars and the last century, namely Alfonsas Nyka-Viliūnas[2*]. Invited to speak about literature at the university, she lamented that the female students, compared to those of our own *Mackenna's Gold* days, were hardened in their ways, they detested post-modernism and were not open to discussion. They were surprised at my friend's attempt to analyse Žemaitė's *The Daughter-in-Law* in a very contemporary and thorough way, as thoroughly as the length of a seminar allows.

'What do you think Katrė's final words "please forgive me" mean?' she once asked the class. Without a doubt, they could not identify with the final, submissive gesture of a rural character oppressed by the family patriarch and unable to come to terms with this. Probably Old Vingis had got Katrė pregnant and when she begs forgiveness from Jonas and Mrs Vingis, instead of being accepted along with her good fortune to be with child (the source of which should not matter to a woman), she is scorned as worthless. During her last weeks, my friend became entirely disillusioned with literature. She would hum the song 'I am so alone, so hellishly alone...' claiming that the forgotten, slightly snobbish twentieth-century Russian writer had a perfect sense of language and solved ingenious linguistic puzzles: '*Ya nikak ne ponimal, kak sovetski veter ochiutilsia v veterinare. Shto delayet slovo tomat v avtomate. I kak*

2*   Here the author/speaker combines two similar sounding names: Alfonsas Nyka-Niliūnas is a well known émigré poet; Giedrius Viliūnas is a contemporary literary scholar.

prevratit zubr v arbuza.'[3*] He had intentionally avoided novelistic narrative, playing a sophisticated game of cat and mouse to taunt readers who understand plot to be simply a sequence of intriguing events.

When – it's no longer relevant how – my friend's cat disappeared, I worried that the kids in her yard, deprived of their daily pleasure of patting its head with the strangely folded ears as it peeked out of her bag, might decide to play some nasty prank on my friend. They might decide to kick a ball through her only remaining cracked window. They might cover the window with the newspaper *Lietuvos Rytas* from the outside at night. They might fill a paper sack with shit and leave it on her doormat. In winter they might race past her on sledges up the hill. Towards the Gates of Dawn… They might grab her by the shoulders, shouting 'murderer, murderer!' and what could she do? Wade through the soft snow as if through that short-haired fur with her dry eyes fixed on the railroad tracks? What's most painful about this is that the disappearance of her pet undoubtedly contributed to the fact that my friend never finished her second book or the essay she was writing. It's true that I can't prove that she was in fact undertaking these particular creative pursuits, but every living person leaves something unfinished when they depart. Sometimes those things are great, sometimes banal and sometimes even obscene. My mother's work colleague's sixty-year-old husband, for example, died with his mistress. To be more precise, he died *on* her. The frightened young woman, before dialling the emergency service, rolled her boyfriend over onto his back, dressed him in his suit, and, completely illogically, put on his shoes. If that wasn't enough, she pressed a book into his hands in order to further neutralise the situation. Stories about this nonetheless tragic event would not have

---

[3*] The wordplay referenced in these sentences (which are Nabokov's) is based on the presence of root words in other, unrelated words in Russian. 'In no way could I understand how the Soviet wind (Rus. *veter*) found itself in the word 'a veterinary surgeon' (Rus. *veterinar*). What the word *tomato* is doing in an *automated* machine (Rus. *avtomat*). And how does a bison (Rus. *zubr*) turn into a melon (Rus. *arbuz*).'

spread as quickly as a good joke if it weren't for the book's title: it was the then popular novel by Hemingway, *A Farewell to Arms.*

And the aforementioned unfinished essay that my friend was writing was supposed to be called 'The Last Time'. You know, my friend used to say to me, there are volumes and volumes written about the mysteries of the first time. We could both recite by heart the McCullough that we'd read in our childhood: 'Bowing, she gently pressed her lips to his wound, her hands slid down his chest towards his shoulders, slowly, intoxicatingly caressing them. Surprised, frightened, trying with all his strength to free himself, he pushed her head away, but somehow she ended up in his embrace once again – like a snake that had ensnared his will and was holding tight. Pain, the church, even God were all forgotten.' We must admit that from a literary angle, the last time has been unjustly neglected.

After all, there are thousands of women who have experienced, contemplated the act even-handedly, without emotions, from… let's say a three-year distance. I can formulate for you precisely, she said, how the last time differs from the first. It's unique, because it is unrepeatable, in the literal meaning of this word. The first, you know, will be repeated, unless of course at the end, as in the famous case in our town, you die. But the last time can only be repeated in memory, dreams and essays. In principle, it's all one and the same – formulas without structure, as the contemporary literary critic Jūratė Sprindytė-Baranova[4*] would say. I know that when she wrote, my friend would recklessly base her work on her own – and sometimes my – experience. Her experience of the last time was with a guy named Vitka – a painter and not the estate agent representing her, as one text has stated. She preferred self-conscious, strong, but painfully sensitive, sexual, even bashful, cement-spattered labourers who ate canned fish imported from Asia with a spoon and cursed expressively. Vitka was so self-conscious that he scraped and planed the corridor walls until he'd removed half of the wall. 'I'll finish

[4*]   The speaker/author combines two similar sounding names: Jūratė Sprindytė is a well known literary scholar; Jūratė Baranova is a philosopher and essayist.

tomorrow. My word is solid,' he said to my friend, stepping back two metres from the wall, constantly evaluating his work; but he did not finish for another two weeks. They became intimate in that unheated corridor to the melody of the long, drawn-out meow of the jealous cat.

Her second book, *The Beauty of Death Strikes*, also remains unfinished. This was supposed to be a book of *prêt à porter* funeral wear featuring colour photographs of the highest quality and short descriptions, the text was going to be white on a black background. Clothing created for the final journey was supposed to be affordable for any relatives of the deceased, but the projected coffee-table book was not intended for the average book buyer, because it was to be priced at a hundred and fifty litas, otherwise the cost of the photographs and the models' fees would never have been covered. I saw some of the completed photographs. The models lay inside coffins, dressed in specially created suits. A businessman who had committed suicide. A motorcyclist who'd been killed on the road. An émigré who met his end in Ireland – a man rendered an abstract statistic. A politician. An ordinary guy – a beekeeper. A beautiful woman. A homeless person. A poet. A florist. A child. Each got their own page with a short caption underneath the photograph. Only the New Lithuanians and sexual minorities received two-page spreads.

'Death,' my friend claimed, 'must be public – like sex, chastity, indigestion and shoe inserts that guarantee quality of life. It's no accident that funeral photographs adorn the front pages of all the best newspapers. I saw a shocking television show about a fire, which had destroyed a home in a village. The cameraman was filming the burnt corpse of a baby. People long for images of death and burials. Flipping through such pages, they crave cheese and beer. Their children frolic and shoot at one another. I wouldn't want to fall behind the times with my naïve work and turn into a pitiful anachronism. Why is it that for birthdays, weddings or divorces, even when we go to the theatre, we dress up, never begrudging the price of stylish accessories; yet we allow ourselves to get buried in galoshes and dresses that don't even zip at the back and in a colour that we wouldn't be caught dead in?'

I remember a photo of a dead prostitute in my friend's book. The model lay in a white coffin littered with pink feathers dressed in only a corset and azure stockings attached to garters. The corners of the coffin were stylishly decorated with pleats made from the same material as the stockings. The model's head rested on a stuffed poodle. Her perfect legs and breasts were frivolously covered with several issues of *Stilius (Style)* magazine. In her hand the woman was holding a pink... mobile phone. I expect that the book would have been successful. I also expect that someone will make good use of this barely exploited idea, if not this year then in a few years. Shrouds don't burn.

And now, Ladies and Gentlemen, you can turn your mobile phones back on. I am coming to the end. And during this part of my speech, nobody has the power to stop me. I am hurrying like everybody else. I see how several women are crossing their legs, afraid, like I am, that they will not make it to where they absolutely must go. Besides, I want to buy some grapefruit and wine today. If anyone were to ask why I drink, I would answer like Jerzy Pilch: 'I drink because my character is weak. I drink because something in my head is turned upside down. I drink because I am too anaemic, and I want to be rejuvenated. I drink because I am nervous and I want to calm my nerves. I drink because I am sad and I want to clear my soul.' To conclude, if I really consider myself honest, not wanting to make you too sad, I have to explain who inspired this talk. One of my many close friends – among whom I consider all of you, especially those who came here by accident – is always asking: 'Why aren't you writing anything anymore?' I answer very directly: 'Because the narrator in me has died. Or perhaps it would be more convenient to say that she has gone missing in action.'

Although I am extremely shy and she was a real live wire, we had some things in common. Some people, usually at public events like bookfairs or book signings, when we would appear together – more precisely, we would meld into one – would confuse our faces, tastes, and opinions. It's true, we were born in the same town. The same day, the same hour, during the same snowstorm. However, we became friends at university – we met during our first year. Because that was exactly when I started to write. Until then, if I still remember correctly, I was staring out the window at a little goat, which from a distance looked like a rock.

In a few years the field at the edge of town was developed with identical houses. Each one of those houses soon became home to people who dressed the same, liked the same food, and who opened their French locks into the very same rooms. Nobody would even have suspected that one sunny June morning one of the many Veronicas – and all love stories about women named Veronica are sad, both in literature and in real life – abandoned by her lover, would have the courage to jump from a three-storey house. She would jump and soar all the while holding, as I recall it, pressed against her armpit, not crutches, but two little boys. Her twin sons, like two drops of water, resembled her past lover even though thirty-five years had passed since their break up... The woman in black, whose relatives all died of starvation in Siberia, is buried in the cemetery on the outskirts of town. I found her abandoned grave by accident in late autumn when I was attending someone else's funeral – a former elementary school teacher. November was turning into December and the leaves were frozen. The aster blossoms on the square patch of black soil had turned brown and the ordinary stone monument, built by the unknown good Samaritan, resembled the arched back of a cat. It was located in the shameful section of the cemetery devoted to suicides; the monument leaned to one side, nearly touching the cemetery fence, and was crafted out of field stones stuck together with veins of cement... The sugar factory worker, she flushed her baby down the toilet and spent seven years in jail. She never married. She moved to Vilnius. I always buy grapefruit at her kiosk, which is called 'Marlen', but I don't know why. It's not even on my way home; it's right next to the former railroad-workers' hospital. The woman, who I still easily recognise, puts on green fuzzy fingerless gloves at the beginning of winter so that her fingers are bare and able to move unhindered. I watch as, somewhat agitated but always polite, she weighs my heavy golden-coloured fruit; she places the grapefruit carefully into the open plastic bag, as if afraid of harming the babies' heads.

Sometimes I tire of reworking other people's fates. Your relationship with a text is similar to your relationship with a man you love with whom you connect deeply, body and soul. (One should really say clinically, because it verges on poisonous.) Thinking about sentences, punctuation and words, you connect with them as with a blind and impossible to remedy, yet brief, love affair. The dependence is quite similar to hatred. Later, you distance yourself from the text, sinking into it in your thoughts as if into sweet syrup, until in the end it turns into nothing. Recently I have been occupied with something else. A very secret thing. Just like a particular, somewhat snobbish, twentieth-century Russian writer, I decipher linguistic puzzles. He would intentionally distance himself from his narrative with sophisticated games of cat and mouse in order to taunt his more stupid readers, who understood plot as a sequence of events. I imagine him comfortably seated in a mismatched chair, wearing a silk robe and a nightcap made of butterfly netting. Between his porcelain teeth, which he had put in during the years that he spent in America, there would be an ever-smouldering cigar.

I think while standing in line at the post office or grocery store, while riding the trolleybus, while drinking nettle tea diluted with white wine, while staring into the dark of the night, while stroking my cat. My head hurts as I try to imagine the solution to the riddle. What does the Estonian kroner have in common with my grandmother Ona, who lived under President Smetona? (She would spin yarn from two skeins into one, on paper spools made out of old letters written to another woman.) How does a false tooth, fastened onto a rotten root barely holding on to one's jawbone, became a crown? How does a news agency like ELTA become TALENT[5*]? Why do style magazines always appear stolen to me? And finally, and most

---

[5*] This wordplay between the word talent and the name of the news agency is likely a criticism of the increasing focus on entertainment and celebrity in the news industry [Ed. note].

importantly, who is this asshole, and on what grounds did he dare to call any penis Dick?

First published in Giedra Radvilavičiūtė, *Nekrologas*, *Šiaurės Atėnai*, 2006–11–18, no 821.

Translated by Jūra Avižienis from Giedra Radvilavičiūtė, *Šianakt aš miegosiu prie sienos*, Vilnius: Baltos lankos, 2010.

Giedra Radvilavičiūtė (born 1960) studied Lithuanian language and literature at Vilnius University and lived for some time in Chicago. Though she published her first prose works in the 1990s, she only came to the fore as an essayist in 1999. Since then she has published several impressive collections in which she blurs the lines between short story and essay. She is one of the most well-known women prose writers in Lithuania.

Colour and Form

Birutė Jonuškaitė

There is a fire of nasturtium that lies in the eyes of cats. I agree with Leśmian: the redness of the nasturtium is truly fiery – inspirational, dangerous and fiery – while its leaves are a luxuriantly healthy green. That is until the small, repulsive larvae appear in great numbers.

All the flowers from mum's garden, found in the space surrounding the house that comprises the mosaic of my childhood, were interesting to me in their own way, with certain memories clinging to them, encoded in my brain according to colours and smells, connecting me with the name days of people close to me, with holidays, or with particular family events.

Peonies stand for the end of the school year. With their enormous white and pink heads, they represent huge bouquets for everybody, even for the teachers one liked the least – after all, there were a couple months of freedom ahead.

Dahlias stand for the beginning of the school year. The rigid blossoms, seemingly crammed with petals, went only to the class teacher. During all of those eight years, there was not one female teacher who was also a tutor. There were only male tutors in the following order: a bent-over, deaf bachelor; a crazy half-wit alcoholic bachelor still searching for a wife; and a well-kept bachelor who flirted with everyone, but who loved boys. You wouldn't have brought those happy dahlias to any one of them yourself, but mum would order you to, and she would pick them herself. It was no skin off her back as the whole area near the fence was full of them. In

Lithuanian one says that the woodpecker is colourful, but dahlias even more so.

Lilacs stand for the violet name day of my mother. Isn't it for this reason that she died so young? After all, violet is the colour of sorrow and anxiety. The Crucified Christ is covered with violet tulles before Easter while the priests wear violet garments...

Lilies stand for the white, sweetly fragrant anniversary of my cousin's death – an aberration of fate: he was run over by a train on the eve of his eighteenth birthday, in July, right as they were blooming.

Rue stands for first communion, and a crown that never seems to stay on my head. So what if the back of my head is still not particularly sinful; my hair is thin and short, and even with a number of hairpins I can't manage to keep that somewhat heavy green halo on it. It slides to one side, then the other, while the hairpins stick out like the thorns of a briar patch.

Before chrysanthemums had come into fashion, the violet, dark blue little suns that I now know to be called blue felicia were used on All Saints Day and All Souls Day, and it was as if all the constellations had fallen from the sky onto the graves. Pansies also stand for graves, graves and more graves. From spring to autumn, in all possible colours and on all possible occasions, we come to weed them and water them on feast days. It's an occasion to ask about grandparents, none of whom I ever saw.

Sage was one of my mum's favourites: the little red soldiers of Napoleon, and that's all.

Snapdragons, which we knew simply as dragons, stand for the awfully funny lips of rabbits in all warm colours. 'Make one, make one, don't you know how to make a crown out of *dragons*?' the children would say, annoying one another. It was an enormous source of shame if you didn't know how to weave them together.

Cowslips make me think of the sunny shores of the lake. Smelling of wild strawberries, they are always close to hand; you only needed to snoop around a little among the tall grass to find them. During a sweet hour or so of oblivion, you would stretch out among the bent grass and tear the yellowish bells off the cowslips one after another, and suck and suck with your eyes closed, disappearing beyond the borders of dad's fields, beyond the border of the blue lake, even beyond the nearby forest. You are suspended somewhere in the most pleasant point of the universe, light and formless, able to become anything you want, floating between strange galaxies, feeling no danger at all, no fears whatsoever, neither the flow of time, nor a feeling of belonging to a planet, community, or family of some sort. You don't even care about the ants climbing up your legs – even those brown ones that painfully pee on you. Cowslips are the harmless narcotics of childhood summers, leaving only an unforgettable love for sunny colours.

Marsh marigolds belong to the same category. A cold wave of air would rise from the earth. All puddles would turn to stone at night, and in the morning it would be impossible to break them, even with the hardest of shoe heels. And in the evening the ducks quacked loudly in the swamp belonging to the neighbour Jankauskas; the lapwings (pewits) just having flown home, greeting everyone. I would put rubber boots on and head straight for the huge puddles and ditches from which each year they surfaced from the water. You would find yellowish little clouds and would immediately wonder how to reach them, how to pick at least a little bouquet without falling in all the way up to your knees with your boots on. You would either manage to do it, or you didn't. You would march home victoriously with dry feet, or in shoes smelling of swamp, because you had a fistful of flowers, full of dampness, the very first flowers to conquer the departing winter despite their fragility and tendency to wilt quickly. You needed them as proof that *it has already started*, that you are bringing it home and that the entire house will wake up and will overflow with spring.

***

If it was only the fire of nasturtium that burned in the eyes of a cat, it would be a cat that walked alone and returned in the night only when the consequences of war become unbearable: torn ears, swollen eyes, wounds festering over its whole body. Who knows if it is due to such an ability to make use of freedom that the Egyptians embalmed cats after they died, burying them in enormous necropolises and mourning them just as they did people. Who knows whether that is why killing a cat was sacrilege to them, and a degenerate who did just that was sentenced to death.

Why was a Sphinx built in Giza in 10,500 B.C.? Perhaps they knew something we don't know today? Perhaps they understood something essential? That's what I ask my cat, Geisha, in whose eyes I most often see a calming tenderness. And just so I would fully believe in her, the cat begins to purr.

Before Geisha, there had been various cats in our house. Generally, they aroused contradictory feelings in me: love and anxiety. Warm, soft and pleasant strokes, blissful purring on long winter nights somewhere near your feet, your side, or even on your lap. But it's enough to look into the eyes of these animals and feel how everything inside them is totally the opposite: a proud independence, worthy of respect, their form and their elegance when they move. So where does this insurmountable feeling of danger come from? The feeling that the cat will sneak up and attack, that it will become a huge black panther? That in the night it will crawl into your bed, or the bed of your child, and suck the life out of you or him? In contrast to a dog, you can never trust a cat – who knows what century that belief, alive and well, comes from. Dogs rip, bite and tear the faces, shins and arms of their owners, maul their small children, but the harm cats do to people is never reported. So why does their gaze scare us? Maybe a legend somewhere in my subconscious that gives me no peace is responsible, a legend about a Sphinx that lived on a rock near the road to the city of Thebes that would offer a riddle to travellers, and those who could not solve it were torn apart? Do we still fear that we will be unable to solve the riddle? Did this question torment the painter Gustave Moreau, who depicted *The Triumphant Sphinx* with the elegant face of a proud woman adorned with a crown?

Geisha was nothing like a big-eyed, big-eared, wrinkled cat-sphinx. She didn't have any documents showing her lineage, but according to my small daughter, she had 'a pedigree'. Perhaps it was her genes which determined that when growing up in a flat – a rather small, enclosed space – she was affectionate and tidy. Even when she was young, she didn't crawl up the curtains, didn't push the flower pots off the windowsill, didn't pee on the carpet, on the bed or in someone's shoes. Rather, she would lap up water from the sink or tub, and not her own dish. She particularly liked to take part when the children had a bath. They splashed around in the tub, giggling with delight at all the foam, and she'd sit on the edge and, it seemed, could not look away. Or she'd walk on the edges of the tub, back and forth, back and forth. Her curiosity would even get the better of her, and she would slip and fall into the water.

She slept in the funniest of poses: with her legs stretched out, two to the front and two to the back, just like a piglet. One paw would cover her eyes and she would twist all around like a little number eight. All four legs were raised and curled up into a little ball in such a way that at first glance, you couldn't distinguish her head from her tail. She walked extremely gracefully – in a way only Russian blue bloods can – and her smooth fur allowed her to express herself in the most refined, cat-like shapes. She was a flirt – a quiet, elegant flirt. She would reveal her voice only in very exceptional circumstances: when she was left alone for a long period of time, she would give a few meows in greeting to those who had returned. Otherwise she would meow when she was very hungry – for instance, when she didn't get frozen sprats for three days or so. 'What, am I going to live with just dry food?' she complained angrily, having gone to her little dish for the umpteenth time to find nothing. But these complaints stopped when we moved from the flat to live in a house. She discovered mice and little birds. That was a new dessert.

She was of course confused at first by the increased amount of space. Going outside for the first time in her life, she still didn't understand what freedom meant. The appearance of any other animal – be it a dog, a cat or even a crow – frightened her. She hurtled toward the tree like an arrow and got to the top in an instant. You had to coax her patiently for a long time to come down. She didn't stick her nose outside for a few days after such adventures. But one day, just as I opened the door, she shot out to the yard like a bullet.

She didn't come back for three days. We had almost gotten past our stage of mourning when she reappeared acting as if nothing had happened, but looking at her gait, you could see it was much freer and somehow full of satisfaction and self-confidence, I understood that Geisha's way of thinking had totally changed. She had become the master of her house and her territory. She went past the other cats like the new Lithuanian elite went past people living in a landfill. All she was missing was an Armani purse on her shoulder and Swarovski crystal in her hair. And perhaps she had them – who knows what style-cats like. She was like an elegant, pretty girl who had just married well – to a good, rich, older man, of course. She even stopped being afraid of our bitch dog. Our wolf-dog bitch was of a meeker type and tended to get along with all living creatures, thus the appearance of the cat most likely amused rather than annoyed her. She would run up, smell the cat and then run off. But if that smelling lasted a little bit longer, Geisha would smack her on the nose in such a way that the poor thing cowered in pain. When the cat, having jumped on the windowsill, sat in its favourite sphinx pose, it raised its head high and educated the bitch with the glare of a queen: no familiarity whatsoever, miss! Don't stick your nose where you don't need to! You'll get the white bow-tie on my neck dirty!

However, spring, like the marriages of trophy wives with old men, has a happy beginning and… a much more serious end. She walked around the yard for a whole month like Musetta from *La Bohème* wearing a sexy costume and high heels made by the famous Lithuanian designer Juozas Statkevičius. Geisha started becoming lazier and slower, snoozing on the chair and hiding under the tablecloth for days on end. She would go outside only to perform the necessary duties. It seemed that she started to become disinterested in the world beyond the borders of the house. The round, flirty eyes full of devilishness lost their nasturtium fire; anxiety churned in them more and more often. Every touch, and now she needed them more and for longer, was cause for long, monotonous mantras.

After some time, she hardly left my side. It was summer and each morning I went to the nearby lake to swim. Geisha went along. She sat on the shore and waited patiently until I finished swimming and got out of the water. We would both return home and together weed the gardens, walk and pick strawberries. She rubbed up against me, jumped on my neck, poked me with her nose, and in the evening when I sat at the computer, she tried to lie down on my lap. The cat constantly underfoot sapped my patience. Her walking between my feet led to 'accidents' on more than one occasion: dishes would run out of my hands, I would spill soup on myself, step on her tail or paw, but she still refused to stop.

Geisha's last, fateful day was in the beginning of August. I was weeding the strawberry patch. The cat didn't only snuggle up to my legs and my gloved hands – she would always approach me from the front, look straight into my face and meow. She meowed like she was crying, with an undisguised fear; she meowed like never before, full of an unspeakable concern. Then I remembered my fateful day – when I laid next to screaming women for an entire day. They were also afraid. They also felt pain.

The box lined with soft little blankets had been prepared long ago. Emergency medical care had also been prepared, in the form of my daughters and me. I tried to explain all this to Geisha, but she was not put at ease. She accompanied me to the house with the same ear-splitting meowing, most likely lamenting her situation in the name of all the works of God of the feminine gender. She begged for help. But how could I help her?

We talked. She meowed, I told her about my experiences, the experiences of my girlfriends, I tried to joke around, said that it's like that for all of them, that it will pass, that we are able to endure everything, that I won't leave her – just so she wouldn't worry and concentrate better on the unavoidable process. I worked as a cat psychologist until 2 am. She didn't want to be alone for one minute in the little box, which to me appeared so comfortable, safe and sufficiently spacious. If I sat next to her and petted her, it was fine, but if I got the idea to snooze on the sofa and pulled my hand away, the cat screamed even louder and jumped on my lap. I had to endure until the end, with one hand on her back, and that's how we awaited the first kitten.

Then she fell silent and calmed down. Raising her head, she very clearly told me to go away: I'm not afraid anymore. I will continue on my own. Thank you, you can go to bed.

In the morning, there were four little ones in her cosy embrace. I never saw a better mother than Geisha. She would have ripped to pieces any intruder who would have thought to harm her children, just like that Sphinx of Thebes. She even changed her eating habits because of them. She started eating meat, chewing it with a mouthful of her favourite grass in the yard; she tried soups, cheese, pancakes – everything we offered her. Like the wisest of dieticians, she chose only what a nursing mother needed so the children would grow up to be healthy and strong. And that's how they grew up before going on to other owners, and when the next spring came, Geisha once again became an elegant flirt, eating only dry food, tinned cat food from the shop and frozen sprats.

And that's how it is every year, and that's how this work of God amazes me with her wisdom and sacrificing motherhood, her passion and independence, with her fiery furry and audacious elegance, her tenderness and savage hunting instincts (even when she wasn't hungry, she would bring home small birds and mice and put them near the door on the welcome mat). What awed me most was the fact that everything fitted together harmoniously – everything that is within us, from the most amazing to the most horrible, all basic instincts, all of the most beautiful shapes and the most secretive depths. Maybe that's why cats arouse such anxiety in us? Maybe that's why they make films about cat-people? Maybe that's why there are so many of them in all sorts of artwork? What is it that cannot give us peace? How did it happen that what was once the defender of motherhood and home, a protector from demons and other bad spirits, became the embodiment of the devil's works and witches' spells during the Middle Ages? The fate of cats and of women accused of witchcraft was the same – they were burned in town squares, and not just in any old town but in 16th century Paris, where live cats were thrown into the bonfire in the Place du Châtelet. The cats will burn, thus the seed of the devil will as well? Why do we spit, even now, when we see a cat, especially a black one and all the more if it has the gall to cross our path?

Witches perceived more than the average person. Perhaps cats discern things better? And those who see, know and understand more – for them it's easier.

So what is it in the eyes of cats that bothers us? Is it the flame of nasturtium, or something that has been interpreted in various ways over thousands of years, but which is still an unsolvable riddle?

Translated by Jayde Will from Birutė Jonuškaitė, *Kregždėlaiškis*, Vilnius: Versus aureus (2007).

Birutė Jonuškaitė (born 1959) is a prose writer, poet and essayist. She was born and raised in the village of Seivai, in the Punskas region of Poland and studied journalism at Vilnius University. After graduating from university she lived in Poland, Lithuania and Canada. She returned to settle in Lithuania where she now works at the Lithuanian Writers' Union. She is the author of the novels *The Great Island* (*Didžioji sala*, 2 vol., 1997–1999) and *The Tango of White Zippers* (*Baltų užtrauktukų tango*, 2009), the short story collections *The Bridge of Grass-snakes* (*Žalčių tiltas*, 2002) and *Zip Me Up* (*Užsagstyk mane*, 2011). Jonuškaitė has also translated poetry, novels and essays from Polish into Lithuanian. She has been awarded several literary prizes and her work has been widely translated.

Christmas with a Stranger

Danutė Kalinauskaitė

Kolya came all geared up: hair combed, the face of a fifty-year-old, the dyed 'chestnut' hair and eyebrows of a thirty-year-old with a bottle of *Sobieski* in his inside pocket. He cradled a three-litre jar of marinated bell peppers in his arms like a month-old child. This wasn't emptiness wrapped up in a raincoat, you'd say at once, but a body full to the brim with the warmest of blood. And that body wore a fake leather jacket, a Turkish sweater covered with rhombuses, and, as was fitting when going to visit someone, bright red socks and the pointiest of shoes with a raised heel. What's more he had a gold signet ring. And Kolya's scent is not one of fear, or the dampness of shrouds and mouse fur, but of tobacco, garlic and Adidas.

During the first hour we got to know one another's 'general contours'. According to my horoscope, I'm a Scorpio whereas he's a Cancer. I hail from Kaunas; he's from the outskirts of Moscow, but up until he was eight years old, before his father, an anti-ballistic missile defence officer, brought him to Lithuania in 1960, he grew up with his grandparents in Siberia. What does he remember from those times? The sound of trees uprooting when the winds picked up in Siberia and the birches would flex like bent grass. He remembers how grandpa and grandma, living in a log cabin, would chase each other naked through the snow in the winter and would both go to the forest to wrestle bears, with grandma piling in first. She smelled of manly sweat, knew all the herbs, smoked a pipe and would always shove the tobacco into the belly of the pipe with her little finger, the nail of which was long and yellow. He also remembers the trees cut

237

down in mid-winter and the white flesh and red heart of the wood steaming in the snow. He recalls the tracks of wolves, weasels and black grouse as well as cedar nuts and boiling snow in the round aluminium teapot. Kolya is immune to everything – both in body and in soul – because *privivki*, the Russian vaccines from those times, still work perfectly. Suddenly – perhaps so that his words were made flesh – he rolls up the sleeve of his shirt right there in front of my face and exposes a muscular, hairy forearm with a tattoo of the name 'Lyosha' and a snake curled around an anchor. Look, he says…

In turn, I also tell him this and that. It seems that he genuinely likes my story from yesterday, but that kind of 'humour', in his opinion, is common in divorced, lonely men. By the way, he is also divorced, more than once, and now he has decided to live with just a cat for company – a fire-coloured cat named Bill (second name: Clinton). Once he brought it to work and while Kolya was plastering, Bill sat on the windowsill with narrowed eyes and, understandably, could not avoid accidently pressing Siamese hair fossils into the corner of the window – to a future sea and Devonian period. Generally though, Kolya was not some steppe wolf, God forbid; he has a girlfriend named Lelka, twenty years his junior, and she, as they all are, is full of womanly whims: clouds of perfumes, hot chocolate, natural silk and furs, reading only the 'odes' written on the left side of restaurant menus, but not the ones on the right. When he, paying for all of this, once decided to test her feelings and asked what three things – hinting at the fact that they should be people – she would take with her to a desert island, she replied without hesitation: *Gone With the Wind*, fishnet stockings and a manicure kit, because without work she would die. Kolya was not among those things. Still, one could understand the manicure kit – but you could sense the resentment in Kolya's voice and along with it the seriousness of a justifiable exception: *she's a manicurist*. She attended not only to the hands of the average Olya and Liolya, but also to the hands of two government ministers: the minister of agriculture and transport, and not long ago the minister of defence joined him.

And right this minute it was her, his woman, who was phoning.

Having gone out into the corridor, Kolya covered the receiver with his palm: 'Lelka, I am with a client right now. I'm with a client. Well, you could say it's an exceptional case... I'll buy it. I'll bring it home... *Nadeysia i zhdi* – hope and wait.' Finishing the words of his song, he deftly and secretly tried on my *ushanka* that was hanging on the coat rack, and then, crouching down in front of the mirror and hunching his shoulders, he then began springing up and down on his raised heels and, squinting, threw a few jabs into the air – boxers have a special term for this: shadow boxing.

So what, for Pete's sake, is bothering me, a man of intellect, he asks me when he returns. He asks tactically. He can see when people are being dragged down by worries even though they try to crack jokes. For some reason, especially during the holidays, people like to jab forks into their throats, slip nooses around their necks, jump from bridges or out of windows, and their guardian angel, unfortunately – and it really is a pity – cannot manage every time to slide a fluffy pillow under the head of a good person in time. I don't want to explain anything besides what I've already told Kolya, but slowly, and I don't know why myself – I only invited him over for his presence after all – I begin to talk to him...

I tell him how the other day I went to my mailbox and how I did not find the typical junk mail inviting me to buy *Jysk* flower boxes and sets of packing tape as well as ads promising a 'cheap and quick divorce' or to 'reach spiritual harmony (call Irena at 223...)'. Instead, someone had accidentally thrown a piece of paper into the mailbox – a blank piece of paper. But it was the colour of skim milk. And suddenly, in a thin thread of association, came the realisation that this was the emptying of being, I told Kolya. It struck me: *Finita la commedia*... Feelings, the heart, how could I have thought that taste, smell, touch and even sight could end like an ink cartridge or a bank account. When my wife moved out it seemed to me that not only did she take *her* Singer, not only did she make off with the fine china dinner set and the 'soft' furniture, but she also stole my autumn, my winter. My Christmas. I was left with bare walls, morning and afternoon. She even took the non-essentials –

the grey evening ashtray into which the day waned and for which she, I know, certainly wouldn't have any use. And on top of all that, Kolya, my mother dies and I end up... an orphan. Afterwards, as if deliberately, the telephone and door bell start to forget you. Someone with manicure scissors, the kind Lelka uses to cut the nails of the government ministers, cuts your links to the world one by one. Air becomes increasingly rare until one day, under the bell jar – again, this isn't my invention but a classic for suicides – there's no oxygen left. You lie in bed in the early morning, the air around you feels heavy and though it may seem that there are many more amazing things to see, you see only one: the reflection of the pathologist-faced moon, shining above you as if viewed from the dark water of the bottom of a river. What else could be reflected there when your big toe has a morgue number attached?

Kolya listened, frozen, with a poppy seed *kūčiukas*[1] in his mouth. He glanced furtively at my foot under the table. Afterwards he looked again, as if he wanted to be certain of what he saw, i.e. that he didn't see a morgue number. Having contemplated this for a little while, and clearly feeling that he needed to, Goddamit, seize the initiative into his own hands, he asked, unhesitatingly: 'Kostas, do you have both kidneys? You haven't sold one to pay your debts, have you? You don't have cirrhosis of the liver, do you? Your bile's in order? Your hips, and especially your knees, they're not screwed on? Your eyes aren't made out of plastic, are they? I don't even need to ask about your heart. I can see that you have one. So in other words, you have everything! You're not lacking anything!'

Visibly annoyed, he got up to walk around the room. Well, if that's the way it's going to be, then he'll have to tell his own story, I say. A story for a story – a tooth for a tooth. So he begins: a few years ago his youngest brother met a schoolmate by chance in Russia. They hadn't seen each other for exactly twenty years. They met, drank, embraced and kissed one another, bared their souls and, as the Russians say, *naraspashku*, which means they had a heart-to-heart

1 A sweet, crouton-shaped biscuit traditionally eaten during the Christmas season.

and promised never to separate again; then they got into a fight and later the criminal investigators counted twenty-six stab wounds in his brother's body inflicted by the schoolmate – just a few less than the amount of litas he had left over from his disability pension after you subtract the alimony payments. During the trial the schoolmate got quite lost in the numbers. The courtroom buzzed angrily like a hive of bees. 'Mathematics had always been my weak point,' he replied to the accusations, blushing, 'but I want you to know that I was always strong in my native literature.' Putting his hand to his heart, he stooped and asked for forgiveness from the court and from all the people sitting in the courtroom for the fact that up until now he had not learned 'to count honestly'.

His favourite sister... oh, Kostas... At the time she was unemployed and living in Ust-Kamensk when one day a display board honouring 'outstanding workers' fell on her and broke her back. The responsibility for the fact that that particular memorial plaque in the centre of town was hanging by a thread, as is always the case in Russia in these circumstances, was 'carried' by the wind that blew that day from the northwest... His other sister left work at the end of her shift during a blizzard and froze to death in the snow... He was also, by the way, an orphan. He had buried his mother a year ago as well. A gypsy fortune-teller once foretold that she would drown. His mother believed it. She had already nearly drowned a few times but always escaped her watery fate. The last time she got very ill, she was delighted when she was taken to the hospital: 'In other words, Kolya,' she said, 'I won't die yet. I won't fall into the water, the sea is far away, and I also won't drown in the river or a lake so this means it isn't time for me yet.'

'However when your time comes,' and now Kolya's voice, and especially his face, struck a fatalistic tone, 'the water starts to appear from out of nowhere, from within yourself. Water started to come out of my mother's chest and legs and the nurses sat her up at night so she could breathe out from the tops of her lungs, but they also filled and she drowned. Dropsy. She drowned in water, which, with *that hour* having come, if there is neither a river nor a lake around you, you have to get up and turn it on. When the nurse brought her personal things, I saw what had swum out of my mother: reading glasses and a pipe... twelve graves...' Nicholas opened up his arms, measuring in the same way fishermen show the size of the pike they have caught, most often exaggerating a little. 'And now they all need to be cared for. But would someone stick their head into a cement mixer because of this? Between the wheels? Lay down on the tracks?'

A call comes from a colleague at Totally Windows. 'Gerard, I'm with a client.' Kolya, now totally at home in this foreign home, no longer goes out into the corridor. He has removed his 'skin' and familiarly placed his pointy dress shoes near the door next to mine, and now with his shirt untucked he's in a half-collapsing armchair: 'No, it's okay, I can talk... Well, call Mečikas, let Mečikas call Nazaras. Don't release the 'Nightingale', and catch the 'Mushroom Pickers'. Great, Gerard. All in order. Gotcha. I'll give you a call.'

And, whether you want to or not, you hear the minutiae of life entering into your empty life – the hushed telephone calls, the subdued clinking of dishes, the echo betraying your steps, even the silence – it comes in from the street, appears out of nowhere and soon takes over living your life for you. Kolya is stuffing himself, snacking on *kūčiukai* with bell peppers, drinking Sobieski vodka while sticking the gnawed chicken bones underneath the table without looking into a polythene bag he placed earlier between his legs, for the benefit Bill Clinton... It's with bitter longing – as though I'm chasing Kolya on the running track in a stadium when I know that I won't catch him – that I remember how I had once filched a brandy glass from a bar before giving it to my wife. And I even promised to get the whole collection. I remember how I used to tuck her in during the early morning and how I warmed her 'gangrened' toes. I remember many details; they returned to me when Kolya appeared. You could argue that they mean nothing, but there was a whole world made from them – content, and not form, like now: the smells of wood, fresh sawdust, woodchips and sap under the bark lying in your memory like the strata of minerals in an iron ore mine. The core's redness is similar to fire and blood; the steam from our kitchen mugs and the round teapot without which, I am still certain, no new world can be established and the old one cannot be resurrected from the dead; and much more. And it seems to me that Kolya is like a longhaul driver – those types would never wrap a rope in a newspaper, only sandwiches, and how tasty, for those sandwiches of theirs smell of the printing press and lead! – who has returned from my life, a place I have not visited for quite some time already. And he tells how everything is back there. Are the windows nailed shut, Kolya? Would anyone remember me if I returned – the wind, whatever its species, or the snow, whistling on the stove from the pain of a little spring cleaning? They say the memory of suffering is long...

A call. Well, of course, it's Lelka. Women... And again he's in the corridor talking with his palm covering his mouth: 'Lelka, you, my child, are already testing my patience because right now I really don't care about that nail you are polishing for *her*, got me? I am with a client now. The same one. We're not drinking because this is a *special case*. Dangerous? He's most dangerous to himself. Or maybe to you, stupid, if you keep asking... If you've already finished one of her hands, then take the other, am I, Goddamit, supposed to tell you when and whose nails to cut?!'

Kolya has been talking in a raised voice. He returns furious. He is becoming a real man who has set things straight. Those women... But I see that he's even looking at me all cockeyed, raw – like that Siamese cat. Because when somebody steps on Kolya Afanasyevich's calluses and he gets worked up, he really gets worked up – like a week ago with that house with the pool outside the city where he, Mečikas, Nazaras and some others were putting in additional hours – not working for Totally Windows – fixing plumbing, digging trenches, putting in windows, plastering and painting. Having finished work and taken a shower – Nazaras even shaved, having carelessly singed his moustache while welding pipes, reducing him almost to tears because for him his moustache was everything and because 'a real man should be able to have an eagle perch on his moustache' – they joined the owner to 'break the ice' with a little Smirnoff. The owner had already laid out a spread next to the pool; he put out some tinned sprats, onions and a little herring, everything served in a refined way.

He even took care to provide toothpicks, but the hostess, taking her husband to the side, said: 'Did *they* already finish work? Felix, make sure I don't ever see their mugs around here again...' Kolya squinted like his fiery cat, though his eyebrows and fur were a ripe chestnut colour: 'Ah, you see, our intellectual friends, our little brothers,' I hear all of his tension in his voice, 'if it weren't for us, the Dimas, Mečikases, Slavikases and Kolyas, you wouldn't have any windows, any walls, any shitholes, and even, it seems, any of your goddamn heads...'

...Sometimes it is only the very faintest of feelings that can communicate with you. For example, when, for whatever reason, the only thing that remains of you is a frame, the outlines in a colouring book titled *Colour Yourself*, because all the colours have gone elsewhere (perhaps, like everything these days, to where they are better paid) and the desire and strength to colour deserts you once again, there comes a gift of fate. Even if the sky drops red socks into the space between the lines, of course, it's not enough – Nicholas Belochvostikov must be inside those socks. Having buried our small misunderstandings, Kolya and I spoke, *naraspashku*, and it seemed that there were no topics that could not be broached: fear as one of the basic states of man; the soul and how much it weighs; the prostate, which Kolya explains is a man's secondary heart and without a doubt the more important one and one for which pumpkin oil is its best friend as the years pass...

There was an un-Christmas-like minor key to Kolya's voice: he had entered into his middle years, but had been almost nowhere, so what was the point of living, dammit, if he was going to die without having seen the bedouins of Africa or the aborigines of Australia. He had heard that a businessman in Russia had gotten rich just before he was shot and very nearly didn't manage to see the world; but, having sensed something like this might happen, luckily he wrote the following in his will: 'I want to travel, even after my death.' He did so in a glass coffin, so the world would be clearly visible from both sides. His nearest and dearest, cursing him but carrying out his posthumous wishes, took him across Europe: he was transported to the Alps, lugged up the snaking roads through the fjords of Norway... Nicholas was deep in thought. He had on occasion seriously thought about such a possibility in the event that things didn't work out while he was alive. Of course, he wouldn't burden Lelka with such an obligation. She was not the kind of person who would lug him, dead, through fjords. It wasn't clear if she would lug him around much longer alive. Besides, he was beginning to suspect her of infidelity. It was possible that it was even with Gerardito. But she wouldn't lay her head down for Mečikas too...

'So have you travelled a lot?' he asks and the greenness of his eyes moistens. At the very bottom of the greenness there is an emerald that could have crystallised, you hazard a timid guess, either from a mixture of faith, hope and love for a dear one, or equally as likely could well have crystallised from stupidity.

'Almost around the whole world. Kolya, tell me, do you really think that when you're travelling you're escaping? You can't escape yourself anywhere, not in Norway or by dyeing your eyebrows...'

'The whole world...' Kolya answers with an echo from the fjords.

We fall silent for a moment. Each of us with our own burden, each with our own Sisyphean task. And suddenly panic overtakes me, thinking that this silence might linger too long. Just a little longer and Kolya will leave because he is already bored with me. Because having fired off all of my merry gunpowder – the hats and black leather gloves, little saws and chisels – I have nothing else of interest for a person that would make his blood course through his veins. And when Kolya leaves... When he reaches that critical distance away from my home...

I read somewhere that Russians, when talking about the phenomenon of the 'modern Russian' (which no one, not even they themselves, are able to explain), sometimes call themselves wet matches – hard to light and quick to go out. But Kolya... all of my senses, which were on standby, are now signalling – no, they're not signalling, bells are going off, my heart is beating – that this is the one who you'd manage to light a cigarette with. And you'd light it up on the first try, even in a northerly wind. It doesn't matter that, when trying to talk you out of sticking your head into a cement mixer, he doesn't offer up the arguments for 'the positive side'. What for? You yourself are an argument. Besides, the real argument is about wearing socks that are the colour of a presidium's tablecloth. In the end – and this is most important – it is the argument that will survive a catastrophic tsunami hanging on to a python and, look, he'll reach back and pull someone along and drag them by the hair, and why not, Goddamit, if they were just lying around uselessly on the way. Just listen to him, go with him...

'But we don't even need to knock on any more doors,' Kolya says, calm again and lit up by an inner serenity (or maybe it's the emerald?). 'If we can't go out into the world, that world, Kostas, will move in with us, right into our room or even into our palm, just take it and use it...'

And sure enough, when the television screen scatters its snowflakes across the room, after a long pause the world once again comes into your home. What happened in it while you were sticking your head in a noose?

On Channel 1 there's a report about Christmas around the globe. Dire news from Naples – the church nativity tableaux were stolen. It appears, you see, that the white dust of Jerusalem's roads kicked up in clouds of dust while cows, sheep and donkeys were herded off in groups. St. Josephs, Virgin Marys, shepherds and wise men were taken away – whole episodes of the memory of God – all drastically purged. But the most worrying, at least for Kolya and I, is the sky emptied by the thieves who carted off its wind-shaped arches, took down and extinguished the moon, the sun and the stars, and left all of us under the wide-open holes of the cosmos, each and every one of us the most orphaned of orphans... Still, and this is the real Christmas miracle: baby Jesus was not touched in any of those nativity tableaux...

'Thinking logically,' Kolya wrinkles his brow severely: 'Can Jesus be stolen? Casper, Balthazar, Melchior, even St. Joseph, sure, but even then, clearly, only if you're in a really tough spot, but Jesus?! In the end what can you do with him, stolen? Sell him? Keep him hidden in a shed and use him for your own purposes? Continuously make demands and more demands? Export him as contraband along with Saint George cigarettes? No, no,' he shakes his head with his eyes closed, and suddenly he hits the top of his head on the wall, 'we all know that cursed state of mind when the burden of logic sits on you with all its force, and you can't run or scream...'

On Channel 2 there are orphanages and old people's homes. There is the tear of an inebriated old man in close-up in one of the latter. He found himself there, in the 'Grey-Haired Club', after he signed over his flat to a nurse who used to massage his back but also 'tenderly grabbed my buttocks'... We see a family with twelve children – 'the backbone on which today's Lithuania relies, despite the governmental controls, despite the stolen millions' – sitting at the Christmas table on which all the plates – including the soup bowls, the appetiser trays, the platters usually filled with herring – are full of apples. Apples, everywhere there are only the apples that they grew and which, from the time they are small until the time they are grown, they chew with great perseverance. Maybe for that reason they have such strong backbones. But their teeth – when the camera zooms in, Kolya manages to get a look – they're made of steel...

On Channel 3 the wife of the Belarusian sausage king is singing. We both assess the vocal material sceptically, and even decide that she, most likely, doesn't have a voice at all but only impressive silicon. Nicholas doesn't like it when silicon squeaks between his hands. It squeaks, beg your pardon, like cheap potato starch. 'You've tried it?' I ask him. Many times! He's too lazy to talk about it. He's allergic to it – as soon as he touches silicon he immediately develops a rash. And boy do they explode in the crematorium when they're put inside. He's heard it himself...

But on Channel 4 it's all serious – tragic numbers, how many people went gaga this year and chose the unfortunate fate of wandering among the trees and the bushes until their appointed time on the earth passes. 'Lithuania is once again among the leaders,' a psychologist walks around the studio with a piece of unpolished green amber hanging on her chest and stops next to a window frame, which to her clearly symbolises the link between this world and the next. 'In Europe, we are like a zoo... We have crossed all boundaries... the consequences of the Soviet era... Unfortunately, from all this the press and journalists only titillate us with sensationalism...' After her factual analysis, a lyrical interlude ensues: the narrator's voice, imbued with a worried metaphysical tone, is accompanied by images: clouds, pine needles and pine cones, a shoe rinsed out by snow and rain nestles in a bed of moss, the remains of a shirt, the end of a rope swinging romantically in the wind, and a line runs by underneath: 'Christmas sale with manufacturer's prices...' Nicholas turns his head toward the television: 'All the same, it's good that you're here, and not dead among those pine branches. Right, Kostas?'

And in that moment you feel how, little by little, this and that is weaving together in your home – mostly from the absurd and the grotesque, somewhat less from mercy, and even less from sympathy. Who? And then the slow sensation – is it you? Or is it someone else *for* you? A moment later, is there SOMEONE at all? Regardless of what it is, that textile is abrasive, 'stinging', because Kolya is working on it, weaving it, and before weaving it, he readied the threads in his own unique way, and when trying to wrap and warm yourself in it, you might be bloodied if at that time you've shed your skin and thrown it on the back of the chair, or someone else has flayed it off. However, God sees – late on Christmas Eve we really are something or other...

Translated by Jayde Will from Danutė Kalinauskaitė, *Niekada nežinai*, Vilnius: Baltos lankos (2008).

Danutė Kalinauskaitė (born 1959) studied Lithuanian language and literature at Vilnius University. Her first short-story collection, published in 1987, made her overnight success and marked her as one of the most important authors of her generation. However she shunned the limelight and it was only in 2008 that she published her second short-story collection, *You Never Know* (*Niekada nežinai*, 2008), which won the Lithuanian Writers' Union Prize.

Acknowledgement

The International Cultural Programme Centre extends its gratitude and appreciation to all the authors, translators and consultants who made a valued contribution to this project by devoting their time and energy. A very special thank you to the publisher Dedalus Books, Dr Almantas Samalavičius for his all contributions, and the language editor Medeinė Tribinevičius.